ON W

# ON WEST GREEN

by Robert Rosenthal

First published in 2024 by Wrate's Publishing
ISBN 978-1-0686952-1-6
Copyright © 2024 by Robert Rosenthal
Typeset by Wrate's Editing Services
www.wrateseditingservices.co.uk

Wrate's Publishing

For my family, past, present and future

# Significant characters in order of appearance

Lucas Fairbright: known as Spikey in 1979. London estate agent, husband of Mollie, father of Ned and Joe in 2002.

Benny: Cornish gang member 1979.

Vince: Cornish gang member in 1979.

Dale: owner of *Mousehole Cat,* Cornish gang member in 1979.

Steve Jerrish: Cornish gang boss in 1979, small-time criminal in 2002.

Frenchie: drug trafficking mastermind.

Hasan Güney: Arjan's uncle and Rasheed's father in Mardin.

Mustafa Igli: young man in Mardin in 1979; Topkapi gang-boss in London in 2002.

Bulent Igli: Mustafa's brother, career soldier.

Cetin Zaman: young man in Mardin in 1979. Husband of Dilek and father of Mehmet, Onur and Emine in London in 2002.

Dilek Zaman: young woman in Mardin in 1979. Wife of Cetin and mother of Mehmet, Onur and Emine in London in 2002.

Arjan Barzani: thirteen, child refugee from Qamishli, friend of Mark and Ned in 2002.

Fatima Barzani: Arjan's mother.

Kalil Barzani: Arjan's older brother.

Rasheed Güney: Hasan Güney's son, Arjan's cousin and guardian.

Dymphna Güney: Rasheed's wife, Shereen's mother.

Shereen Güney: fifteen, daughter of Rasheed and
  Dymphna.

Jack Job: owner of Stanhopes estate agent.

Ned Fairbright: thirteen, friend of Mark and Arjan. Son of
  Lucas and Mollie.

Mark Durrant: thirteen, friend of Ned and Arjan. Son of
  Lloyd and Brenda.

Joe Fairbright: eleven, brother of Ned, son of Lucas and
  Mollie.

Mollie Fairbright: wife to Lucas, mother to Ned and Joe.

Mehmet Zaman: thirteen, son of Cetin and Dilek, brother
  of Onur and Emine.

Necip: thirteen, Mehmet's friend.

Brenda Durrant: mother to Mark, wife to Lloyd.

Lloyd Durrant: father to Mark, husband to Brenda, friend
  to Lucas, Dwayne and Ellis.

Emine Zaman: fifteen, daughter of Cetin and Dilek, sister
  of Mehmet and Onur, friend of Shereen and Tulay.

Tulay: fifteen, friend of Emine and Shereen.

Grey: thirteen, 'cousin' of Mark, son of Dwayne.

Onur Zaman: twenty, son of Cetin and Dilek, brother of
  Mehmet and Emine.

Denzil: twenty, friend of Onur, cousin of Kemal.

Kemal: Topkapi gang lieutenant, cousin of Denzil.

Dwayne: Jamaican gang member, father of Grey, 'uncle' of
  Mark and friend of Lloyd.

Ellis: Jamaican gang member, friend of Dwayne and Lloyd.

Ms Poole: Park School teacher, form tutor and head of
  drama.

Elif Igli: Bulent's daughter and Mustafa's niece.

# The West Green Area

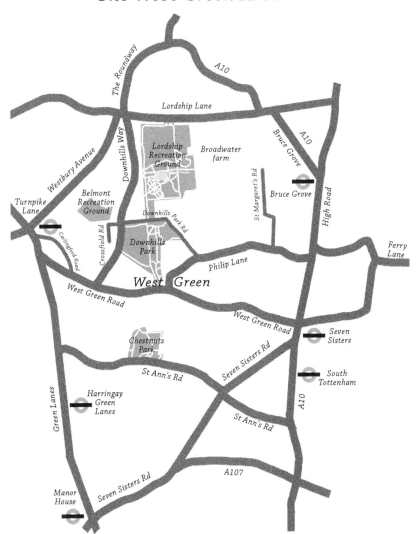

# Part One

# ROADS TO WEST GREEN

**1979–2000**

# Chapter One

Spikey and Benny had been waiting for hours on the quayside of Polperro, a small fishing harbour near Plymouth. At least the cold night gave them a starry sky to look at; the full moon reflected a broad swathe of light across the calm sea. It was 4am. The others were two hours late. They listened for the sound of the returning boat, each in their thoughts, snuggling in their jackets to stay warm. Fishermen often went out at night, so their lights might draw fish closer to the surface. But tonight, it wasn't just fish that their boat, the *Mousehole Cat*, was looking for.

Finally, they heard it. The distant drone of twin 40-horse-power outboard motors, growing steadily louder as the boat turned the headland and then quieter again as the skipper dropped the throttle so as not to disturb the sleeping village. The *Mousehole Cat* pulled up alongside the quay. It was a small boat, a twenty-foot Wilson Flyer with a semi-enclosed wheelhouse but otherwise an open deck for crew, nets and catch. On board, they could see Dale at the wheel and Vince at the bow with mooring ropes in hand. Spikey and Benny caught the ropes as they were thrown and secured the *Cat* to the bollards. Not a word was spoken. Dale shut the power and conducted his closing checks while Vince passed their night's catch to Spikey and Benny on the quay. Tonight, instead of a netful of slippery mackerel there were thirty large black bin-liners. Just as they finished unloading a figure emerged from the shadows.

'All done?' Spikey recognised the hushed voice as Steve, leader of the gang.

'Yes, boss,' replied Benny.

'Let's go then.'

It took two trips to carry all thirty bags quickly and quietly through the village to Dale's cottage. Only when they were all inside and the door shut behind them, did they break silence. Steve was first, his laughter a signal for the others to join in and within minutes they were sitting around the fire drinking whisky and catching up on events. The pick-up had gone smoothly, if delayed. The *Cat* had connected with *Queen of the Sea*, a Guyanese-registered trawler about twenty miles out, but the *Queen* had been late, held up by a mechanical fault. Dale had positioned the *Cat* parallel to the *Queen* about ten metres apart, a zip line had been thrown across and the cargo then transferred in a net.

The black bags now sat piled before them. Job half done. The next stage was to pass them to their new owners and collect their commission.

'What are we carrying this time, Steve?' asked Benny.

The group deferred to Steve. Although there was nothing striking about his looks, his mullet black hair, average height and build, he projected an air of menace and talked a lot about violence. He was their unchallenged alpha male.

'Expect it's some of Morocco's finest,' Steve replied. 'Frenchie doesn't share details; she just sends orders. Don't ask if you don't want your fingers chopped off.'

They all knew that Steve received their order from a

French woman who co-ordinated the supply and distribution of Moroccan hashish into the UK. She offered a niche service to drug producers who did not want the work and risk involved in managing their own distribution and sales, and to distributors who preferred to avoid long-term commitments to producers. She matched them up, arranged the logistics and delivered. No one in the gang apart from Steve had ever spoken to Frenchie and even he seemed terrified of her. The times Spikey had heard him on the phone to her, Steve had treated her with a level of respect and obedience that he afforded no one else. She was a shadowy character, and everyone knew that it would be a fatal error to cross her.

'Can we take a look, Steve?' Benny was always a bit cheeky and usually got away with it. 'Open one up? It's the least we deserve, to know what we've risked our lives for out on the high seas.'

Steve fixed his eyes on Benny who hadn't even been on the boat, his humour vanishing in the long cold stare.

'I'm just sayin',' went Benny, backing off as he realised he had overstepped the mark. The seconds passed, the atmosphere froze, and then Steve freed them all with a belly laugh. Their relief was palpable as they realised that they could all join in. The moment of danger had passed. Steve was like that. He could switch in seconds. One minute your friend, the next you could fear for your own life. His unpredictability and the permanent underlying threat of violence cemented his authority. Everyone feared him and there were no challengers for his position in the gang.

'Maybe just a peek,' said Steve, 'but no touching, mind.'

With that he reached for the nearest sack, examined its bindings, and carefully unpicked them. Peeling away the treble plastic bagging he revealed a pile of cellophane-wrapped blocks.

'Looks like you were right, Steve,' said Vince, looking around the group for their reactions. 'There must be twenty kilo blocks per bag. Thirty bags. That's six hundred kilos of hashish at £700 per kilo. That's nearly half a mill on the street.' Vince was good at mental maths.

'Shame it's not ours,' said Steve. 'No sticky fingers, you lot or you might wake up without any. This lot don't pay us to look, just move the cargo. Right? Tomorrow, we move. I'll go early with twelve bags to Bristol. Benny with me. We should be by the phone around 2pm. You've all got the Bristol number. You set off after me. Around 11am. Vince, take six to Exeter. Spikey and Dale, take twelve to Birmingham. Call me when you're nearby. I'll give you the address. Then call me again when you're out with the money. Don't leave the address without it. Right boys, carry the bags up to the back bedroom. I'll stay up there with it. The rest of you kip down here. Thanks for the hospitality, Dale.'

'All right, Steve, job well done!' they toasted him in unison. It was time to rest.

Smuggling was in the coastal Cornish DNA. The Cornish had been at it for centuries, using their rocky coves to bring in goods and avoid taxes. The isolated harbours of Cornwall's 400 mile coast together with the region's remoteness had always made it difficult to police. Steve liked to think that smugglers provided a service to the public: cheap tax-free products, or goods that were not otherwise available. Not much had changed in two hundred years except that instead of rum, drugs were now the most profitable cargo.

Spikey was eighteen. His birth name was Lucas. He'd grown up in Launceston, a quiet Cornish market town but as a teenager got bored and frustrated. He hated school and made the bare minimum effort, but as time went by, he had given up even with that. When he was fifteen, he had punked his hair into a spiky Mohican and dyed it blue, for a bit of excitement. This had upset his family and school even more. Mum and Dad. Always on his case, giving him chores, asking about his homework; they seemed to think he was some brainbox, destined for university. But he hated class-rooms. Recently Dad had been going through his bedroom drawers. Looking for what? If he had had a brother or sister at least the pressure would be shared, and he'd have an ally in the house. But he was an only child. None of his mates had such strict parents, and they all had siblings. His parents just didn't understand him or how the world had changed since they were young. It had seemed like he was the only one with so much to kick back against, so he felt isolated and lonely. He had to get away; to find somewhere that he would be accepted for who he was, people he could relate to. He left school at sixteen, worked behind the newsagent counter to save money, avoided his parents when possible and finally left home, for Plymouth. He'd heard of a squat in an abandoned warehouse near Sutton Harbour. He found it and luckily there was space for him. He introduced himself to his new neighbours as Spikey, cracked a lot of jokes and made himself popular quickly. In no time he had found a new community and unlocked the door to Plymouth's subculture.

He met Benny in the squat. Benny was a couple of years older and originally from Port Isaac, a small fishing village being transformed by London second-homers. They had a lot in common, from what Benny told him about his family. The pair hung out at the Three Tonnes, a pub with live music, popular with young people and with a reputation for the availability of drugs. That's where they met Steve. Steve was older, maybe twenty-eight, worked as delivery driver with his own work van. He had his own flat in town too.

To Spikey and Benny, Steve seemed really cool: properly grown up with money, a job, flat and van; a tough guy with a life story to match. Steve told them that he had grown up in a foster family in Newquay, the sort that did it for the money, not the love of children, and didn't have much time for him. His birth mother was an addict and lost to him. As for his father, Steve didn't even know his name. So, from the age of thirteen he got out whenever he could and spent every spare moment hanging out on the beach with surfers.

Spikey understood that Steve must have felt he belonged on the beach and modelled himself on some of the surfers he met there: he picked up how to banter and impress, how to roll a joint, eventually securing his place among them by finding out how to supply them with gear. At sixteen he was travelling to Plymouth. He told his foster parents he was visiting his birth grandmother. Sometimes he did. But on every trip, he'd visit the Three Tonnes where he'd been told he could score. In no time he knew the Tonnes dealers and was running a line to Newquay. Twelve years later, he had replaced them.

Vince was the only Plymouth-born boy. He still lived with his parents in Saltash and though not the youngest of the crew, he was the least worldly. He'd been coming to the Tonnes since he turned eighteen, six years before but didn't sus that it was a dealers' pub until he met Benny. Sometimes Spikey wondered what Vince was doing in the gang at all, he seemed so naïve. Maybe he didn't have any other friends, anywhere else to go.

Dale was twenty-six and the Polperro connection, born

and bred. Like Port Isaac, it was pretty as a postcard and now dominated by tourism. Off season, there were not enough people to keep shops in business so he would travel to Plymouth once a month for supplies, including those he could get at the Tonnes. Steve and Dale had been the first to meet, a casual encounter at the bar months before. Dale had mentioned his boat and Steve had wanted to know more. When Dale told him about his van and cottage, all inherited from his late fisherman father, Steve wouldn't let him go. Dale knew about boats and the sea. He'd been out fishing with his dad for years before he recently died. For his part, Dale was interested in Steve's seemingly endless supply of weed and was happy to stick around so long as this continued. Steve always had weed and over time the others had drifted into his orbit, making small talk and sharing a puff in the pub garden. This was what Spikey had been looking for, people who respected him, who he could grow to trust, a crew he could roll with. One night they were all there together when Steve caught everyone's attention.

'I know you all like a bit of blow. How would you like to have your own regular supply and make some cash?'

And so, the gang was born. If there was a pecking order, Steve was at the top, Dale close behind, Vince at the bottom leaving Benny and Spikey bobbing in the middle. They might be young, but they lived in the squat and were in constant touch with the Plymouth drug scene. To Steve they each had their uses.

The next morning started according to plan. Steve and Benny set off at 8am, the others at 11am. Spikey had never sat so close to anything so valuable as the pile of bags in the back of the van. What if they got pulled over? What if they were in a crash? Dale listened to Radio 1 while Spikey tried to suppress his anxiety. He always felt it on these jobs. After two hours Dale took the slip road, pulling up in Michaelwood service station.

'Sit tight, I'll phone for the address,' said Dale slamming the door shut and heading for the telephones in the service station. Five minutes passed. Then he returned.

'Got it,' he said, waving a piece of paper. Spikey took a stretch but was quick and they were soon on the road again.

This was their fourth job together. Same game plan. Steve handled everything and gave them precise orders. They knew they were small cogs in a big logistical operation, but that was fine so long as there was enough reward to be worth the risk, and there certainly was. Each of them was promised £500 per operation which took place over three or four days. This was a lot of money for Spikey, even if the cargo was worth hundreds of times more.

It was mid-afternoon as they approached their turn-off, Junction 8 of the M5. They threaded through the suburbs for fifteen minutes. Their destination was an innocuous 1930s suburban semi-detached house. Dale reversed on to the paved drive, the van's rear doors facing the front door. A net curtain twitched. They got out of the van as the front door opened.

'Hello John, how good to see you,' said a man they had never seen before. He had the physique of a rugby player, a neat haircut and unfashionable leisure wear.

'Come on in. Let me help you with your bags.'

In seconds they were inside the front room with the cargo. It was a typical knock-through with a kitchen at the back. The sofa was positioned facing the fireplace with its back to the hall door and a coffee table before it. There was a kitchen off to the right. The bags were piled up on the other side of the coffee table.

'I'm Prop. Take a seat.' He gestured them to the sofa. 'Afraid I'm outa teabags. Right, let's look.'

Prop squatted by the bags. He carefully unwrapped the plastic to reveal a pile of cellophane bricks within each of the twelve bags. He picked one at random from each bag and put these on the table. Spikey was aware that other men had appeared, two from the kitchen and two in his peripheral vision standing at the hall door.

With a scalpel he pierced each block and scraped off a small amount, drawing in its odour with a deep breath, rolling it in his fingers and sampling it with his tongue. Giving nothing away, he weighed each block using a set of scales that already sat on the coffee table. Finally, he emptied the bags of their blocks and counted them. The room was silent except for the noise of his movements.

After what seemed an eternity, Prop looked up, turned his head from kitchen to hall door making sure he had his associates' attention and then turned his gaze on Dale and Spikey.

'It's short. Missin' a brick.'

Spikey turned his head to Dale. Dale didn't return the glance. He stared straight at Prop.

'Look mister, we've just done our job. We've brought it on shore, and we've brought it to you. We don't get to weigh and count between boats, and we don't get to open the bags. Maybe it went missing on the boat or even before that. I can just tell you it wasn't us.'

Prop stared.

'Wait here, I've got to make some calls.'

He left the room and went upstairs leaving them guarded on the sofa. No one spoke. The tension was palpable. Time passed. It was hot and stuffy. Spikey could sense the perspiration breaking on his forehead. As minutes passed, he felt droplets forming and slowly trickling down his face. Finally Prop came downstairs.

'Frenchie's not happy. You can go but we ain't payin' your fee.'

Spikey wasn't sure whether to be relieved that he might walk out in one piece or indignant that they weren't being paid. Steve would go ballistic. He had insisted they not leave until the fee was paid.

'You better speak to Steve,' said Dale. 'He told us not to leave till you've paid us the fee.'

'Frenchie will talk to Steve. You boys can go.'

No one moved. It was a stand-off. But it didn't seem like they had any options. Five hardened players against two minor cogs. After a few minutes Dale got up, Spikey followed and they left. It was ten minutes before Dale spoke.

'That went well, didn't it?'

They fell silent again, each in his own thoughts about how they would tell Steve what had happened. They were nearing the M5, but still in suburbia.

Dale pulled over by a phone box and rang Steve. Spikey sat in the van and watched Dale's facial expression as he spoke down the line.

'What's going on?' asked Steve.

'Don't know, Steve. The package was short. They held us responsible. Must've been skimmed at source or in transit. Maybe on the ship.'

'Or maybe you two thought you'd be clever. On the motorway.' Steve was fuming, looking for an explanation or a scapegoat.

'As if that's been the only window for it to disappear. Maybe Vince already had a look on the boat. Or maybe you had a little sleepwalk last night. It was all in your bedroom.'

Dale retaliated. He was the only one who dared stand up to Steve. He could read Steve's thoughts. Steve wouldn't want a fight with him, he was too valuable. He would be looking for another scapegoat.

'What about Spikey? Has he been alone with the package? Did you stop for a piss on the way up?'

Dale thought about it.

'Yeah, when I rang you for the address.'

'Listen up. Frenchie's not pleased. You're short-handed and our contract has been cancelled. We'll be lucky if that's the end of the story. These people take rip-offs very seriously, deadly seriously if you know what I mean. I've seen her make a man dig his own grave and put him in it. You better get back sharp and over to the Tonnes, soon as…'

Dale got back in the van, and they got back on the road.

'What was that about?' asked Spikey.

'Steve wants us back sharp. I think he suspects us. Or maybe you.'

'Don't be daft, Dale. Why would I rip Steve off?' asked Spikey feeling a rising panic. In a matter of minutes his sense of belonging and loyalty towards his mates had turned into fear as he felt the spotlight of blame landing on him. 'And if I had skimmed a block, where would I have hidden it?'

The rest of the long journey continued in silence. How could this have happened? It was an occupational risk that the gang were never able to stock-take on collection or delivery. So, there was no way of being sure that it had not been skimmed upstream: on the ship, or even before, but not even Steve could suggest this. It would be the end of his business. The gang would have to take the blame and in turn Steve would need a scapegoat. Spikey only knew for certain that he had not done it.

So, who else could it be? Benny was the one who had suggested opening the bags. Did his curiosity make him so obvious as to rule him out? Dale and Vince had been alone with the cargo on *Mousehole Cat* at sea. Each had a day bag they could have used to hide a block. They might have acted together, or alone when the other wasn't looking. Dale had also been alone in the van at the Michaelwood service stop. Or could it have been Steve himself? He had spent half the night alone with the stash in the back bedroom.

Whoever it was, even if it was an elaborate scam by Steve himself, he would be looking for a scapegoat. He would have to demonstrate internal discipline to maintain the confidence of customers up and down stream. Who was the weakest link? Not Dale. Steve needed his boat, cottage and van. What about Vince? Spikey couldn't imagine him having the nerve for a stunt like that and imagined Steve wouldn't either. The more he thought about it the more he felt the finger pointing at Benny and him, the younger and more expend-able members of the crew. And between them, Steve liked Benny's cheek. He would be safe. Spikey knew, he was for it. He felt devastated. He had just found his tribe and now faced expulsion. He wondered what Steve would do. Cripple him? Kill him? The more he thought about it, the more likely it seemed. He had to get away.

It was dark by the time they reached Plymouth.

'I gotta go to the squat before the Tonnes,' he said to Dale. 'Drop me and I'll meet you there'.

Dale nodded.

Ten minutes later, Spikey ran through the squat to his room. Panic gripped him as he rummaged through his stuff, cramming his few clothes into a holdall, pulling some photos off the wall, and leaving quick as he could. He reached the coach station. The last coach to London was leaving in ten minutes. Steve wouldn't find him there. The ticket queue was slow-moving, and he only just made it onboard.

As he watched the darkness roll by, he made a plan. He would find a pub scene, a punk crew, and ask for a sofa to crash on for a few nights, till he could discover a squat with a room and then pick up some hours of work. He had done it before in Plymouth.

The coach arrived in Victoria before sunrise. London still slept. He left the terminus and ventured along Buckingham Palace Road where a poster caught his eye. It advertised a free punk gig that night in the Salisbury pub, Green Lanes, near Manor House tube. He didn't have any better ideas so as soon as the tube opened, he found his way there. He emerged from Manor House station to find Finsbury Park located immediately next to it, through a tall red-brick pillared gate. With the whole day to kill, he went in and looked around. The sun was just rising. That early, he had it to himself. He saw a boating pond and cafe, broad tree-lined walkways, lots of open grassland and benches. He found one in a quiet corner and laid down to rest.

It was mid-afternoon when he woke. He hadn't meant to sleep but had been so tired. A group of teenage school kids were standing around him whispering dares about how to mess him up. He opened his eyes, swung his legs to the ground and stood up, making himself look as big as he could. They scattered. So, this was London. He needed to get off the streets and pinned his hopes on the gig. He wandered up to the cafe. A group of punks sat inside. Going in, his spiky hair and ripped jeans won him a couple of nods which he took as an invitation and joined them. Some were going to the gig that night, so he told them he had just arrived in

London and had nowhere to go. They invited him to come back to theirs after the gig. They lived in a squat nearby, in Wightman Road.

The plan had worked. He had escaped Jerrish and landed in Green Lanes, a bustling high street, buzzing with the sound of foreign languages, black, brown and olive as well as white skins, and colourful shop displays. It was so different to Plymouth: drab, monocultural, depressing and edgy, where to look different risked violence from musclebound sailors and skinheads who dominated the streets. Here he felt safe, exhilarated, and free. He hoped that this time he really had found his tribe.

# Chapter Two

**MARDIN, EASTERN TURKEY, 1979**

It was only 8am, but the modern town was already heating up. Its concrete buildings, glass-fronted shops and wide, car-filled roads, absorbed and radiated the heat, unlike the old town with its closely packed mud and stone houses and shaded narrow alleys that climbed up the hill to the castle. The modern street was busy with people making their way to work. Hasan was among them, in his mid-forties, average height and build, neat side-parted dark hair, a modest neatly clipped moustache, self-styled to go unnoticed. He went into a tobacconist, plate glass doors, glass-fronted counter, postcard carousel, marble floor to retain the cool against the day's rising heat.

'Good morning, Mustafa. A pack of Birinci please.'

'Morning to you, Hasan, last of the big spenders! Twenty Birinci coming up,' replied Mustafa turning from the counter to reach for these budget cigarettes from the floor-to-ceiling shelves. Though of similar age, Mustafa's appearance could not have been more different. He looked like a big, flamboyant hairy bear. He seemed to have modelled himself on some North American music star, maybe James Brown, with his gold chain and rings, blow-dried quiff and colourful, feminine clothes. It was almost comical, Hasan thought as he wondered if the man was homosexual. Hasan admired the courage that must be involved in choosing to stand out in a small conservative town. Hasan tried to get on with everyone and liked to think he was successful with this cigarette seller. Sometimes Hasan wondered if cigarettes were the only thing Mustafa sold from under his counter; maybe other things were available on request? Hasan's desire to get on was often tempered with caution and he sensed that behind his flamboyant appearance, Mustafa was not someone to trust or to cross. So, he always tried to keep their chats on safe ground. Football was safe. Today Mustafa beat him to it.

'Did you watch the game last night?'

'Oh yes,' Hasan replied, 'we gave Samsunspor a proper kicking!'

They had developed their acquaintance over recent months through football small-talk and their common passion for the nearest League team, Diyarbakirspor.

Another man joined them, appearing through a door in a corner of the shop. In his early twenties, tall, thin, with neatly clipped hair and crisply dressed, with a pallid complexion, an expressionless face and unsmiling mouth. A cold, hard young man, thought Hasan, forming his first impression.

'Hasan, this is my baby brother Bulent,' Mustafa explained.

'Some baby,' joked Hasan, nodding at the full-grown man. Bulent wasn't laughing.

'Good to meet you.' Hasan offered his hand.

Bulent took it. Hasan forced himself not to recoil from its cold, limp hold.

'Bulent just returned from military service.'

'Yes,' added Bulent. 'I am helping Mustafa in the shop until I work out my next move.'

'How did it go? The service?' asked Hasan, expecting the

moaning reply that most people would give.

'I really liked it. The camaraderie, discipline, sense of purpose, serving the motherland. We did our bit in the mountains fighting the terrorists.'

'Bulent is a patriot,' Mustafa added, as if some explanation was required. 'When I did my military service, we couldn't wait to get out, me and my friends,' he laughed. Bulent didn't join him. Hasan felt the tension.

'Well, yes, it is important to find purpose in your work, to feel it is worthwhile,' Hasan replied, feeling uncomfortable with this conversation and hoping to bring it to an end.

'You're not from round here, are you?' Bulent picked up on Hasan's accent. 'So where are you from? Your accent. It's...'

'Qamishli, over the border, friend,' interrupted Hasan, trying to avoid the possible direction of conversation.

'Hasan's a mechanic, working in Osman's garage,' Mustafa chipped in, as if to authorise Hasan's right to be there.

'Oh right,' continued Bulent. 'I am thinking perhaps to sign up again, as a career soldier. It is more meaningful to me than sitting in a shop all day,' taking a poke at his brother.

'Well, it was nice to meet you, Bulent,' Hasan extricated himself, 'Mustafa,' he gestured his farewell, closing the tobacconist door. How different these brothers were, he thought, reflecting on how wrong it is to assume all Turks were the same.

Hasan Güney was a Kurd from the small town of Qamishli just 67km away. He had travelled to Mardin two years before looking for work with his teenage son, Rasheed, after his wife had died in a car accident. Both towns were in Kurdistan, the region where Kurdish language and culture were prevalent among a majority, but they sat on either side of the Syrian-Turkish border. He found his own situation curious: to be a Kurd in Kurdistan but considered foreign on the Turkish side, undesirable on the Syrian side and a terrorist suspect by both state authorities. He was one of twelve million Kurds in Turkey. Here in Mardin they were in the majority.

Twenty metres down the road was Saladin's cafe where he often stopped for a coffee on the way to Osman's garage. His apprentice, Cetin, was already there; Turkish, eighteen, boyish face, curly black hair, athletic physique sitting at a pavement table sipping his coffee. Hasan joined him. He liked Cetin, his cheerful honesty, enthusiasm, the charming naivety of someone who had never travelled from the place of his birth; he reminded Hasan of his own eighteen-year-old son, Rasheed. They were both so young yet ambitious. It astounded him that even at their tender age, both were already engaged, Cetin to his teenage sweetheart Dilek and Rasheed to Dymphna, a young Irish nurse working in Mardin who he had recently met. He remembered himself at eighteen being excruciatingly shy with girls. He had been twenty-seven before he got married. He admired Cetin's ambitions: to qualify, get a good job, earn better money, and support a family. He was certainly proving to be a reliable, efficient, and competently skilled mechanic. His own son, Rasheed, wanted to be an engineer. He was enrolled at the Technical and Vocational High School and hoped to go to university.

'Another good night for Diyarbakir, eh?'

'Seems to be the morning's headline,' replied Hasan. He enjoyed watching football but the real reason he talked about it was that he had learnt it was a safe way to create bonds with other men. Even when it got heated, say with supporters of other teams, it remained within safe bounds, unlike his earlier exchange with Bulent. They often talked about football, families, relationships, music and movies, topics of no consequence. But as Hasan had grown to trust Cetin, they sometimes talked about politics too.

The encounter with Bulent was on his mind. It had reminded him that Cetin was a young man and that sooner or later he would get called up for his military service. This would disrupt the young man's dreams.

'Cetin, have you heard anything from the army recruitment office yet?'

'Not yet thankfully. I don't want to take a break in my apprenticeship here. And I don't want to end up fighting either. I don't understand the war or why these terrorists are fighting us.'

Hasan thought about how to respond. This was a sensitive topic, and he could find himself under arrest if he said the wrong thing but felt he could trust Cetin.

'You know, the government say that Kurds are 'mountain Turks' but in some ways, we are not Turks. We have our own language and culture.'

'But we are all Turkish,' Cetin replied, 'equal under the same flag. Why do Kurds dwell on differences rather than what we have in common?'

'My friend, many Kurds believe this was their homeland long before we had modern Turkey, that it was occupied for centuries by Ottomans, Arabs, Persians and now divided by Turkey, Syria, Iraq, Iran. Should our culture disappear? Should we become just like them? Imagine now if the Greeks invade Turkey and tell you the same. "There is no longer any Turkey, you are all equal Greeks under our government" and arrest you or worse for still speaking Turkish.'

This gave Cetin pause for thought. Conscious of Cetin's silence, Hasan decided it was time to change the subject.

'How's Dilek? You two love birds got any romantic plans for the weekend?' Hasan joked.

'I'm hoping for a picnic in some shady spot. She wants to make plans for the wedding.'

'Lucky man. She's a treasure. Don't lose her.'

Cetin and Dilek had met in school. He had liked her straightforward and down-to-earth approach, her self-belief which gave her confidence when she was asked to speak up in class by the teacher or needed to stand up for herself in the playground. He had finally worked up the courage to ask her out when they were sixteen, and they had been together ever since. Like Cetin, Dilek had known no other place but Mardin. She had enjoyed a happy childhood in this town where her parents ran a leather tailoring business. They made leather jackets and coats, selling them from their own shop premises as well as supplying wholesale to others. The business had been in the family for three generations. It was a comfortable life. She loved Mardin's cosmopolitan culture, the Kurdish and Arabic influences that she could hear in street chatter and taste in the food. The town had been a Silk Road trading post in between Ottoman and Persian empires and felt connected to worlds beyond, set amid the arid beauty of the surrounding countryside. Since leaving school Dilek had been working as a bank cashier. They dreamt of having their own home and raising their own family in Mardin. Dilek's parents were impressed by Cetin's ambition, drive and honesty, and imagined the family's growing reputation and influence in future years, when he eventually established his own garage. Her father secretly hoped that in time Cetin could be persuaded to abandon the garage plan and come to work in the family business. The family succession meant everything to them. For his part, Cetin secretly thought a lot about moving abroad – maybe Germany or the UK, where he could earn more money – but he had not yet dared suggest this to Dilek.

'We're setting the date for September, in four months,' continued Cetin. 'She's got so many relatives scattered across the country, even some abroad. Her parents want to invite them all. Not like my family! Just my uncle and a few cousins.'

Cetin's family was indeed small and beset with tragedy. Both his parents had also been from small families, and he had been an only child. By the time he was fourteen he had lost them both, first his father to a heart attack when he was ten, and then his mother to cancer. Since then, he had been taken in by his uncle. Cetin could not wait to get married and build a new family of his own.

'September is a fine month, getting a bit cooler. What you need for dancing,' joked Hasan.

They got up to leave, put some money for the coffees on the table and headed towards Osman's garage. They were half-way down the block when they were stopped by a patrol of three soldiers coming towards them, an officer and two others. Soldiers had been part of the daily street scene for as long as Cetin could remember, but in the last few months there had been a lot more of them and they had become much more active: patrolling, checking people's papers, operating roadblocks. Being so close to the Syrian border, Cetin had always suspected that Mardin must be a centre for smuggling. He had thought this increase must be a response to an increase in crime, that the army must be trying to arrest criminals and terrorists.

'Good morning,' the officer greeted Cetin and Hasan. 'Your identification cards, please.'

'Yes of course,' said Cetin as they both reached in their

pockets and produced their cards. The one in charge scrutinised the card photos and looked up at their faces, one by one, spending longer on Hasan's.

'You're Syrian? Kurd?' he asked.

'That's right, sir,' he replied, 'just on the way to work.'

'Empty your pockets.' The officer directed at Hasan, turning his back now on Cetin.

Hasan obliged and held out for inspection a wallet, the Birinci cigarettes and a lighter, some keys. The officer passed them to one of the soldiers.

'Turn around and put your arms against the wall,' the officer ordered, proceeding to frisk Hasan. When he had finished, the soldier returned Hasan's things.

'Stay out of trouble and remember you're lucky to be here,' said the officer, giving Hasan a hostile look.

'Yes sir, of course.'

The soldiers moved on. Cetin felt shocked. He looked at Hasan.

'You alright?' he asked.

'Of course, why?'

'The way he talked to you. It was like you were a criminal. And he left me completely alone.'

'Ha, Cetin, believe me. I'm used to it.'

Cetin had been asked for his ID card many times before but never searched, so this was his first close-up encounter. Hasan was not a criminal. At school they had learnt how Kemal Atatürk, whose portrait adorned every public building, had made everyone equal in the new Turkey; it was to be a stable, modern, secular state. With each school year they learnt more about these achievements: freedom of religion, equality for women, adoption of the Roman alphabet, democracy, and the importance of the army to protect these advances. So it jarred to see this prejudice.

'Cetin,' Hasan replied, 'the soldiers can see I am a Kurd, so they think maybe I am a terrorist. This is not the first time I have been stopped by soldiers, Turkish and Syrian. But life must carry on. Enough of this. It is better not to talk about it. Come, to work.'

The weekend came and Cetin picked up Dilek, picnic basket in hand. They headed for a shady grove close to the old castle which sat above the town. It was hot and noisy walking along the streets of the modern district, but once they started climbing the narrow alleys and stairways of the old quarter they were cooled by the shade of old, overhanging, mud-rendered buildings on either side. They were not the only ones with this weekend plan and plenty of other couples and families were already settled on blankets, under trees where they could find them, around the castle grounds. In places, children played hide-and-seek or football. There was a happy, holiday atmosphere. They found a spot and settled down.

'Mama and Papa have made a good deal with the best restaurant for the reception,' Dilek began, 'you know, the one with the roof terrace and amazing views. Is that good with you?'

'Yes of course, that's a great choice… Dilek, something happened this week. It unsettled me.'

'Tell me.'

'I was with Hasan, walking to work and we were stopped for our ID cards. Hasan is a good, law-abiding man. But the way they treated him… emptied his pockets, searched him, told him he was "lucky to be here". He had done nothing. Anyway, it upset me. You know I respect the army. But this was harassment.'

Although they were in love, they had not talked much about politics and now that Cetin had raised the subject Dilek opened up.

'I have noticed a lot more army on the streets recently. Maybe there's an increased terrorist threat. You know, the PKK.' she said.

The PKK or Kurdistan Workers' Party was a separatist organisation that had been fighting the government for years.

'There are loads of Kurds in Mardin,' said Cetin. 'Doesn't make them all PKK. Hasan is a Kurd and not a terrorist. Is that the way they treat all Kurdish people … like terrorist suspects?'

'I know. Sometimes it looks like a military occupation. If I was Kurdish it would make me angry. I would expect my Turkish friends to stand up for me. We have lived here all our lives, and now the tension is growing. Getting worse.'

Until now, Cetin had avoided sharing his thoughts about migrating, but the way the conversation was going, this seemed like the moment.

'Dilek, there is something I need to ask you. Would you consider moving away? I have been thinking for a while that we could make so much more money in Western Europe. So many have gone to Germany, Scandinavia or England. Look at the cars they bring back, the houses they can build with the money they send back. I could find work as a mechanic anywhere. I have been thinking about this for a while, but the army, the searches, the talk of terrorists all tell me to think harder… to make it a real option.'

Dilek was taken aback and sat in silence for minutes reflecting on his words.

'This is a lot to think about, Cetin. Maybe this is the beginning of a conversation. It would be a big shock for my parents. We can talk about this again. But now we should focus on the wedding.'

Through the following week Cetin carried on with work as usual and tried to think of other things, but the idea of moving away and starting a new life kept coming back to him. He noticed army searches now, each time he went out. Were they becoming more frequent or was he just more aware of them? He didn't know. It seemed that most of the people he saw being stopped were wearing traditional Kurdish trousers or hats. He knew it was only a matter of time before he would receive his own call-up papers from the army conscription office. He did not want to be one of these uniformed recruits sent out to stop and search ordinary Kurdish people. Until now he had accepted his civic duty to serve. But now it worried him. Meanwhile, he was more and more excited about the money they could earn abroad.

Then, on Tuesday, the peace was shattered. Cetin was in the garage pit, draining old oil from a car and Hasan was changing a tyre when they were startled by a loud thud. It had to be an explosion in the middle distance, loud enough to shock, far enough not to break their glass.

'A bomb,' Hasan called out running to the garage office. 'I must call the college to check Rasheed is safe.'

The aftershock of the explosion was now filling with the distant sound of sirens as emergency vehicles began to respond. A few minutes later Hasan came back.

'Rasheed is alright. The college is undamaged. Quickly. You must call your family and Dilek, make sure everyone is alright.'

It was Cetin's turn to run to the office.

When he returned, he nodded to Hasan with relief.

'Thankfully, all ours are safe,' said Hasan, 'but this is bad.

Probably the PKK. The war has come down from the mountains now and to the town. It will make life more difficult for everyone.'

'Is this why there have been so many soldiers and searches? Do you think the army knew this bomb was coming?'

'Cetin, the things we say must stay private. You can get in trouble for talking about this.' Hasan spoke quietly and with a sense of weariness and despair. 'It's a vicious circle. The PKK shoot soldiers and bomb the town. So, the army treat all Kurds like terrorist suspects. So, more Kurds turn cold towards their Turkish neighbours or join the PKK. Now, this bomb. Will it help the PKK or just increase army searches? Will it help anyone or just harden more hearts on both sides? How do we get out of this circle of discrimination and violence? Some want to leave the country altogether. My son Rasheed wants to go. He has an Irish girlfriend, a nurse, and he hopes they will go to her country. She wants to be closer to her family and now maybe away from bombs.'

'And you, Hasan, will you go too?'

'No, Cetin, I have learnt to keep my head down and smile. I will stay here and put up with the army searches. I have nothing to hide. I know who I am. If the soldiers want to search and humiliate me, they can get on with it without it touching my soul.'

The next day on the way to work, Hasan stopped as usual at Mustafa's to buy his cigarettes. As last time, Bulent was in the shop with Mustafa. Hasan gave his polite greetings, but the bomb overshadowed any attempt at small talk.

'It's not good for business,' grumbled Mustafa. 'People are scared to leave their homes for the shops.'

'It's bad for everyone,' agreed Hasan.

'The army will get them,' contributed Bulent. 'We just

need more patrols and searches. The terrorists cannot overcome the might of the Turkish army.'

'At times like this,' Mustafa continued, 'I think about moving on. Maybe abroad. Some import-export business in Europe and trade with connections here in Turkey. Running this shop, I've met plenty of people running all sorts of businesses in and around Mardin.'

'Where would you go?' asked Hasan, hoping Mustafa might give out some ideas that he could pass on to Rasheed or Cetin.

'I have to say, London always appealed. A centre of international trade and finance. An established Turkish community. A great music scene, you know I love all that. Yes, Bulent, you could run the shop for Papa.'

Hasan could see that Mustafa was playing with his brother and was only part serious about London. Bulent's was visibly bristling as Mustafa talked.

'But you know I'm going back to the military,' spluttered Bulent, seemingly unable to recognise Mustafa's teasing. 'Now more than ever, I am needed to help defeat these terrorists.'

'I need to be off to work. Good day gentlemen.' Hasan excused himself and slipped away, having no interest in their family games.

Cetin and Dilek met the following weekend.

'What a week, Cetin. That bomb. Thank goodness no one was killed,' she said.

'It's been difficult. I've been thinking a lot about our conversation, you remember, about maybe going abroad. And the bomb has magnified everything. I mean, we've lived here all our lives. Kurdish, Turkish, I never thought this mattered till now. But the military, the fighting in the mountains, now the bomb…will it be the last? I don't want to start our life together in a war zone with Kurdish and Turkish neighbours turned against each other.'

'You know, Cetin, sooner or later they will call you up.'

'Yes, and I am frightened of that. I do not want to fight. Hasan told me his son wants to go maybe to Ireland, his girl-friend's country.'

Dilek felt unsettled by this talk. Until now, her horizon had been the prospect of a settled family life close to the support of her extended family network in the beautiful town of her birth. But she understood exactly what Cetin was saying. Perhaps he was right, and their future really did lie overseas.

September approached. The couple spent their weekends making wedding plans and dreaming about their fami-ly-to-be. Dilek would work as long as possible before having children to save money for a house while Cetin would estab-lish himself as a skilled motor mechanic, eventually opening his own business. In their imaginary plans, they would have three children and at least one would go to university. But they could do all of this in another country.

The wedding was fantastic. Dilek's family hired the whole restaurant for the evening. Its spectacular rooftop terrace had views across the town and up to the castle. A sumptuous buffet was continuously available downstairs while people danced to live music on the terrace into the small hours. Cetin's guest list was modest given the smallness of his family and circle of friends, but Dilek more than made up for this through her extended family. Cetin estimated there were probably sixty guests, and he was grateful that her father was paying. He had invited Hasan and his son Rasheed, who quickly disappeared into the dancefloor crowd and was not seen for hours. Cetin circulated among the guests making small talk but soon found Hasan who sat alone downstairs close to the buffet.

'So, you finally did it, eh?' Hasan congratulated him.

'Yes, the beginning of our new life. I wanted to tell you, Hasan, we have decided to go. To England. We think it will give us more opportunities. It took a lot of discussion, but Dilek agrees that there will be more opportunities for us and, inshallah, our children.'

'I understand. There is a time for everything. And now is the time for you two love birds to leave your nest. The world is waiting.'

Cetin was always impressed and comforted by Hasan's calm and wise words.

'What is your plan? Where will you stay?' Hasan continued.

'Dilek has an aunt, Selma, who lives in London. We hope to start there.'

'How are Dilek's parents taking this news?'

'We haven't told them yet and they will be disappointed. We thought it would be better to wait until today is over before we tell them. They will say we are too young and worry what will happen to us. They may think they will never see us again and that they will miss their grandchildren growing up. But in the end, they will accept our decision. We can come back to visit them, and maybe we will come back to live here in the future.'

'Perhaps one day I will visit you too.' replied Hasan. 'I am thinking about leaving the garage and becoming a lorry driver. Long distance.'

'My home will always be your home, in whatever country. For certain we must keep in touch.' As they spoke, neither could imagine how their paths might cross in the future.

# Chapter Three

## HARRINGAY, LONDON, 1979

Selma and her Cypriot husband Cesme lived in a one-bedroom flat on Hermitage Road, near Finsbury Park and ten minutes' walk from Manor House tube station. Cetin and Dilek slept on their floor but got up before their hosts to be out of the way. From the first morning, Selma made coffee before going to work and offered them her local knowledge.

'This is a good area for Turks. Go to the end of the road, then turn right, you will see Harringay Stadium station and then the Green Lanes. You will see, Turkish bakers, halal butchers, mini-markets, social clubs, and if you ask around, job opportunities.'

'Thank you, Selma, we will use every minute of the day,' said Cetin.

'Meanwhile, Cesme and me, we will ask around for you too.'

Cetin and Dilek left the building with Selma and Cesme. At the end of Hermitage Road, before turning right, Finsbury Park caught their eye beyond busy lanes of traffic and behind concrete fence posts. The grass was a deep tone of rain-fed green, while huge ancient plane trees spread their branches over the road and shed their browning autumn leaves.

'Maybe we can visit the park later,' said Dilek remembering

their picnics together in Mardin, 'on the way back.'

'Yes, that would be nice.'

They turned right and soon found the Green Lanes. At first glance, it presented an English urban landscape: looking up they saw tall, redbrick buildings, some with elaborate white stucco features around the windows. They seemed old and had been quite grand when they were first built, but most were now quite shabby, with peeling paint, dirt-stained walls and grimy windows. At ground level, every building had a shop front. Walking up the road, more and more of these looked and felt Turkish. How amazing to see shop signs in their language. A supermarket brightened up the pavement with a fantastic colourful display of fruit and veg-etables, so beautifully arranged it could have been entered for a design competition. The familiar smell of fresh, warm Turkish bread came from Yaşar Halim, an enormous bakery, so popular it took up two whole shop fronts. And now they could hear Turkish being spoken around them: snippets of conversation from passers-by.

'Dilek, this is amazing,' said Cetin, 'here we will find com-munity. Here we will not be strangers.'

Some shop fronts were heavily curtained but with shop front signs with the names of Turkish football teams or towns. On these doors, other signs hung at door level in English, 'members only'.

'Wait here, Dilek, I'm going to see what goes on.'

Cetin stopped at one and went in. It felt immediately familiar, a men's social club like many he knew from Mardin. No women in sight. He was glad he had left Dilek outside. A wall-mounted TV played a video tape of some Turkish soap opera he didn't recognise, while groups of men sat at four or five tables, some playing backgammon, some drinking tea and chatting. The fug of tobacco smoke filled the room. Some looked up as he entered, one or two returned his nod of greeting. He quickly withdrew and closed the door.

'Men's club,' he reported to Dilek.

Walking on they counted seven such clubs, each behind a similarly abandoned-looking frontage. Cetin knew that one of these would welcome him and provide the openings he needed to get a job, but which one? Behind their doors, men came together around a common past: a hometown, a football team or political leanings and he expected it would not take long to pick up clues of these from overheard conversations, regional dialect, wall posters or the choice of Turkish newspapers on the tables to find where he would fit.

Within two weeks of sleeping on Selma's floor, Selma helped Dilek find work as an office cleaner. Dilek liked getting paid in cash and the job meant she did not need to speak to anyone. She could listen to her English lesson tapes on headphones while she worked. Meanwhile, Cesme found Cetin work in the Turkish supermarket where he stacked shelves and carried boxes. Two months later the couple had saved enough to put a deposit down with Stanhopes estate agent and moved into their own one-bedroom flat above a bookmaker on the West Green Road, close to Green Lanes.

Every day after work, Cetin would visit another of the men's clubs on the Green Lanes. After visiting all seven he had narrowed down his choice to Topkapi or Anatolia. Both had members from around Mardin, but he finally decided on Anatolia because the people seemed more friendly and there was more interest in talking about football. The club offered a place to meet others, the beginning of all opportunities.

In Anatolia he met Erhan, who told him about his work as a driver for the Turkish Food Company, TFC, and how to get a driving licence. Driving would take him one step closer to motor mechanics. Cetin thought of his old friend Hasan in Mardin and wondered if he had left the garage yet to become a driver. He smiled to think that once again they might be sharing the experience of their working day, albeit thousands of miles apart.

Over the coming months Cetin took driving lessons after his supermarket shifts, got his licence and with a good word from Erhan found work driving for TFC. While the Green Lanes was a Turkish hub, they delivered to shops scattered right across the city. With the help of his A-Z, he quickly got used to driving in London and loved visiting different shops. Each gave him new ideas for how to lay out produce and organise displays. He got to know many of the owners and managers too. Some never went beyond polite greetings, but others became friendly. The friendliest was Atalan who owned a supermarket on the West Green Road, not far from the Green Lanes. Atalan's shop had expanded to occupy three shop fronts and employed four people. Cetin was impressed by this success.

Meanwhile, Dilek moved on from office cleaning through a connection of Selma's. She found work sewing garments together at home for an Islington-based fashion company. They called it 'piece work' and she was paid for each finished garment. Every week a van would deliver boxes of pre-cut cloth sleeves, jacket bodies or bodices and she would sew them together using the machine they supplied. The boxes used up a big corner of their cramped living room and the machine took over their table. It was not well paid, but it contributed, allowed her to decide her working hours and didn't involve having to speak English in a workplace.

The months passed. When Dilek was not working, she

liked to walk the streets of West Green around the flat. The absence of armed police or soldiers made her feel safe. She knew there were gangsters and thieves here, just as in Mardin, but if the police were not frightened enough to carry guns, why should she be? She was fascinated by the cultural and ethnic diversity, how London was like a magnet drawing other different-looking people from all around the world. She felt something in common with all of them. This was a melting pot of foreigners, outsiders, who were all in it together. Somehow it made it easier to feel she belonged.

She liked the look of the houses, street after street of Victorian and Edwardian terraced houses, bay windows and porticos, red brick, and painted render. Here and there was a modern building where an old one had come down, but by and large the landscape had a feeling of heritage and solidity compared to the concrete of modern Mardin.

Her favourite place was Downhills Park, the sky so open, the grass so green, the trees so big and beautiful, so many facilities and free for everyone. There was nothing like this in Mardin. Whenever she had enough time and the weather allowed, she would walk there and spend time looking at the trees and flowers, deep in her thoughts and feeling close to nature, and through nature, close to her hometown. It was most beautiful in spring. She loved the pink and white blossoms on the fruit trees, the sticky pollens blowing off trees and then bright colourful flowers blooming in the planted beds. The natural beauty and the spring weather drew people into the park in numbers. The buzz of chatter, the laughter of playing children all reminded her that life was good.

Their first child, Onur, was born in 1982. Although this gave them joy, it increased their financial needs. The piece work allowed her to keep working, sewing whenever Onur slept while Cetin continued driving for TFC. Their second child, Emine, followed in 1986 just as Onur started at nursery school. Cetin was tiring of the driving job, but returning to a mechanical apprenticeship would leave them short of money. He imagined there was more money in retail and he now dreamt of setting up his own supermarket. He knew he would be successful. Through his delivery visits he had seen a lot of good and bad ideas in shops and was confident he could apply the best of these in one place. His chance came one day 1987 during a delivery to Atalan.

'Come in for a coffee, Cetin,' the owner insisted.

In the back office Atalan told him, 'Cetin, I need more help running the shop. All my relatives are already here or working elsewhere. I have run out of family! But I think you are smart, and I like your ambitions. So, think about it and let me know.'

The next day Cetin gave notice to the TFC and the following week joined Atalan in the shop. 'Moving on, Hasan,' he thought to himself, imagining he was in telepathic communication with his old friend in Mardin, 'perhaps you have too.'

In 1988, Dilek gave birth to their third child Mehmet. Cetin worked hard for Atalan and had begun to feel like his business partner. He contributed to the shop's success by bringing in ideas he had seen in other shops. He rearranged the shelves, improved the colourful displays of fruit and vegetables outside the shop front, introduced a loyalty card and weekly special deals for regular customers. As the shop prospered, so he earned more. He felt proud and rewarded by his work. His youthful garage ambition now seemed a distant dream.

One day in November 1989, almost exactly ten years after arriving in Britain, Cetin brought home a gift for Dilek.

'My love, come sit, I have something for you,' he said.

They settled together on the small sofa. Cetin had never been happier in his life. Before him, seven-year-old Onur was doing kick-ups with a plastic football on the carpet in front of them, trying to keep it from touching the ground with small, controlled foot flicks; Emine pushed some little cars across the floor getting under Onur's feet. Family chaos. At least Mehmet slept peacefully in a crib next door in the bedroom.

'What is it, Cetin? You should not waste your money on gifts for me,' she said, but was secretly thrilled.

He placed a wrapped gift in her hands.

'Open it,' he said.

It was a teapot.

'That's lovely, we can all enjoy this together,' she smiled. 'Shall I put the kettle on?'

'Yes, but first look inside.'

She took the lid off the pot. Inside was a key.

'Our new home,' he said, 'Three bedrooms and a small garden. Room for the children to play. For us and our daughter to have our own bedrooms. I collected the key from Stanhopes today.'

Dilek was lost for words, brimming with joy. Tears came to her eyes.

'Remember our dreams?' He continued, 'To have work, three children and a home of our own? We have done this, in a new country with a new language. It has taken the last ten years. Just imagine, what we can do in the next ten.'

The next day Cetin took Dilek and the children to visit their new home, a three-bedroom house in St Margaret's Road, a quiet street of terraced houses like the ones Dilek admired during her walks off Philip Lane, not far Downhills Park. Each house had its own front door and a little front space, some with hedges or flowerpots, others just dustbins.

They would have a whole house, their own front door, and a garden for the children to play. They were planting roots in this new country. Cetin was so happy and proud of their achievement.

'Here we are, children, our beautiful new home,' Dilek said as they went through the front door. She offered them smiles and reassurance that a better new life would begin. But her inner voice was troubled. Could they earn enough to keep up the rent on this bigger place? And the more comfortable life became, the more rooted they would become. What would it mean for her children to grow up without grandparents, so far away from her culture or knowing their hometown of Mardin?

# Chapter Four

## KURDISTAN TO LONDON, 2000

Arjan was at school when he heard the shooting. Gunfire. Some children started screaming with fear. Others seemed to go into a paralysed daze. Arjan felt fully functional but experienced a strange sense of detachment from his body, as if he was now looking down upon the classroom scene from above. It was like watching an action movie but scarier. The teacher told all the children to get under the tables while he closed the window shutters. The gunfire got louder. More of it. Separate shots, continuous shots of machine guns. Then there were big bangs, explosions in the streets. One very loud and close. The window glass shattered. The walls shook. More children were screaming. Some sobbing.

'Stay under the tables,' the teacher shouted, 'you will be safe.'

Ten minutes, half an hour, forty-five minutes, it continued. And then it stopped almost as suddenly as it had started. Dust seeped through the shutters and filled the warm air in the classroom. The teacher cautiously got up from under his desk and walked to the shutters, opening one a fraction, then fully.

'You can come out now, children, from under the tables. Let's call our names and see if everyone is alright.'

As they gathered around him and he checked each of them for injury, anxious parents were arriving at the school door to collect their children. One by one they left. Then Arjan's brother, Kalil, came. His clothes were covered in dust. Arjan ran to his arms and Kalil hugged him. Hand in hand, they went out onto the street. Arjan saw some houses were destroyed but the school was miraculously untouched. He could see people moving around the streets. Some carrying stretchers, some with spades digging in the rubble of destroyed houses.

'It is very bad, Arjan,' Kalil said, with a lump in his throat, 'the worst.'

Without asking, Arjan understood and emotion flooded up from a deep inner well. When they got home, they found their mother, Fatima sitting on a chunk of rubble, once part of their house wall, grey with cement dust, wailing hysterically, holding her hands to heaven. Kalil and Arjan hugged her, attempting to console her, supporting her yet holding their own grief. Somewhere beneath the rubble, their father and sister. In that moment, eleven-year-old Arjan was robbed of his childhood.

Their sleepy Kurdish village was close to the border town of Qamishli in northern Syria. From time to time, it warped into a war zone under attack from army incursions by Turkish or Syrian national armed forces, looking for Kurdish separatist fighters. Both governments thought this necessary to prevent the creation of an independent Kurdistan which neither wanted. This time the army had shelled and shot at the village without entering.

Within days the dead were buried in the hilltop cemetery on the edge of the village. After the funeral, Arjan lingered, looking at the rows of graves. In a deeply spiritual and revelatory moment, he saw not just his own loss but that of others, generations of elders who had lived and died here, many dying by violence. He saw his tragedy as part of a long historical trajectory. As he looked out beyond the cemetery, the arid landscape stretched out as far as the eye could see. A patchwork of fields, scorched by the sun to shades of yellow and brown. Every so often a grove of trees broke the monotony in the shimmering heat. How small we are and how short is life, Arjan thought as he scanned this vast landscape.

Their neighbours offered them shelter. They all slept on the kitchen floor. They survived by the kindness of others while Fatima and Kalil talked through what they could now do. Their priority was to make sure Arjan would be safe from anything like this happening again. They decided to send him out of the country. Fatima would ask her brother Hasan to help. He had moved to Mardin, over the border in Turkey many years ago, and his son Rasheed, Arjan's grown-up cousin, was now in London. They would ask if he could go there. Hasan could help arrange the journey. He knew people who could fix it. And Rasheed could take care of Arjan once he arrived. Fatima rang Hasan who in turn rang Rasheed. She knew it was a lot to ask of them. Rasheed and his wife had only met Arjan once, many years ago. But they were family. In a few days it was agreed, and Fatima went into Qamishli to transfer all her savings to Hasan's bank. She would be eternally grateful to them all. The following Monday, Arjan travelled by bus, north to Mardin.

He arrived at dusk. It was a warm May evening. Mardin was bigger than Qamishli and much bigger than his village. The old town spilled down a hillside from a high castle, a warren of narrow alleys and stairways, built centuries before the invention of cars. The ancient buildings on either side created welcome shade from the summer heat. Spread out below the hill was the modern town, looking much as in Syria, a mix of older houses and modern apartment blocks, shopping streets and small factories. The main difference was that all the street signs were in Roman script instead of Arabic so he couldn't read them. And the money was different too. He carried his school back-pack with a change of clothes. Hasan met him at the bus station. Arjan wasn't sure if he would remember his uncle, it been so long since they last met.

'Arjan, my boy, how you have grown,' he heard in Kurdish and turned to see a man approaching him on the bus platform. His uncle Hasan.

'Good journey? Come on, let's get you home. How is your mother? And Kalil? I have a truck, not a car so I have borrowed this one to collect you.'

The borrowed car had seen better days and seemed out of character with this neat and tidy uncle. It was bashed, dented and badly needed a wash. The upholstery was ripped and sticky. The windows were jammed, leaving only a narrow open gap. Exhaust fumes seeped into the cabin and Arjan craned towards the gap for air.

'Sorry about this crate. It belongs to a friend. Another truck driver. I think he spends too much time in the truck and forgets how to look after this little darling!' he joked.

Fortunately, they soon reached Hasan's apartment. They could have walked. He didn't understand why Hasan had brought a car at all. Maybe he expected Arjan would have more bags. The apartment was small and cramped but Hasan seemed content living alone. Arjan slept on cushions on the living room floor. For the next few days, while Hasan went to work, he wandered around Mardin, exploring the alleys of the old town, watching life pass by, traders in the market, craftsmen in their workshops, the social buzz of street cafes, children walking to and from school. Communication was not a problem since many people spoke Kurdish and some even spoke Arabic being so close to the border. But he was scared, just a child, barely eleven years old, who had lost his home, school and family. He felt alone in a dangerous and unknown world. Why had his mother sent him away? He wanted to be at home, even if he had to face the dangers of war. At least he would be with his family.

Meanwhile Hasan arranged Arjan's transport to Britain. Arjan had been told that Hasan started out as a mechanic but then bought his own truck, driving cargoes all over Europe including Britain, before buying more and setting up a business. He had developed many connections and left the driving to others these days.

Fatima had told Arjan about an accident. Hasan had been driving the family in a car when the driver of an oncoming bus had suffered a heart attack at the wheel. The bus had crossed into the opposite lane and forced Hasan off the road into a tree. The accident had widowed him and he had never forgiven himself, although everyone told him it had not been his fault. He had been left to bring up his twelve-year-old son, Rasheed, alone. That was twenty-seven years ago. Since then, Rasheed had gone to Ireland, married his Irish girlfriend, had a daughter, and then they had all moved to London. Arjan knew that was where he was going.

'What's Rasheed like?' asked Arjan. 'And his wife?'

'Rasheed is a kind and decent man. Hard-working. He is an engineer now, fixing trains and railway tracks around London. It gives him good money. He will look after you. His wife is a nurse. Also, kind and decent. Maybe that is why they love each other. She was working here in Mardin, in the hospital, when they first met so she speaks some Turkish and Kurdish. And they have a daughter a little older than you. They will be your new family. Shereen will be your big sister. You will be safe, have a better education and more opportunities than in Qamishli.'

In the evenings Hasan took Arjan to street cafes to eat, in the cooling air.

'You will like London,' Hasan told him, 'I have been there many times. I have carried melons, almonds, olive oil, even livestock to Britain. London is a place of opportunity if you are brave enough to look for it. In Tottenham there are many Turks and Kurds. West Green, Wood Green. Green Lanes. You will find friends.' Arjan felt reassured.

After two weeks Hasan told him it was time to go. They drove in his friend's battered car to a walled, gated enclosure on the edge of town. The gate was opened by a man, Fahid, who greeted Hasan and then with a hug they said goodbye. Arjan felt so alone as he watched Hasan drive away. Inside the enclosure, a house, and some outbuildings. Fahid led Arjan into the house. There he met others, about fifteen men, no women, sitting on low cushions with their backs against the wall, some smoking or fidgeting with worry beads. Most smiled on seeing he was a child. Some introduced themselves and tried to make him feel at ease, while others were more reserved. He tried to remember their names but lost track after Tarik, Ahmed, Mo and Abdul. Maybe he would remember others with time. All were Syrians and some were Kurds like him. Food was brought in and put on a low table in the centre of the room, salad, pitta, hummus, and falafel. Arjan's hunger was muted by fear of what lay ahead.

The next morning Fahid woke them. It was late morning.

'Brothers and sisters,' he said, 'now you take this phone number and this money for bus tickets. You travel separately. You do not know each other, but you, little one,' he looked at Arjan, 'you travel with him,' pointing to Mo, one of the names he had remembered.

The man smiled. 'Hello little brother, my name is Mo.' He offered his hand. 'We will stick together.'

'First you go to Ankara,' Fahid continued, 'It is a twelve-hour journey. The bus leaves at 6pm tonight. When you get there, you buy a ticket to Edirne. Another seven hours. When you get there, you can meet again in the bus station cafe. Then one of you ring this number. Someone will come to find you.'

At first the Ankara bus felt luxurious. Arjan sat next to Mo. The others spread themselves out among the other passengers. It was a big, air-conditioned coach with plush upholstered seats. There were two drivers who would take turns. They played loud Turkish pop music over the speakers and every couple of hours one of them would walk up the aisle with a cologne spray to freshen up passengers. They chatted as they sat together.

'So, what's your story, Arjan?' Mo asked. 'How does a child come to be travelling to London alone?'

Arjan told Mo about the attack on the village, his father and sister, and his family's plan to send him to safety.

'I am sorry that children so young must experience these horrors.'

'And why are you travelling to London, Mo?' asked Arjan.

'Well, if I do not go, life will be dangerous for me. It is not safe to speak against the government in Syria, and I have done too much. I am a journalist. It has been my job. But now the police want to arrest me. If they find me, they will make me disappear.'

'So, you will make yourself disappear first,' joked Arjan. Mo laughed.

'Exactly.'

'And what of the others? Do you know why they are here? What about Abdul, Tarik and Ahmed?'

'Everyone has their reasons, Arjan,' said Mo quietly, 'Abdul says he hopes to make money in London, to send back to his family. Tarik's like me, he fears the police. He told me he was arrested five times this year. He is a trade unionist.'

'What's that?'

'Trade unions try to get better wages for their members in factories. And Ahmed's the same as you, a Kurd escaping war in the north.'

Arjan quietly reflected on what he heard. He had not realised that there were so many reasons that people wanted to leave Syria. He hoped he was going to a happier, safer place and that he would not have to escape like this again.

After four hours it was dark as the bus stopped at a roadside pit-stop, a wooden stall shaded during the day by a canvas canopy hanging from a wooden structure and illuminated at night by a string of lightbulbs. They could buy lahmacun pizza slices or watermelon and use a toilet. Back on the road, the glamour of the bus was wearing off. Arjan couldn't lie down and couldn't sleep sitting up as they rolled on for another eight hours with just a couple more stops.

The sun was rising as they reached Ankara, huge compared to Mardin. He had never seen so many tall buildings, roads, and cars. At Ankara bus station, they bought tickets for Edirne on the Greek border, seven hours away. The bus left at midday. They arrived in the early evening and gathered in the bus station cafe as instructed. One man rang the telephone number for the group. After an hour they were collected in a minibus and driven to a warehouse on the edge of town. They slept on the warehouse floor. Arjan was so happy to lie down and stretch out, he did not notice the hard ground. In the morning two women came with food and coffee. They ate and then washed in the warehouse toilet. They didn't have to wait long. An hour later, a lorry pulled into the warehouse, and all fifteen were herded into a hidden compartment, a smuggling chamber behind a partition in the back of the lorry.

'How will we all fit in here? Where can we sit? How will we relieve ourselves?' Arjan whispered to Mo, feeling panic rise within him.

'We use the bucket. It is only a few hours,' replied Mo pointing to a metal pail. 'Think of the safety that waits at the end of the journey.' And with that Arjan squeezed himself into a tight space between the adult travellers. The lorry set off. It crossed the border into Bulgaria and, four hours later, reached Sofia.

They stopped in another warehouse on the outskirts of the city. This time they waited for nearly two weeks, time enough to recuperate and prepare for the next leg of the journey. Arjan and Mo spent time together talking and he started to think of the older man as a father figure.

'You are lucky to have family in London,' Mo told him. 'They will look after you'

'What of you, Mo? When we reach Britain where will you go?'

'I have connections. London has many Arab and Kurdish people. I have addresses to find them.'

'I hope we stay friends,' said Arjan.

'Always,' replied Mo reassuringly. Arjan wondered if Mo

had children but was afraid to ask.

Eventually another lorry arrived, and they were guided into another smuggling chamber for a ten-hour journey across Serbia and Hungary to Austria. This chamber was more spacious than the last and as it was not his first, Arjan was more relaxed as he nestled into a corner and mentally prepared himself for the journey: the cramped immobility, body heat, terrible ventilation, minimal food and water, the bucket toilet. The driver stopped every few hours to rest and if he found a secluded spot he opened the doors, emptied the bucket, and replenish their supplies. This journey ended at another warehouse, somewhere in Austria, where they waited two more days for the next transport.

By now they knew exactly what to expect. This final lorry ride to Calais would take thirteen hours. It turned out to be the worst. As it brought them closer to Britain, conditions in the chamber deteriorated while their emotional journey neared its climax. Their excitement grew as they imagined the lives they would enjoy, high wages and plentiful work, tolerance for religions and political freedom, the cool climate and abundant rain, a land of opportunity. But alongside the excitement, their anxieties grew. The stakes were raised with each passing hour. To be caught and turned away at the last, having come so far, would be more painful than failing at the earlier stages of the trip. They had heard that the UK immigration police used dogs to find stowaways. Would they be caught and sent back? Would the traffickers cheat them?

Arjan listened to his companion's chatter. Some dwelled on hope and others on fears. What Mo had said was true: he was lucky to have family in London. Fatima had told him that he had met his cousin, though he barely remembered. About seven years before, Rasheed, Dymphna and their daughter

Shereen returned to visit Hasan in Mardin, and they had all crossed the border to visit the family in Qamishli. Arjan had been just four, Shereen six. Now Rasheed and Dymphna were expecting him in London. Would Rasheed recognise him?

Then everything happened at once. The lorry slowed to a crawl and as the engine noise lowered, they could faintly hear new sounds outside. The bleeping of lifter vehicles or reversing lorries, clanks and bangs of enormous quayside chains, the faint squawking of seagulls, the scraping sounds of a metal gangway against a stone pier. The lorry engine stopped. It felt as if time stood still. The silence was thick, mixed with fear, body heat and stale air. Each imagined what was happening just beyond the metal partition of the container. An army of officials with all the tools at their disposal, hunting them? Like cats hunting mice? The engine started again, the lorry edged forwards, climbed a ramp and then a new sensation: a slight rocking of a ship in water.

The crossing was awful. What had started as a gentle side-to-side movement became a violent three- dimensional plunging and lurching in the open sea. Instead of the restricted trickle of fresh air, all they could smell now through the ventilation grille was the odour of diesel mixed with the foul smell of their own vomit. But there was no way out, no way back. He tried to focus all thoughts elsewhere. He was in his grandfather's beautiful olive grove. It was hot, around midday, a clear blue summer sky. He saw the olive trees, the beauty of their old, gnarled trunks, looking like deformed and fantastic statues; the gathering ripeness of the olives, and in a nearby grove of oranges and lemons, fruit growing and turning to full colour; the fragrances of wild rosemary and lavender, the background sounds of crickets, of rustling leaves in the stirring breeze. His family were all there, even his father and sister, sitting on blankets in the shade under the largest tree, a picnic spread before them. They told stories, taking it in turns, laughing and clapping each other in appreciation of the entertainment. He got lost in each story, imagining their voices. A beautiful way to spend a summer day. Arjan wrapped himself in this dream as if in a blanket on a freezing night. Hours must have passed. And then the lurching stopped. The sounding of the ship klaxon, the unwinding of heavy chains, the hull clunking against the quay. Waiting. Then the lorry engines started. They moved. Down the ramp, on to firm land... and then the engine was turned off again. More waiting. Everyone was alert. The final hurdle approached, getting past UK Immigration and Customs. They sat still and silent for about twenty minutes, their minds filled with fear. And then the lorry engine started, very slowly moving on through several chicanes as if on a go-kart track until it straightened out and gradually picked up speed.

Half an hour later the lorry stopped, the doors were opened, and they were led out into a warehouse on an industrial estate. It looked old and some of the buildings were derelict. It must have been close to the road as there was a constant background noise of motorway traffic. It was blissful, to stand and walk, to breathe fresh air, to be in Britain. The driver brought them food and water, showed them a toilet they could use. Their long journey was nearly over. That evening they settled back into the smuggling chamber for one last time and were driven for a final two-hours to their destination in London. For the last time, the lorry slowed, the engine was switched off and they heard the clang of closing warehouse doors. The lorry doors opened, crates were shuffled, and their compartment opened.

As Arjan and Mo clambered out of the lorry, stretching their legs and breathing fresh air deep into their lungs alongside their companions, they hardly dared believe they had reached the journey's end. They looked around this warehouse. It was like all the others they had seen, with a vehicle area, a loading bay and, behind this storage space, some rows of shelved boxes and some open crates of watermelons.

'Welcome to London,' said the driver, 'You are in Edmonton, north London. You can use the toilet,' he pointed towards the rear of the storage area, 'and then you are on your own.' He handed out a photocopied map of the area to everyone.

The little group of travellers would forever be bonded by their experience of the journey but now had to go separate ways and follow their own plans. Mo stayed with Arjan.

'I'm in no hurry, little brother, let's see you safe before I go.'

Together they walked out into an unknown city with no English words or money but some coins for a phone call. Arjan had Rasheed's phone number and so they looked together for a public telephone, but when they found one it was broken. So, they just walked. It got dark. The air was fresh and cool. They followed the main road, hoping it was leading towards the centre. Arjan was struck by the number of cars and how mixed up the buildings were: new with old, big with small, housing with shops and offices. After about half an hour they were filled with joy to see Arabic writing above a kebab takeaway. They would ask these people to let them use a phone, and so it was that Arjan rang Rasheed. An hour later they both sat in Rasheed's car driving through the streets to safety, telling him about their journey, switching between Kurdish and Arabic, Mo's mother tongue. Rasheed had been brought up trilingual and enjoyed this nostalgic language switching as much as hearing the drama of their story. He was grateful to Mo for minding Arjan and offered to drive him to his first address on the Green Lanes. When they got there it was buzzing, even at this time of the evening. Arjan felt strangely at home seeing the mini-markets brightening the street with stacked colourful displays of fruit and vegetables, the sight of women wearing hijabs and dark-skinned moustached men, flat caps and even some baggy Kurdish trousers. As Mo got out of the car they promised to keep in touch. Then he disappeared into the streetscape.

Rasheed's home was a flat in Debden, a block on the Broadwater Farm estate in Tottenham. Arjan was so happy and grateful to be with them, and they were pleased that they could offer their hospitality. He would sleep on the sofa in their living room. Shereen was at Park secondary school, a short walk from home, so they planned to enrol him there.

Arjan's first few days were an emotional roller-coaster. There was the huge relief of the journey's end, the gratitude for safety with his newfound family, excitement about this new environment, buildings the like of which he had not seen before, the cooler climate, languages he did not understand. And then there was anxiety and sadness: how would he manage in a new school without speaking English, would people be kind, would he find friends, how long could he stay with Rasheed, were his mother and brother alright? He missed them so much.

Shereen did her best to make him feel welcome too. Although she spoke English, she had learnt some Arabic, Turkish and Kurdish from her father. How was his journey? What music did he like? What clothes labels or trainers did he like? Day by day he opened up to them and felt safe and cared for.

He wrote to Fatima to say he had arrived safely. He was so happy a month later to receive a reply. They were still in the village. Their neighbours had helped them repair the roof and walls sufficiently to move back into their home while a complete repair would take many more months. The Turkish army had pulled back, but Kalil had gone, she didn't write where, but Arjan guessed he had joined the PKK. His old world seemed a million miles away. His new family were kind, but he was worried. How easy would it be to get used to a new school, make new friends, and be happy in this new life? Would he ever see his mother again?

Part Two

# LIVES
# COLLIDE

**2001-2002**

# Chapter Five

**WEST GREEN**

Lucas Fairbright enjoyed his job as an estate agent in Tottenham's West Green. He liked to think he was helping people fulfil their dreams of owning their own home, while helping sellers make a profit from London's spiralling property market. Everyone was a winner while he earned his commission whichever way the market went.

He had eventually got lucky. Back in 1979 and just off the bus, he had spent four months looking for work, going door to door but getting no offers. Everyone said they already had family and friends to work for them, and in any case his hair and clothes seemed to put people off. So, eventually he had trimmed his spikes and bought some smart casuals from a charity shop. His squat mates hadn't recognised him at first and thought it was hysterical. From now on, they joked, Spikey would be the one to talk to the police when the neighbours complained about their loud music. He tried job hunting again with a new level of confidence. Stanhopes estate agency was the third shop he tried on the West Green Road. Jack Job, the manager, liked him straight away and Lucas found himself appointed as a trainee sales agent.

Twenty-two years later he was still there and now a partner in the business.

It was a bright late summer's morning, as Lucas left his house in Crossfield Road and walked south through Downhills Park. He loved this time of year. The trees still full of foliage, flowers still offering colour and daylight hours still allowing outdoor evenings. His path ran parallel to Belmont Road, separated from its busy traffic by a border of tall shrubs and a brick wall topped with old iron railings. To his left, he surveyed the expanse of grassy playing field, a couple of goalposts set up for official matches. Sometimes they were replaced by rugby posts. Who put them up? He had no idea. Off to the left, on the northern edge and now over his left shoulder, the old changing rooms, a gloomy, flat-roofed, redbrick structure, metal grilles over the high slit windows, although these were no defence against the more likely criminal danger of getting graffitied. Does anyone ever use it, he wondered? Beyond the field, lines of magnificent mature trees. A few people, like himself, moved across the landscape. He spotted a couple of dog-walkers, someone jogging, an old woman walking slowly with the aid of a stick. Nevertheless, he felt as if he had the park to himself. The sense of space calmed him, the grass and trees connected him to nature. His daily walk to work was a breeze, the hardest dilemma being whether to walk the pavement or the park. Life was good. He smiled to himself.

As an estate agent he had learnt that parks and open spaces were a definite plus for property values and that Downhills was the jewel in the crown of West Green neighbourhood. Its playground and the sense of space and fresh air, were a big attraction for young house-hunting couples and families. The remnants of a grander past, the pillared entrances, balustrades, terraces, and the formal Italian garden of the now-demolished Downhills House added charm and character. According to his mental map, the park sat at the centre of the area, like a village green, with the network of streets built around it. He had researched the local history. Just one hundred and fifty years before he would have been walking through a landscape of fields, woods, and streams. But the extension of railways from London to Tottenham from the 1860s, including the 1878 Palace Gates line with a station at West Green, had changed the landscape forever. Developers had bought up farmland, streets were laid out and houses built. He had memorised the facts in case a house buyer should ask about the area's history, which they sometimes did. In 1902, Tottenham's Urban District Council, bought Downhills House to preserve some open space for the 'physical recreation and spiritual well-being' of the growing population. It was a Georgian manor with a formal Italian garden, fountain, ornamental trees, balustrades and terrace, shrubbery, rockery, and hornbeam avenue. They had demolished the house but maintained the grounds and woodlands. These now formed the eastern side of the park, together with new tennis courts, playgrounds. Meanwhile, they purchased the neighbouring field as a recreational ground which now made up the western side of the park. The two halves were divided by a footpath, 'Midnight Alley', running north to south between what were now Downhills Park and West Green Roads.

His path reached the end of the park and swung left to follow the southern boundary, beside a tall metal fence and Park School beyond. This led to a park gate and the remnants of the original West Green, a lonely triangle of grass and war memorial, cut off by busy roads. Turning right, he passed the

Black Boy pub – he wondered why the name hadn't changed in this day and age – and an old disused cinema long since repurposed as a shop selling second-hand office furniture. He'd gone inside once. The floor still sloped as designed to help cinema goers see the screen over other people's heads. Other shops came next: fried chicken , a newsagent, dry cleaner's, electrical repairs, a car parts shop. He navigated around a heap of black refuse sacks piled against a lamppost and a dumped armchair sitting mid-pavement like a surreal throne bizarrely washed up on an urban shore. Passing a betting-shop window, he risked a vain glance at his reflection. It gave him a sense of satisfaction, clean-shaven, high cheekbones, strong jawline, hair cut tightly on the sides and layered on the top. Not bad, he thought, for nearly forty. He looked forward to a caffeine hit. Two minutes later he reached the office and stepped inside.

'Morning, Jack,' he greeted his boss. Jack Job, twenty years older and five stone heavier than Lucas, a wry man-of-the-world, pale-skinned with slicked-back greying hair.

'Sorry I'm late, lunchbox issues,' said Lucas, feeling the need to explain himself.

Lucas loved his children, but every morning was a runaround. Parenthood had introduced him and his wife Mollie to the morning routines of getting two children as well as themselves ready for the world: out of bed, washed, fed, given their lunchboxes and sent to school. Now that Ned was thirteen and Joe ten, he and Mollie had it down to a smooth routine...on good days. But there were always curveballs, like getting Ned out from under the covers, child illness, running out of packets of crisps or the occasional midweek hangover. Mollie studied architecture in central London and on lecture days was also out of the door early.

Ned and Joe. He often thought about how children change your life. One day you're young, the centre of your own world, mapping out your own dreams and spending your time doing what you want, looking after only yourself; and the next, your days are filled with the needs of others, especially little people who can't do anything for themselves. Your earlier dreams fade, your centre shifts, though you do it out of choice and love. At thirteen, Ned thought he knew everything, didn't need his parents, pushed every domestic boundary while demanding designer brand casual wear and electronic goods just to keep up with his peers. Ned was hard work, but Lucas understood. He remembered Ned's earlier years: his love of physical play, climbing, football and they had loved to play together in the park. Chasing him around the playground being a scary monster, standing nervously under the monkey bars to catch Ned if he fell, up the climbing frame and down the slide together, knocking a ball around on the vast expanse of field even on waterlogged winter days. Until gradually Ned's friends replaced him as playmates and Lucas found himself playing a different type of parent. Joe was born soon after, but no second-born can shake off the shadow of their older sibling all the way to adulthood. Joe wanted to join in but was inevitably smaller and less proficient at playground games. As time passed, he became a quieter, more thoughtful child and preferred the indoors. Now in Year 6 he was happier than ever before, at last one of the oldest and biggest in the primary school. He was shining and thriving, free of Ned's shadow. Lucas found it poignant knowing that this time couldn't last and next September he would transfer, once again to be one of the youngest and smallest in the big school. Perhaps then having a big brother might prove useful.

'Ah, parenthood,' said Jack, who had never had children, shuffling through some papers on his desk. 'You've got a 9.45 rental viewing at Carlingford. It's a Mr Jerrish'.

'OK, Jack,' Lucas skimmed his Filofax to check his schedule, 'that's good. I'll just get a quick coffee and I'll be there'.

Stanhopes estate agency managed sales and lettings. Sales tended to cater for young professionals putting their foot on the property ladder and Jack saw Lucas's relative youth and style as essential marketing tools for this growing demand. The young, charismatic Lucas was more likely to win the confidence of these customers than an old codger. Meanwhile Jack was more confident dealing with lettings, catering for all those unable to access a mortgage or qualify for social housing. It was ironic, thought Lucas, that the poorest of the poor were caught in the most expensive housing option. Lucas tried to avoid the lettings work. The housing stock was usually grim, the clients were often desperate, and he didn't like playing the officious rent collector. But as a partner he had to deal with both sides of the business, like now.

Lucas took the Belmont Road route to Carlingford Road, a five-minute walk along residential streets, the park briefly visible through its ornate iron railings. He had seen the park go through big changes in the twenty-two years since he had arrived in Tottenham. It had suffered from Tory spending cuts during the 1980s and 1990s: the disappearance of park wardens, decline of play equipment, reduced ground maintenance. Sometimes it had felt a bit scary, like a no-man's-land. But since 1997, he had watched as residents had campaigned and won government money from what the New Labour government called the Single Regeneration Budget to make improvements. New play equipment had just been installed and new tarmac paths laid. These were the first gains and others were planned. Above all, the campaigners wanted to see a cafe in the park with toilets, something that would draw people in and keep them there, that would create a permanent presence and make all users feel safer. He knew the area was on the up as rising prices in Camden, Hackney and Islington pushed many young house-hunters further out. Tottenham had remained one of London's more affordable areas to buy since the events of October 1985 at Broadwater Farm, 'disturbances', 'riots' or 'uprisings,' depending on how you looked at it. But whichever way, they had given Tottenham a negative press. Lucas remembered it well. Cynthia Jarrett, a Black woman, had died during a police search of her nearby home in South Tottenham. Just a week earlier in Brixton, the police had shot Cherry Groce, another Black woman, and the community had reacted to the news with indignation and fury. Demonstrations had turned to violence and a police officer, Keith Blakelock, had lost his life. The media's negative branding of the area still lingered after sixteen years, but now the property affordability gap was narrowing.

Lucas reached 15a Carlingford Road to find his customer waiting. He felt uncomfortable as soon as he saw him. He looked more like a typical buyer than a renter, White, smartly dressed and in his mid-to-late forties. He scanned the face, square jaw, thin lips, high cheekbones, high forehead, neatly styled black hair, nothing particularly striking or unusual about his looks. But he felt a glimmer of recognition that he couldn't quite place.

'Mr Jerrish, pleased to meet you, I'm Lucas Fairbright from Stanhopes. I understand you're interested in renting 15a.'

Lucas avoided eye contact, tried to keep his composure, and averted his face as he fumbled with the keys.

'Mr Fairbright. Pleased to meet you. Well, renting depends

on what it looks like. Let's take a look, shall we?'

As they shook hands, Lucas looked up, and it clicked. His stomach turned. Mr Jerrish. Steve. Steve Jerrish? He had never known Steve's surname. This was a ghost from the past, someone Lucas had left behind twenty-two years before and hoped never to meet again. The way Jerrish looked at Lucas was unnerving, those eyes drilling into him with that persistent stare.

'Have I met you before?' Jerrish asked, 'you look very familiar.'

'I don't think so, Mr Jerrish. Shall we go inside?'

'Here we are then.'

They went through the street door into the narrow hall which had been partitioned when the two-floor house had been converted into flats. Fumbling for a second key, Lucas led the way into 15a. Another narrow hallway, a bay-windowed front room facing the street, two smaller bedrooms off the hall and a kitchen and bathroom at the rear. There was a small garden beyond this.

'It's a lovely flat,' offered Lucas, 'great for a young family. It has its own garden but better still, you're just two minutes from the park and playground. Or for a dog.'

Jerrish looked around the room in silence and then led himself off to look in more detail. Lucas watched him checking the windows for aspect and security, the skirting boards for electrical points, and the meter cupboard.

'And you're asking £600 a month, with a month's deposit?'

'That's right Mr Jerrish. Two months in advance. Do you like it?'

'Yes, I think it will suit me fine. Let's go to your office and do the paperwork. Will cash do?'

A result thought Lucas. It was unusual to reach an

agreement on the spot and without a quibble about the rent. Jack would be pleased.

'I'm sure we've met before,' Jerrish picked up again on the walk to the office. 'Maybe on holiday? Spain?'

'Sorry, Mr Jerrish, I've never been to Spain. I've just got one of those common faces people think they've seen before.'

'It'll come to me. I've got a good memory.'

Lucas smiled, although he churned inside. They walked back to the office in an awkward silence. Jack had gone out. They completed the paperwork. Jerrish paid in cash and took the keys. Two months in advance rent plus a third month deposit, £1,800 in cash. You would have to be stupid or a hard nut to carry that kind of money around in Tottenham. He knew Jerrish wasn't stupid.

'I'll be seeing you again,' said Jerrish, looking over his shoulder as he stepped out.

Lucas sat in shock, exhausted by the effort of maintaining his composure. He had come here to escape this face from the past and built a new life. He was happily married, had beautiful children, a good job and his own home. He had found his place here in West Green, put down roots, made good friends. Now, the appearance of Jerrish threatened to bring it all back and destroy everything. Running was not an option this time. What was he going to do if Jerrish remembered who he was?

## DOWNHILLS PARK AND PARK SCHOOL

Ned, Arjan and Mark wore the same school uniform and were of similar height, but physical similarity stopped there. Mark was a well-built Jamaican, Arjan a slender Kurd with Middle Eastern olive skin and Ned a pale, white-skinned

English boy with an average build. Each of them lived close by, Arjan on Broadwater Farm, Ned on Crossfield Road and Mark on Downhills Park Road. Mark and Ned had spent many hours and days of their childhood in Downhills. It was a place of freedom from the four walls of home and being told what to do by family; freedom to stretch out your arms, run, shout, throw things and go wild without bothering anyone or getting told off. It felt like their space, their park. The school bordered the park and many classroom windows looked out onto it. No wonder the school had taken the name Park School. They talked as they walked to school.

'How was your weekend?' Mark asked.

'Dry,' said Ned. 'Jus' stuck at home with Mum, dad, 'n lil' bro'.'

'Ha. No gamin' then?' went Mark. 'I completed Donkey Kong. My dad vexed me so much. He's always sayin' too much gamin' makes you stupid but I say it makes me sharp.'

'You ain't sharp,' went Ned, 'just loud.'

'Allow it,' said Arjan. He didn't like his friends poking each other even though he knew it was just banter. He always did his best to broker harmony.

Ned and Mark had come up from primary school together. In Year 6 they got to name one friend they hoped would be in their new school class and they had named each other. Arjan had joined their new class 7CP in Year 7 but didn't know anyone in the year or speak any English, though he had an older cousin, Shereen, in Year 11. She looked out for him. Their form tutor Ms Power had asked Ned and Mark to be Arjan's 'buddy'. At first, they didn't know what to do with him and felt awkward having him follow them around. But eventually they warmed to the role and now, two years on, were all good friends. They went to all their lessons and hung out together in the school yard. They taught him English words and tried to learn a few Kurdish and Arabic words from him. Before long they were tight friends and always had each other's backs.

'Quit beefin,' man. We're bros, innit?' said Arjan. He had learnt English quickly from the boys around him and spoke like them but with a strong accent.

Arjan didn't have a computer or games console at home, but he loved books with pictures. Every fortnight Dymphna would choose some at the library and he would spend hours looking at them, speaking the words aloud and making sense with the help of the pictures. One old and tattered book, *The Three Musketeers,* was about men from history with swords and floppy hats riding horses and having adventures. He imagined himself and his friends to be like those men, a brave band of three.

Monday morning in school was always a shock to the senses after the weekend and it took Arjan a good hour to acclimatise. 9CP's first lesson was Maths with Ms Strand in Fo6, close to their tutor room, bottom of the stairs just off the atrium. Every day involved the same routine: door squeeze, corridor and staircase melee, door squeeze into Fo6. Ms Strand had a traditional attitude to discipline and lacked any warmth for or interest in her pupils. Everyone shrank themselves to avoid her attention and wrath. She gave out some textbooks, set them to page thirty-five and told them they had forty minutes to do the work while she sat at her desk to do her marking. No one bothered her, however much they needed help. Those who struggled just contained their frustration and doodled graff tags on their exercise books for thirty minutes. A few who understood the work got on for thirty minutes of quiet concentration, finally broken by the tannoy buzz, Ms Strand collecting the textbooks and dismissing them row by row.

Next was French. From the orderly silence of Ms Strand's class, they passed back into the teenage jungle: corridors filled with pupils walking, running, milling, pushing, shoving, the hubbub of chatter and shouting, rucksacks bashing. Out of the building, into the covered section of playground. More elbow room, less crush or echo for two minutes, then back indoors and a repeat of the corridor shove, until the space opened out into another wide atrium area and staircase. Room G24 was two flights up. They started climbing, dozens going up, others coming down or just hanging halfway up chatting and narrowing the passage. The smells of body odour and Lynx Africa. It felt like they were forcing their way through a steamy undergrowth of hormones. Moving between lessons, like lunch and breaktime, was an education of another kind. By the time they reached G24, their adrenalin levels were high. And they weren't going to get lower.

Mark and Ned hated French, though Arjan liked learning new languages. He already had a lot of experience, most recently learning English, and had the idea of how each language put words together to make sentences. Structure. Patterns. Rules. He liked to use these skills with French. But not today. Ms Deason was off sick, and they had a supply teacher. Everyone knew Mr Awanle and that the hour would be mayhem.

'Sit down, sit down 9CP, sit down... be quiet, be quiet 9CP... you over there, sit down... hey, hey I know your face... I will your name.' He tried to settle the class down but with little success. No one feared him, and most felt no reason to listen to him. No one wanted to know what work Ms Deason had left for them. Supply teachers weren't real teachers, they were sport.

'What's that smell, sir?' Mehmet was calling out. 'It's terrible sir, I think Arjan needs the toilet,' looking for a laugh from the class.

Mehmet had a pretty-boy face and curly black hair, looks that had drawn doting attention from adults through his childhood. Now thirteen, he was an arrogant bully who liked to clown around. He enjoyed being the centre of attention and getting a laugh at others' expense. He thought it made him popular and powerful with the Turkish boys. Most of them laughed because they didn't want to be his next victim.

'You be quiet,' said Mr Anwale, trying to maintain his authority. A game of Whac-A-Mole. He would stand over one group of teenagers until they sat down but as soon as he moved across to the next the first group would be up again. After thirty-five minutes the class got bored with pranking and were mostly sitting, receptive enough for him to hand out a worksheet. Fifteen minutes later, the tannoy sounded for break and they all ran for the door before Mr Awanle could give an orderly dismissal. Arjan had joined in with his friends but felt sorry for Mr Awanle and could not understand this attitude to school and teachers. In Syria, teachers were respected, schools seen as a means to improve your life and family's prospects.

Out in the playground, the friends headed for the edge of the covered area which other Year 9 boys used for football. They passed Mehmet, his lieutenant Necip and a group of others, sitting around the edge of the concrete ping-pong table, chatting in Turkish and laughing.

'Hey, Arjan, how's ya goats?' he called in English as they walked by, adding something in Turkish to his mates and making them all laugh.

'Up ya mountain Farm?' Necip chipped in with a laugh, making fun of Broadwater Farm where he knew Arjan lived while taking a swipe at his Kurdish background.

Arjan hated them for running down Kurds. He knew only too well that many Turks looked down on them, called them ignorant mountain peasants even though there were twelve million Kurds in Turkey. His brother Kalil had told him the Turkish government was even worse than Syria to its Kurds, banned their language, songs, and festivals. He remembered the Turkish army crossing the border and attacking his village, killing his father and sister, destroying his home. But he knew better than to respond to the goading. This was not enough horseplay for Mehmet. Followed by his mates, Mehmet slid off the concrete table and walked towards the friends, turning now to Ned.

'Got somethin' for me in ya bag?'

'Ya wan' my lunch, huh?' Ned replied lightly, standing tall but hoping to defuse the bullying with humour.

'What about a phone?' went Mehmet. This was taking a bad turn. Mark intervened, trying to divert the drift.

'Yo Mehmet, I hear your bruvver Onur got some peng wheels.'

'True dat,' Mehmet looked up to his twenty-year-old brother and bragged about him a lot. Onur was a big name in the area. The word was he was connected to bad people and had a fancy car. It was Onur's reputation that gave his little brother Mehmet his swagger. Do wrong by Mehmet and Onur would pay a visit. Or so Mehmet liked to say.

'Yeah, pimped his ride, innit,' Mehmet said, bringing them all together in a laugh. The moment of danger passed.

The friends walked on. Every break-time was filled with such moments. Arjan saw his cousin Shereen with her friends

Emine, Grace and other Year 11 girls standing in a circle, moving side to side, some clapping, dancing; looked like they were taking turns spitting bars. Every now and again a giggle or a cheer would come from them. Arjan didn't understand how Shereen could be friends with Emine, Mehmet's sister. He had told her about Mehmet's bullying, and she had just shrugged and said she didn't understand boys' egos. He knew of course that Emine was a different person to her brother, but he had hoped Shereen might be able to exert some influence on him through her friend.

'Come, Shez,' Emine said quietly to Shereen, 'let's walk a bit.' Shereen and Emine peeled off. Shereen understood her friend wanted some private talk.

'I'm worried for Tulay,' said Emine, 'She's in bare trouble with her fam, y'know, they found out she was seein' Walton and they got mad vexed. 'Cos Walton's Black, innit.'

'Tulay's parents, they're well traditional.' said Shereen.

'Like, they told her fifteen's too young for boyfriends and anyway she should be with a Turkish boy.' continued Emine.

'Yeah, I know those ways. But this ain't Turkey. I mean, this is Tottenham, UK twenty-first century, hello?' joked Shereen. They both laughed. 'My days.' she continued. 'Tulay's in bare trouble.'

'She thinks they'll send 'er back to Turkey to get married.' said Emine. 'Arranged. She's never been there. Like us. Born here. British. That can't be legal, can it?'

'She should go out with who she wants, 'course.'

They went quiet, in their own thoughts.

'Your bro, Mehmet,' Shereen started. 'Did ya know he bullies my bro' Arjan? And he's a racist. Always running down Blacks, Kurds everyone who's not a Turk? I mean, look at us. I'm half-Kurd half-Irish, you're Turk. Does it matter?

'Course not. We're friends for who we are, not where our families come from, innit.'

'He's an idiot,' Emine replied, 'he's a pain at home too. All he cares about is lookin' big to impress Onur.'

'But Onur is so nice,' said Shereen who had always fancied him, 'Hey, maybe you could introduce me.' They both giggled. 'Oh yes, sister-in-law!'

'But you got no idea, sis, he's such a pain!'

Meanwhile, the boys reached the grassy slope and the safety of their other friends. Fifteen or so boys and some girls from different Year 9 tutor groups, chatting in twos and threes, joking and laughing, a typical playground scene. Everyone was speaking English. The teenagers were a mix of Black, White and Asian kids.

'Yo, cuz,' Mark greeted his cousin Grey, who was at the centre of this group.

'How's French?' joked Grey.

'Cover teacher, innit. Waste of time. That idiot Mehmet pickin' on Arjan.'

'Mehmet... he's a donkey,' said Arjan. He always made them laugh when he directly translated Kurdish insults. 'In my town, my brother cut off his balls.'

'Yeah,' went Ned, 'Thinks he's proper gangsta. Man needs to hush his gums.'

'Mehmet, Necip, dem Turks is mad,' went Mark. 'Dey t'ink dey can boss everyone. T'ink we're scared.' He felt buoyed by the strength of numbers around him, all aware of how the Turks dominated round here.

When it came to gang trouble round West Green, it was always Turks against Blacks. It could be brutal. Last year, some Turks had attacked a Black kid just because he had knocked over a Turkish kid's can of Coke at school. The

Turkish kid's big brother came back with a machete to find the Black boy in the park. The Black kid's arms got severely cut and scarred from protecting his face from the blade. The threat of big brothers and cousins was what frightened all the teenagers the most.

'Turks run the shops these ends, their gangs run the street,' went Ned.

'Turks invade my country, kill many, burn houses,' went Arjan. They all knew that two years before Turkish troops had crossed into Syrian Kurdistan, attacked Arjan's village.

'Yeah cuz,' Grey was Mark's cousin, 'my dad says dey take liberties on da street. Word is, da Turks wanna rub all d'other gangs out. They may run West Green but not Tottenham. Our crews won't take dat. Comin' soon, they'll reach too far and get a hand chopped, innit.'

## LORDSHIP RECREATIONAL GROUND AND DOWNHILLS PARK

Brenda Durrant had a full day ahead. Her husband, Lloyd, had left for work, Mark was off to school and all the domestic chores were done. She took a moment to count her blessings. How lucky she was to live in this house on Downhills Park Road. To the front, across the road lay Downhills Park while just behind her small garden lay Lordship Rec with its shrubs and saplings taking hold just beyond her garden fence, providing a habitat for nesting birds, field mice and passing foxes. To live in London and be surrounded by parkland! She loved the sense of space and connection with nature, the green vistas, and the sounds of wildlife.

She was going out. She turned left out of the door and in

twenty seconds turned left again into Lordship Rec, down the sloping path and veering right towards the community centre. Today she and her friends were sorting out donations for a jumble sale at the weekend, raising money for a new basketball court. The council had told them that the more money the community could raise, the more the council would contribute. Basketball was important. Youngsters loved it, it brought them together, gave them skills, confidence, and bolstered their sense of purpose and with the inspirational leadership of coach Dwayne, Lloyd's friend, this was a community project that was going to win.

'Good mornin,' Brenda,' greeted the other five volunteers in chorus, already sifting through bin liners of clothing, toys, books, knick-knacks and other paraphernalia.

'Good mornin' to you ladies,' she replied, wondering to herself, not for the first time, why there were no male volunteers. The men would help with some things, she thought, like sports coaching, collecting money, tending the barbecue, but why was there this division of labour? Even in their small back garden, the most she could get Lloyd to do was mow their small patch of grass every couple of months.

'Busy, busy I see. What you wantin' me to do, Gladys?' she asked.

Gladys enjoyed being in charge and although she had never been elected or appointed, had emerged as the group's leader. No one minded, happy to let her take the role if it made her happy, while they all just got on.

'Maybe sort by size and hang some o' dem dresses on da rail.'

Brenda got to it. Sifting, sorting, hanging, chatting. She liked to do what she could to help. This was both her Christian duty and a way of life, a moral code she tried to live by.

She loved to go to church not just for the sense of spiritual transcendence that it gave her, but also to be part of her community, of something bigger. Working together, helping each other, social solidarity, these were as much part of her religion as singing hymns on Sunday. She had been brought up that way in Jamaica and her parents had carried these values with them when they had brought her to England aged twelve. But she knew it was hard. Everyone faced adversities and sometimes she felt as though her community was an isolated island within a vast and frightening ocean, and that rising tides and storms constantly threatened to wash them away. She feared especially for the youth trying to find their path in life, with the least level of experience or resources to face the world, yet the greatest challenges and temptations. She knew the mothers had to keep strong, for the youth and each other. They all knew it and they depended on each other. Before she knew it, it was midday.

'Gladys, I have a date at twelve, so I'll be goin' now, but I'll be back in da afternoon, OK?'

'Thank you, darlin'. Have fun with your fancy man!' Everyone laughed.

'Yes, I will, he's called Mollie.' She joshed back and they all laughed.

Brenda and Mollie had first met at the gates of Belton primary school nine years ago, fetching and carrying little Ned and Mark on the daily school run, even after the boys started protesting that now they were in Year 6, they were old enough to walk on their own. After that, Mollie still had to escort young Joe while Ned insisted on walking ten metres ahead. For her part though, Brenda had insisted on continuing to escort Mark because she simply enjoyed the time spent walking and the social contact with other parents. The school gates were common ground. Parents from all walks of life and backgrounds came together for a few minutes each day, drawn together by their children, the common purpose in all their lives and the future of the neighbourhood.

On this late September day, it was still warm enough to enjoy the outdoors and so Mollie had offered to bring a Thermos of coffee and meet in Downhills Park. The Italian garden, with its formally laid flower beds and benches was their favourite meeting point. Brenda arrived first and enjoyed sitting alone for some minutes, listening out for bird-song amid the background traffic hum and looking at the roses, mostly now sadly shabby and in need of deadheading.

'Sorry I'm late.' Mollie's apology gave Brenda a start, but she laughed and soon they were settled together on the bench.

'How are you?' Brenda asked, as Mollie poured from the Thermos and offered her a cup.

'Oh, fine, you know. Kids. Work. Lucas. Thank goodness for jogging. It keeps me sane. How about you?'

'I'm busy wid da church. It fill my week wid jumble sale, food collection, coffee mornin's, choir, home-visitin' some house-bound brothers and sisters. Lloyd has more business dan he can manage. Der's always huge demand for plumb-ers. He moans about his knees! Some days he can be hours on dem reachin' under sinks.' Brenda always spoke with her Jamaican accent, unlike the rest of her family who would drift in and out of it according to the conversation and who they were talking to.

'He should get his apprentice to do that, with his young agile body!'

'True dat! What 'bout your studies, Mollie? How dem goin'?' Mollie was four years into her seven-year architecture training. People often asked her how it was going, and she always answered in the same way.

'Yes, it's OK but long. Sometimes feels like a prison sentence, and it's easy to forget why I'm doing it.'

'Well, you'll be doin' a good job dat helps other people, designin' buildings and spaces dat make people happy. And how's Lucas? Does he have any tips on da West Green property market, not dat I'm expandin' my property empire jus' now!'

'Ha! He says the sale prices just keep on rising. I guess we're lucky to have bought our house ten years ago. He likes the job, but he does it to keep the family. You know Brenda, actually I wanted to talk to you about Ned. I am worried about school.'

'What's worryin' you? Tell me.'

'Well, I don't know if it's the school or his age. It's difficult being thirteen of course. But Ned won't tell me about school like he used to. He shows me his homework when I ask to see it. I don't understand some of it, but it always looks a bit short, you know, done as quickly as possible. He doesn't like to tell me much, but he says there's a lot of messing in some of the classes. Stops them learning. And he says this tribal thing in the playground is getting worse. It didn't happen in Belton. You know, Turk, Black, White. Does Mark tell you anything?'

'It's da same, Mollie, I worry bout dis too. Mark tell me der's bullyin' in the playground but won't say if he gettin' pick' on and he get angry wid me if I say he should tell da teacher. Da children have strong honour. To get call' a snitch is da worst. So, dey protec' even da worst bully with silence.'

'Sometimes I wonder if Ned would be better off in another school. Do you ever think of moving Mark?'

'Hmmm,' Brenda said thoughtfully. 'I wan' Mark t'do well in school. Get qualification dat open doors. For a better life dan me and Lloyd, 'appy though we are. Successful, you know, professional. A doctor or architec' like you. But you know, da next school may be jus' da same. It's jus' da worl' dat our children livin' in. Dis school is our community, Mollie. It's where we live, our family and friends. Mark is part of it. Inside he'self, 'e know what's right and wrong.'

Yes, Mollie thought, you're right. We planted our roots here. For better or for worse.

# Chapter Six

**BRUCE GROVE**

Dilek listened to talk radio as she worked her sewing machine. She liked Radio 4 because the English was usually clear. In the early days, she had struggled to understand, but felt sure that exposure to radio English would help her to improve her own, and it had. It was Woman's Hour. She liked the idea of the show: an hour for women presented by women in a world where men controlled everything else. It reminded her of home and those wonderful times when she would get together with her women friends. No men allowed. What good times they were. How they would laugh, sometimes until she cried.

'Eighty-one,' she said to herself, adding the latest finished jacket to the growing pile. Every day the piles of sleeves and panels shrank while the pile of complete jackets grew. It was such a satisfying moment to see the completed work. But it only lasted a few days until the van came round to collect it and deliver the next batch of parts. Dilek had been a home-worker now for twenty-two years, since soon after arriving in Tottenham. It still suited her. She could earn money from home, cash in hand, and mind her children at the same time.

And of course, it suited her employer who didn't need to pay rent and overheads for a factory. Her boss said it was the only way for British fashion to compete with cheap factory labour in developing countries. There were enough people wanting to homework around Tottenham to provide an ever-lasting source of competitive labour. The two rooms of their ground-floor had been knocked through to make a larger living room and her 'factory' occupied a rear corner. The children had grown up with it. Cetin was used to it. It was a fixture of their lives.

'It's just coming up to one o'clock and time for the news,' said the radio. Dilek rose from her workbench. She had fixed up to meet her friend Dymphna. This is why I am a homeworker, she thought with a smile, taking pleasure in her occasional use of this freedom and flexibility. Cetin had encouraged her to get a better-paid job away from home, maybe in a bank or office. She had bank experience from home. But she had grown comfortable with this, didn't have to travel to work and was at home when the kids came back. She had also earned a good reputation for the quality of her work and won pay bonuses.

These days she was worried about the boys. Sometimes she felt like they were not hers, but some English imposters who did not behave well, did not respect their parents or share her culture and values. She worked so hard for the family, but the boys treated her as if they thought she was a nagging old woman. She always remembered when they were little and would sneak into her bed in the morning and then jump up and down until she or Cetin were forced to get up and make breakfast; how they loved to sit on her lap and ask for stories; to put their little arms around her and say, 'I love you, Mummy'. Such happy days. How long ago.

These days she wondered if she had lost them to the dark side. Sometimes she regretted that they had ever come here and mourned what they had left behind in Mardin. She had agreed to it, but it had really been Cetin's idea. He had had no ties to keep him there, while for her, it had been a sacrifice to leave her family. If they had stayed, how different it might be now for the boys. They would have had an extended family of uncles, aunts, cousins and grandparents, all positive influences. Wherever they would have gone in town, there would be someone who knew the Zaman boys and would keep an eye on whatever they got up to. But they had made their choice and were here now.

Dilek had met Dymphna at the school gates, just as Mollie had met Brenda, nine years before when Emine and Shereen had both been seven. Dilek had been unconfident in English and had been delighted when Dymphna had spoken to her in Turkish. They had remained friends and Dymphna had helped her become a better English speaker. Now that their daughters walked themselves to secondary school, they had less contact. But they still made arrangements which usually involved a walk in the park. After all, it didn't cost any money. Late summer was turning to early autumn. Some leaves were tinged brown or red as the chlorophyll retreated into woody branches in readiness for the winter. The flower beds were looking tired and depleted. Nevertheless, she still found it beautiful, an oasis of calm and nature.

'Hi there, Dilek,' called Dymphna from her bench in the trees as she saw Dilek walk past and nearly miss her.

'Oh, hi, I didn't see you. How are you?'

'Fine thank you, come sit down. How are you?'

Dilek settled on the bench.

'OK but I am tired. I have so much work now, so many

jackets to make. But I am happy to see you.'

Dymphna could see she was agitated and upset. She bore a weight of worry on her face, her earlier ruminations still lingering on her mind.

'You look worried. What's wrong?' asked Dymphna.

Dilek sat silently for a minute, not sure how to start, but sure that it would help to talk to her friend.

'My Cetin work so hard also. He come home sometimes ten o'clock in the evening. I feel alone with children, keeping the house and my own work on top. And now my boys. They should be helping. But instead, they bring so much worry. We come to England to give them better life. But what they do? They not try hard at school, now Onur has a low-paid, dead-end job and spend all his wage on car. What next? And Mehmet. Only thirteen and he is carrying on like the big mouth Turk man. Mehmet follow his brother. Why they not both follow their father, a good hard-working man? The boys think honest hard work not good for them. They end up with nothing or in prison.'

Dymphna listened and when Dilek had finished she put her hand over Dilek's and squeezed it gently.

'Come on, let's go for a walk,' she said.

They got up from the bench and left the shade and underfoot litter of the small woodland, emerging onto Midnight Alley, which their children walked each day to school, heading south towards the West Green Road. In the middle distance on the playing fields to their right, some men were playing football with jackets and bags for goalposts. Occasional shouts or calls drifted across. To their left the playground came into view, a couple of parents in there with pre-school children just collected from nursery school.

'I'm sorry, Dymphna, too much of me. How are you?'

asked Dilek, keen to move the focus from herself and offer support to her friend.

'Not bad, you know, I am lucky. I don't have the same child problems. Shereen is a great help. Like your Emine, she has a motivation to do well and get a good job. Don't forget the blessings of your daughter. And Arjan, well he is such a tough little cookie. After everything he has gone through, he knows how lucky he is to be here and does what he can to help. But the flat's small, you know. Arjan sleeps on the sofa, no space of his own. The living room always feels a bit like a bedroom with his clothes and things in there. Shereen's been great with it but it's tough on her too having Arjan stay. I know it's the right thing but sometimes... you know.'

'I think I understand, this is hard for you. You have good hearts. Good people.'

'Everyone has their cross to bear,' said Dymphna. They walked a while in silence. 'You know, this isn't the poshest bit of London, but we do well for open space. Lots of it. Down-hills, Lordship, Belmont, Bruce Castle, River Lea. If you know where to go you can really get away from the urban vibe. You know. The city feeling,' she added, realising 'urban vibe' might be beyond Dilek's vocabulary.

'Yes. Park is very beautiful. Very special. In Mardin, nothing like this. It helps me to remember our reasons for coming here, for a better life. Our hope. It still give me hope. Sometimes, I think park is talking to me!'

'I hope it speaks Turkish!' joked Dymphna, and they both laughed.

Dilek carried on.

'I hear this voice tell me "All your problems will pass." And that makes me feel calmer and safer, that my problems are small.'

It was 5pm when Onur came home. Dilek was long back from the park. He gave her a cursory greeting, went upstairs and flung himself on to his bed in the room he shared with his brother. He was tired after the day's work at the warehouse in Edmonton where he moved crates as deliveries came in or orders went out. Some crates were closed, others – for example, the watermelons that came from Turkey – arrived in open crates. Mehmet was already there, lying on his bed looking at a football magazine.

'How's school?' he asked his younger brother in English. Although their parents usually talked to them in Turkish, they talked English to each other, the language of young Londoners.

'French were sick,' Mehmet replied without looking away from his phone. 'Cover teacher. We proper messed 'im up. He couldn't do nothin'. Useless. Shit school. Ha!'

'Pity cover teachers, bro'. No one takes them serious. Imagine *wantin'* that job!'

'And there's these kids in my class, really annoyin', man. One's a Kurd, and his mates, a Black and a White boy always stickin' up for 'im. T'ink I'm gonna make dem my hobby.'

'What 'ave they done to you?'

'Nothin' yet, just disrespectin'.'

'A man's gotta have respect, Mehmet. Look at me. Where would I be without it?'

The boys had lived in Tottenham all their lives. Onur had also gone to Park School. He had enjoyed it. Not so much the lessons, which he didn't really remember, but the school yard and social life. Every day had been a lark, messing with teachers and dodging the blame, hanging in the school yard at break-time, bunking to the park most afternoons. He had made good friends like Denzil and a few enemies too. They had been good times. Now it was Mehmet's turn. Onur always wanted to know about Mehmet's day. It took him back. Brought back that feeling of respect. Gave him a chance to chip into Mehmet's stories with memories of his own. He often exaggerated to impress but Mehmet loved his stories and always passed them on to his school mates. Mehmet knew this bigged him up. Big brothers were legends. Everyone looked up to them. More than that, Onur was Mehmet's role model. Onur had money, a car, respect, he was part of something bigger, something powerful. He was no slave. All Mehmet's school friends knew Onur's name. One day, Mehmet thought, I'll be like Onur. His thoughts were interrupted by their mother calling from downstairs.

'Mehmet, Onur, Emine, come down and help, please,' Dilek called up the stairs in Turkish. She was frustrated with her children and increasingly often thought England had corrupted them: many English children seemed to ignore their family duties. But then she tried to remember that they were teenagers and how she had been at that age; Emine and Mehmet had age as an excuse, but Onur was twenty and still behaved like one. He lived at home but thought himself the big man, above doing family chores. While Emine and Mehmet were coming to the kitchen, Onur was heading for the front door.

'I'm gonna meet Denzil, then I'll tidy and help,' he said.

'It's not fair, Mum,' said Emine, 'you and Dad shouldn't let him get away with it. Just because he's the oldest and a boy.'

Your oldest son should give you pride and hope, Dilek thought to herself, but Onur had lost his way. It was that school. That no-good friend Denzil. It was England. If only they had stayed in Mardin. She suppressed her thoughts and rounded on Onur. She flashed at him in Turkish.

'Are you a man or a boy, Onur? A man faces his responsibilities, only a boy runs out to play. Denzil can wait.'

He blushed while Emine smiled with satisfaction that her mum had made a stand.

'First you work, then you go out to play,' Dilek continued.

Onur rushed through his jobs, emptying the rubbish, washing up and cleaning the kitchen while Emine tidied the living room and Mehmet the hall and stairs. A few minutes later, Mehmet slammed his bedroom door shut while Onur was revving up his car. If it had a silencer, it wasn't very effective. But Onur loved how the noise turned heads. His car was his pride and joy. He had bought the black Ford Focus six months before and every penny went into pimping it up. So far it had violet under-chassis light strips, sport wheel hubs, a massive bass speaker in the boot and tinted window film. You would have to be blind as well as deaf to miss him driving by.

'Mum,' Emine started in Turkish. The children knew their parents found it easier and always used it when they wanted to be close to them, just as they would use English if they didn't.

'When you lived in Turkey, did you and Dad choose each other? Or did your families match you up?'

The question took Dilek completely by surprise. She turned to Emine and replied.

'We met in school and chose each other, my heart. Why do you ask?'

'That's like here in UK, right? Women should get to decide, shouldn't they? So, my friend Tulay, her parents want to stop her seeing her boyfriend 'cos he's not from their culture and want to send her to get married in Turkey. Isn't that terrible?'

Dilek knew of many such stories and all too well how strong such traditional, old-fashioned ways remained even now among some immigrant families in twenty-first century London.

'Yes, terrible. Of course, she should choose her own husband.'

'So why did you leave Turkey?' asked Emine. Dilek had answered this question from her daughter many times before but knew that each time Emine asked she was a little bit older and perhaps looking for answers to a slightly different question.

'We left to find better lives. We hoped for more money, a safer place and better opportunities for you children. And then the fighting started. Army searches. The PKK. The bombs in the city. And yes, in part because of old-fashioned ways of thinking, against women and prejudice against other cultures. Here in London, I see racism, but not from a police gun. We want you children to be friends with all: Kurd, Turk, Black, White.'

Emine seized the moment.

'Yes, Mum, you know my friend Shereen is half-Kurd. Mum, I have to tell you, Mehmet is always dissing Kurds. He's bullying Shereen's bro' Arjan 'cos he's a Kurd. Arjan can't tell his family. How would it look if they came to school about it? And they are gentle people so they will not come to our door either. So, I'm telling you. Can you tell him to stop?'

Dilek was shocked and took a moment before replying.

'We must remember Mehmet is thirteen and at this age every child does foolish hateful things that they think are exciting and funny. I will speak with him. But you know sometimes I think all you children, especially your brothers, would benefit if we sent you back to Turkey for a few months. To understand what you come from, what we did for you, the opportunities you have here. Sometimes I wonder did we make a mistake coming here?'

'Mum, don't talk like that. Never mind the boys, I want to make you proud. I'm gonna smash my GCSEs, go college, uni and be an accountant. Then you will see it was worth it.'

Dilek hugged her daughter.

Emine, Onur and Mehmet each knew they were Turkish as well as British. They spoke their heritage language at home. It was a common bond with other Turks and provided a basis for solidarity and strength, whether in the school yard, high street or among street gangs. But none had ever been to the mother country. Born and raised in Tottenham, they were London Turks. They spoke English like native north Londoners, wore the 'threads' and followed the 'beats'. Like so many second-generation migrants they lived, moving between their cultures. It wasn't always easy at that age to know who you were.

## LORDSHIP LANE

Onur drove by Denzil's home, a terraced house on Lordship Lane. Like many only-children, Denzil had always been doted on by his parents. He had been their first-born, but having experienced two miscarriages and a cot death, he was their only surviving child. After these tragedies, his parents had treasured him, always let him do whatever he wanted and given him whatever they could, even though they were poor village-people with little education who had come from Cyprus during the 1974 war. So, he had grown up to be self-centred and arrogant, well suited to being a school bully in his day. But now he was worried. His father was starting to experience mobility problems and the doctor had sent him for tests for multiple sclerosis. Was he facing a life in a wheelchair? Denzil knew that if his father could no longer do his job as a school caretaker, he would become the main breadwinner. He had a plan for this.

'My lucky space,' Onur smiled to himself, seeing a gap in the line of parked cars and manoeuvring into it.

'What's 'appenin', bro?' Denzil greeted Onur at the door.

They had been mates since schooldays. They had sat together in class, hung out together in the school yard and got up to mischief together just about everywhere. They bossed the school yard. Denzil had been the leader, although he was ordinary-looking, average height and build, with black hair which was never cut with style; his mother trimmed it to save money. He had built his power through his guile, a radar for weaknesses in others and ruthlessness. Onur had been his lieutenant, preferring to hang a couple of steps back where he didn't have to make decisions. He just wanted to swagger, incite fear, and demand respect. He was the one with the stylish clothes and cut. Appearances mattered to Onur. Together, they had a built a reputation and a crew. Everyone respected toughness and feared violence. If anyone started on one of them, the whole crew would pile in. As more and more Turkish families moved to the West Green, playground power had shifted. The school yard used to be run by Blacks, mostly from Caribbean families, but Denzil and Onur's gang had changed that. As more and more Turkish families moved to the West Green, playground power had shifted.

That was school. Four years later, they had both found jobs so they could contribute to their family's bills. Onur had his warehouse work, thanks to Denzil. His cousin, Kemal, knew the owner. Denzil had put in a word for him. Denzil didn't want to work there himself. He liked fixing cars and so got a job at Kwik Fit in Tottenham Hale. In their hearts, both still sought the excitement that comes with mischief, and the power that comes from a tough front, no longer in the school yard but now on the streets. Their ambitions lay outside work.

Kemal was big in Topkapi, a Turkish gang with a serious reputation and access to money, built on drug importing and distribution. Their boss, Mustafa Igli, known for his unpredictability and violence, was reputed to keep a machete in his desk drawer, and to use it to punish minor transgressions that fell short of getting capped. Onur didn't realise, but the Edmonton warehouse was a pivotal part of their import operations. The gang took its name from the cafe on the Green Lanes which served as its headquarters. The cafe itself had been named after the Ottoman Pasha's palace in Istanbul long before the gang had taken it over. The gang had adopted the name. Everyone could see that it signalled their control of London's Turkish underworld. Topkapi operated across Tottenham, Harringay, Wood Green, Stoke Newington and north Hackney.

Kemal let Denzil run some small errands. Denzil used this to brag about his connection with Topkapi, much like Mehmet bragged at school about his big brother Onur. Although he was at the lowest level of membership, exaggeration was his art. He thought Topkapi could open the door to a world of easy money and power. Onur wanted to be in Topkapi too, not so much for the money but for the respect that this would command on the streets. Denzil didn't have a car, so Onur always offered to drive him around on his errands, pumping beats from his on-board sound system, showing off his pimped ride. Feeling big. 'Let's go,' said Denzil nodding towards Onur's car, 'got some deliveries, innit.' 'This is my future,' thought Onur, 'not slavin' all hours like my parents. But bossin' the streets.'

# Chapter Seven

**WEST GREEN**

'That Mr Jerrish is coming back,' Jack told Lucas when he arrived at the office. It was two months since Lucas had shown Jerrish around 15a Carlingford. 'He's after another two-bedroom, says it's for his nephew. Seems a reliable tenant. Paid on time, no complaints from neighbours?'

Lucas nodded.

'Can you meet him at 24b Langham, 11am? He specifically asked for you.'

Lucas had dreaded another possible encounter with Steve Jerrish, but what could he say?

Jerrish was already waiting outside when Lucas arrived.

'Mr Fairbright, good to see you again.'

'Hello Mr Jerrish. How are you? Shall we go inside?' Lucas struggled with the keys and soon they were inside, up a flight of stairs and into the flat.

'Well, another nice two-bedroom,' said Jerrish following Lucas into a large front room with bay window, looking as before at skirting boards and electrical points, windows and aspect.

'For your nephew, I believe?' Lucas tried to make light conversation.

'Oh yes, the flat. He's coming to London. From Cornwall. Going to uni. I promised his mum I'd help find him somewhere to live.' Jerrish interrupted his assessment of the flat, turned to Lucas and gave him a long stare. 'Been to Cornwall, have you Mr Fairbright?'

Lucas fumbled for something to say.

'Oh yes, of course. Spent many a family holiday there.'

'Maybe that's where I recognise you from. Newquay perhaps, or Polperro? Or maybe Plymouth?' Jerrish held his stare. Lucas' stomach churned and felt light as a somersaulting butterfly. Steve's eyes burnt into his face like lasers.

'Lucas is a more conventional name than Spikey. It took me a while to think it through. But look now, here you are. Lucas Spikey Fairbright. After all these years.'

Lucas was determined not to show his fear. He forced himself to meet Steve's stare with a light glance and casual smile.

'Mr Jerrish, I'm not sure I know what you're talking about.'

'I don't suppose the Three Tonnes would mean anything to you either then?'

'It sounds like a pub name, perhaps?' replied Lucas.

'Well, you can say what you like, Mr Fairbright. But I know what I know. I know that a certain spineless punk boy calling himself Spikey did a runner on his mates twenty-two years ago leaving a trail of destruction behind him. And I know that Mr Fairbright, a successful estate agent with a lovely wife and two children has been living and working in West Green for the last twenty-two years. What a coincidence in timing and that, when you look past the hairstyle and clothes, their faces are the same. Don't you think... Spikey?'

Lucas could not escape. He had been found out. Steve continued.

'When I finally twigged it was you, I did my research. A proper little happy family you've got now. A picture of success: house in Crossfield Road, wife Mollie qualifying as an architect, Ned at Park and Joe at Belton school.'

Steve certainly had done his homework. Lucas was dazed. His mind slipped through a time warp as the intervening years seemed to evaporate. He felt like that impressionable, unconfident punk teenager he had been again, standing before this powerful older guy. Glimpses of the intervening years flashed through his mind.

He had met Mollie in the park one bright blossom-filled May morning in 1985. It was a Saturday and he had felt like a walk in nearby Downhills. Saturday mornings were like rush hour in the park. Everyone was out sharing a narrow tarmac path, potholed and buckled by tree roots: joggers, walkers, dog owners, cyclists, scooters, tricyclists, children, teenagers, dodderers. Mollie was a jogger. She lapped him twice within fifteen minutes. He definitely noticed her the first time. She was strikingly attractive: a tall, well-proportioned body, long dark hair tied back in a ponytail, a sculptured face with high cheekbones and almond eyes that he noticed even through her thick-frame glasses. Shortly after her second pass, he saw a credit card on the path in her wake. Had she lost it from her Lycra shorts pocket? He picked it up. It belonged to Mollie Anochin. On her third lap past he called out, 'Mollie? Mollie Anochin?' She stopped, turned, and looked in surprise at a stranger who knew her name. And that was how they met. Of course, she had been grateful, and Lucas could forever play that card as her knight-in-shining-armour.

They really clicked together. Mollie was a similar age,

had grown up in a sleepy Swiss village and like Lucas had taken the first chance to get away, coming to England as an au pair aged eighteen. She had moved from family to family through a word-of-mouth North London circuit of yummy mummies and never gone back. Like him, she loved the buzz of London and the diversity of Tottenham after her small-town childhood home. She now lived nearby, and the park was her running track and outdoor gym. She was also an earnest environmentalist and loved the connection with nature that the park gave her amid the concrete of the city.

Lucas and Mollie dated for three months before she decided that the relationship was incompatible with au pairing. She couldn't bring him into the family house and her duties rarely allowed her to stay at his flat, so she left the job and moved in with him. She had always been a talented artist and soon found work with a graphic designer despite her meagre qualifications. Six months later she became pregnant. Their lives transformed as they forged their own family, first with Ned and three years later with Joe. They moved into a rented two-bedroom house in Crossfield Road with Jack Job's help and had never been happier. For the first time in their lives, both felt they had found family; not just the ones they had been born to, grown up with and run away from. They had found new friends through their children: the parents of other little ones at play group, nursery and then the school gates, like Lloyd and Brenda, Mark's parents. It was remarkable how children could blend different families together in a community. They had built their own family, with their own rules and values and made sure they gave their children all the love and support they themselves had missed. This family was the most valuable thing in the world, the purpose of Lucas' life. He would do anything for it, and anything to protect it.

Lucas fell back to earth. Just milliseconds had passed. Words came to him.

'Okay Steve.' Lucas realised it was futile to continue a pretence. 'But you don't understand. I didn't skim the block. I didn't do anything. I ran because I knew you were going to blame and frame me. You needed Dale for the boat and van. You liked Benny. You knew it couldn't be Vince. I was the weakest link. I thought you would hurt me. I had to leave. Anyway, it's a long time ago. I'm a different person. Law-abiding. Straight. A family man. Let bygones be bygones.'

'The past is always with us, Spikey. You can't escape it. And you cost me. I lost business, customer confidence. I lost Dale, Benny, and Vince. I lost reputation by letting you slip away. Public punishment was necessary, and you deprived me of that. It took me years to get back in with Frenchie. But now I've found you again, better late than never. And you're going to pay *me* back as I say, or else I might have to tell Frenchie that I found you, along with the little bonus package of your wife and children. I think she would just love to get her own back, taking what you hold most precious in the world.'

The walls of the room were closing in on Lucas. He couldn't believe how his world had turned upside down within less than ten minutes.

'What do you want, Steve?' He managed to ask through his increasingly dry mouth. He felt as if he was in a nightmare where his ability to produce words was disappearing, despite his effort to move his mouth.

'Well, lucky for you I need your professional services. I need this flat, Carlingford and a couple more two-bedders for some other nephews moving to town, on complimentary terms. Let's take it one month at a time. And I want a refund on what I've paid on Carlingford. I want you to sort that for me.'

Lucas ran the maths quickly through his head. £600 a month per flat, four of them was going to be £2,400. Plus £600 deposit on each of the three new flats, another £1,800. Plus, refunding Jerrish £1,800 that he had already paid for Carlingford. He would have to find the money himself to pay Steve's rents so Jack wouldn't notice anything. But what if he couldn't find the money? £6,000 would clean out his savings and that would only square things for one month. Lucas knew he would do anything to keep his family safe.

'Come on Steve. How am I going to find £6,000 for you?'

'Well, let's call it compound interest on what you took and lost for me twenty years ago. I'm sure you would agree it's a very reasonable price to safeguard your lovely family. Find me two more flats. You'll be hearing from me.'

'But I didn't take anything,' Lucas protested lamely as Steve snatched the flat keys out of his hand and walked out the door. Lucas was left speechless and terrified, everything he valued suddenly under threat from his past.

# Chapter Eight

## 15th NOVEMBER 2001

## WEST GREEN

'So, what's new wi' da Fairbrights?' Brenda asked as they settled down in Mollie's living room. She had come round to Crossfield Road for a catch-up.

'Well, I'm OK. Head above water. Studies under control. Hey, I've got an interesting project, actually. About working with public open spaces, putting them at the centre of architectural design and reflecting the local natural features in the shape of the building frame.'

''Nough wid dem big words!'

'Sorry, Brenda. I've been thinking about our Downhills. And you know what? It's made me realise how difficult it is to separate the park from its surrounding housing. It's like a village green, you know, at the centre of things. Houses built around it. I can't imagine the park without the houses, I mean it would be like an empty open space, countryside, no people. And can you imagine the houses and streets without the park? Just brick and concrete. It would be just horrible. So, I'm seeing how they complement each other, how important the park is to this place. To making it a good place to live. You know what I mean?'

'Well, I'm no architec' but I t'ink I know exactly what you mean. How's Ned? What's he sayin' 'bout school?'

'It's the same since we last spoke. But I'm trying not to worry, like you said it's part of our community and school is not just about qualifications, is it? He is happy with his friends. And Joe is just great. In his element without a big brother outshining him in primary school. But Brenda, I'm a bit worried about Lucas.' Mollie poured some tea. 'He's been a bit distracted the past month. Well, more than that. He's become really withdrawn and agitated. The smallest thing the kids do will set him off.'

'Oh dear. Wha' d'ya t'ink it could be?'

'All I know is that he came home from work one day, about a month ago and went straight to bed. Said he had a migraine. Later, when I could talk to him, he said he'd had a very difficult day because he'd met a "ghost from the past", those were his exact words. But he wouldn't tell me more.'

'We all 'av skeleton in da closet. Sound like one of dem caught up wid 'im. Maybe ask 'im 'gain, now a few week passed. Let 'im know you're on 'is side. Do you t'ink you can forgive anyt'ing from da past dat dis might bring up?'

'I can't imagine anything that I couldn't forgive, crikey, we've lived together for fifteen years, got two kids and mortgage together. If that's not commitment I don't know what is.'

'So tell 'im, and ask what's goin' on. Where he come from before London?'

'Cornwall. Sounds kind of genteel, but he tells me it's not all thatched cottages and cobbled streets. There's plenty of poverty, crime and bad 'uns too.'

'So, if da problem's a dangerous Cornish ghost, your karate black belt might come in handy,' joked Brenda who had always admired Mollie for her fitness and self-defence skills.

'Yes, I guess whacking is one of the skills I bring to our marriage partnership!' joked Mollie. 'Lucas never was one for confrontation. Just let this ghost try it on with this tiger wife.'

## PARK SCHOOL

Geography was 9CP's last lesson of the morning before lunchtime. Mr Lowenthal was at the door to greet them, each by name.

'Did you have a good weekend?' 'Like the haircut.' He tried to build his relationships with his students and wanted to make Geography interesting. Everyone settled quickly as he started telling them his weekend story.

'I went for a walk in Trent Park, up near Cockfosters, you know the end of the Piccadilly line. Well, it was lovely, but I never saw the weather change so fast, and I got caught in the rain. Soaked! Even my dog wouldn't come near me!'

While everyone laughed at the thought, he seamlessly moved into talking about the causes of rain. Still captured by the story, they followed his instructions, looking at the pictures and graphs and cartoons that he handed out. Time flew by and before they knew it, he was calling them all back to discuss and share what they had found out. They could all answer his questions, including the kids who usually messed with other teachers. Even Mehmet behaved himself. They enjoyed the lesson.

Come lunchtime, there was a rush to leave school. The gate was carefully controlled by Dan, an ex-pupil who had come back to work as a learning mentor and controlled the gate as part of his job. Everyone respected him because he was 'ripped', had 'wicked tats' and a good sense of humour. He kept an orderly and trouble-free gate without having to do much. Ned had a red pass because Lucas and Mollie gave permission for him to come home for lunch. But Mark and Arjan didn't, so they joined a dozen others at the 'tunnel', a burrowed gap under the steel fence at the back of the yard leading into the park. Once out, most headed for the chicken and kebab shops on the West Green Road, though some went to the newsagent for sweets or crisps. To the shopkeepers, the school kids were a mixed blessing. They accepted their business while taking no chances. A sign hung on the newsagent's door warning, 'only two school children at a time.' Inside, extra relatives were drafted in to guard the stock every lunch and home-time. Mark, Ned and Arjan met up at the chicken shop. The counter formed a frontline. Twenty teenagers jostled at the front waving their money overhead. 'Special please, boss!' 'Special, boss!' they called, as they waved their money and jostled. Today's special was a box of chicken nuggets and chips for 99p. Bigger kids elbowed their way through, and the really cheeky ones sometimes grabbed the nearest available box without paying. It was impossible for the workers to keep track of the orders; besides, they didn't much care once they had taken the money.

The three friends joined the jostling queue, finally got served and watched the counter like hawks to make sure no one else took their order.

They walked back to the park looking for a bench. But by the time they reached the park, all were taken so they dropped their school bags and ate standing near the playground, a place filled with memories of childhood. It was a beautiful clear autumn day; the gold and brown leaves of the majestic trees were falling steadily. There could be no doubt about the season and the turning of time. The park was calm, peaceful, and buzzing with the good feeling of friends being together, an escape from the concrete of the city streets and school, an urban oasis.

Arjan nodded as Shereen walked by.

'Hi lil' bro,' she greeted him with a smile, walking on with her friends Emine and Tulay. Emine. Mehmet's sister. Arjan could not understand how Mehmet could be such a racist dick when his sister was friendly to him.

The girls chatted as they walked on.

'Your Arjan's a sweet boy,' said Tulay. She was in the need of talking. 'Y' know, I told you my parents went ape shit 'bout Walton 'cos he's Black, innit, and dey wanna send me Turkey t' get married? Dey say dey won't trus' any London boys even da Muslims to be a good husband and dat der's too many bad 'uns here. So why did dey come here, huh? If dey t'ink it's such a cursed place. Bringin' me as a baby. I had no say in dat. And now I'm grown up and got friends, gonna send me back der. I don't know no one or nuffink 'bout Turkey. If dey love Turkey so much, why don't dey go back der demselves and leave me alone? I'll finish school dis year, get a job, maybe move in wiv Walton.'

'Walton's the reason they wanna send you, Tulay,' said Shereen. 'Why not tell 'em you wanna study for A levels, go uni? Maybe teachers here can help you fin' some money from charities to stay and study.'

'Dey say if I see Walton again, dey'll lock me in my room and I'll miss school.'

'They can't do that,' said Emine. 'I saw a thing on TV about a Kurdish girl. Same. But police came and parents were arrested for 'false imprisonment.' If you stop coming to school, Tulay, we'll go to the police to get you out. OK?'

'T'anks, sis.'

'What does Walton say?' said Emine. 'I mean, if he loves you, he should stand by you, stand up to them, show his commitment; or is he frightened of your family?'

'Really, Tulay, you need help,' said Shereen. 'I think you should speak to a teacher. Ms Poole will help you. She will know what to do.' Ms Poole was their form tutor and head of Drama.

'Yeah, she's cool. I'll t'ink 'bout it.'

The hour was up, the girls completed their park loop and turned back to school amid a drifting taggle of others, jostling at the tunnel to get back in. Benches were vacated, litter bins overflowed, food wrappers, crisp packets and drink cans were scattered on the ground around them. The boys decided to bunk and spend the afternoon in the park. They didn't do this often and had not been caught yet. They waited until the park had thinned out before walking away from the school to its furthest northern edge. They found a secluded bench. An hour passed with Ned and Mark taking turns to tell jokes. Arjan enjoyed them but it was too difficult for him to tell any in English. As they were running out of material, they saw they were not the only ones bunking. Mehmet, Necip and a gang of other Turkish kids were coming towards them.

'Bunkin', then?' Mehmet joked as if he was going to grass them up. 'This is our bench.'

'Since when did you own the park, Mehmet?' said Mark.

'We tax the benches, for your protection,' said Mehmet, talking like some gangster he'd seen in a movie.

The three friends were not looking for trouble and, in any case, knew they were outnumbered. 'Whatever. Forget it. We're bouncin', Mehmet, you coch, your bench,' said Ned knowing that the others would follow his lead. They all stood up.

'You can go but you still gotta pay.'

It was like the moment before a shootout in a Western movie. Then a shouting voice.

'Eh, you lot. Get over here now!' Walking towards them from direction of the school, and still a hundred metres away was Mr Stringer, a deputy head trawling the park looking for bunkers. The boys looked at each other, temporarily united by the need to scatter before Stringer could get close enough to recognise anyone. Ned had never been so happy to see a teacher.

Mark and Arjan went one way, Ned went another and reached the park gate at Downhills Park Road. He crossed the road and ran into Lordship Rec. He would hang out there until 3.30 and then go home. He would find somewhere to sit and ring the others. He headed for the play area next to the pond and 'model traffic area', a miniature street system with junctions and crossings laid out back in the day to teach children road sense. The Rec was quiet, almost empty. He spotted a group of Year 10 girls sitting on the climbing frame, passing a cigarette between them. One was painting her nails. They sucked their teeth at him like cats marking their territory. He walked by. Found a bench by the pond and sat down to call the others. As he unzipped his bag, he heard movement over his shoulder. Mehmet, Necip and two others appeared out of nowhere.

'Close escape from Stringer,' said Mehmet. 'But not from us. What have you got for me?' he joked.

'I ain't got nothin',' protested Ned.

'Don't lie to me, fam, I know you got somethin' for me.'

Necip grabbed Ned's bag and took out his bus pass, a

deodorant spray and phone.

'Well, I reckon it's the phone,' said Mehmet pocketing it as Necip passed it to him, 'and remember, snitches love stitches.' Mehmet's friends all laughed.

Necip dropped the empty bag and the rest of Ned's things on the ground and, done, they turned and walked away. Ned felt humiliated. Could he find a way back from this bullying?

# Chapter Nine

## 20th NOVEMBER 2001

## WEST GREEN

Another month slipped by. Stanhopes preferred tenants with bank accounts who paid their rent by direct debit but were used to those who preferred to pay cash like Mr Jerrish. They would usually come into the office to make their payment, but Jerrish had said that he wanted to pay Lucas in person at the properties, so Jack expected Lucas to return from these meetings with cash.

'Collected from the Jerrish flats yet?' Jack asked.

It felt like a moment of reckoning. Lucas had paid Steve back the £1,800 and delivered cash deposits and rent for the new flats from his savings. But this had cleaned him out. He didn't know how he was going to find Jerrish's rent for the next month. The anxiety was affecting his health. He woke several times a night, had lost his appetite, developed stomach cramps, suffered panic attacks and spent most of the time feeling distracted. Mollie kept asking him if he was okay and he had told her that he had difficulties at work. When they had first met, he had already established himself in his respectable job and had never told her everything about his former life in Plymouth. Now he wanted to protect her from the danger, and it seemed the less she knew, the better. Jack had also noticed something was wrong, but Lucas diverted him by saying things were difficult at home.

'Lucas?' Jack brought him back to earth.

'I was going to do a tour today to collect. I think I'll set off now,' he said picking up four labelled spare keys from his desk drawer.

He left the office, turned right along the West Green Road past the supermarket, electronic repairs, bookies and the dry-cleaner's. He turned onto Belmont Road, lined with decaying Victorian villas, fallen from their original grandeur as fine family homes, now converted to flats or bedsits.

A couple of left turns, then a right and he reached 15a Carlingford. The curtains were closed. He rang the bell, but no one answered. He decided to let himself in and check the condition of the flat. The tenancy agreement allowed inspections – although they were meant to be pre-arranged. He opened the door with the spare key, closed it behind him and was immediately hit by a dry heat and the smell of cannabis. Stepping forwards he called out 'Hello, anyone home?' but there was no answer, so he turned to the living room. Heavy plastic curtains had been put across the door. Pushing them aside, the smell and heat intensified. The room was filled with potted cannabis plants, about sixteen of them, each over a metre tall and nearly a metre wide, two-thirds towards maturity. Against each wall, a tripod and stand held a strong LED lamp with a reflector hood. Checking the bedrooms, he found the same set-up with another sixteen plants between them. Shocked but not surprised, Lucas let himself out and headed for the park. He needed some fresh air and space to gather his thoughts.

In minutes he was walking through the park gates into the

wide expanse of the playing field. He went straight ahead, following the path that bordered Park School. He watched the path's surface ahead of him, warped and buckled tarmac distorted by the irrepressible nature of tree roots, while he slipped into deep thought. He had half-guessed Steve was still in that game and he guessed all four properties were set up the same way. Each flat's crop must be worth about £70,000 and with 24-hour lighting he could turn over a fresh crop every three months. And without paying a penny in rent, courtesy of blackmailing Lucas. Steve's business activities had come on a bit since those *Mousehole Cat* days. Turning this over in his mind, he wondered if he could turn the tables on Steve now that he knew what he was doing in the flats. He could go to the police and get Steve busted, tenancies terminated, blackmail over. But Steve might not be acting alone. Big braggart as he was, there might be bigger dogs with him, and trouble would just thicken for Lucas if he was implicated as a grass. He needed to think this through. But first he needed to be sure about the other three flats. They were all within minutes of the park. Within the hour his suspicions were confirmed.

While Lucas was letting himself out of the last of the flats, Steve Jerrish was drinking freshly squeezed orange juice. Since moving to London, he had been renting a flat in Crouch End, a comfortable middle-class area about two miles west of Tottenham, popular with professionals and people who worked in the media. He was feeling very pleased with himself, if he was honest, a bit smug. Not only was his business plan on track but he could hardly believe that he had found Spikey, settled, respectable, solvent and vulnerable to blackmail. Furthermore, as an estate agent, Spikey could source the properties he needed. He deserved this lucky break.

Life had been a rocky road since 1979 when the *Sea Queen's* cargo had been skimmed and he had fallen from grace with Frenchie. She had wanted her pound of flesh. Retribution. She nearly had his head, but thanks to Spikey's runner, Steve had been able to persuade her that the young punk was to blame. She had continued to use his Cornish route for two more years before securing an alternative and finally letting Steve and his boys go. Soon after, Benny went to live with relatives on a farm in Ireland, Vince got a promotion at B&Q to assistant manager and committed to the straight and narrow, while Dale sold the *Mousehole Cat* and cottage and moved to Spain. Steve had experienced being abandoned throughout his life. Each new episode hardened his shell and soured his view of others. He had no family. He wasn't sure what a real one would feel like. He had learnt how to look after himself from a young age and wouldn't know how to really care for someone else.

After the boys left, he had spent years trying different lines alongside his delivery day job. Street dealing, shifting replica perfume at a street market, and then burglary. His third one went wrong. The property was alarmed directly to a response centre. He was caught, and in 1997 got sent down for three years at Her Majesty's pleasure. Learning new tricks from other convicts, he hatched his next plan. The drug scene was changing. Hashish imports were being steadily displaced by high-strength skunk, hybrid cannabis seeds grown under artificial light with a higher level of the psychoactive THC. Skunk could be grown indoors in the UK with artificial lights, without the cost and risk of importation, plus the production was close to its market. He would rent cheap flats and set up skunk grows. Low-cost, low-risk, no-transport cannabis, grown at the point of market. All he needed was some start-up capital.

In January 2000, a little after his release he could not believe his luck when he bumped into Frenchie again. He had moved back to Plymouth and was driving deliveries. That day he was going to Bristol and stopped at Bridgewater service station. It was such a surprise to see her sitting in the Costa coffee shop. At first, he was apprehensive, but he summoned the courage to approach her. He could not say that she exactly smiled at him. He had never seen her smile. But she invited him to sit, and they had a catch-up. She was moving between Bristol and London, running some new businesses though he did not ask what kind. When she got up to go she offered him her telephone number. He was exhilarated by this reconnect.

He decided he would ask her for the loan he needed as start-up capital. It would cover rent and equipment. The worst that she could do would be to say 'no'. So, a week after the chance meeting he rang her and asked for another meet-up to discuss a business proposition. She agreed to reconvene at the same Costa. He presented his business plan, asked for a £30,000 loan, proposing to repay within two years at 10% annual interest. She had asked about the plan, just like a bank manager would: how many grows, who would manage them, how he would market the product, who to and where, what threats he foresaw from competitors. To his surprise she agreed, there and then. Steve left the service station feeling elated. Was Frenchie giving him a second chance for old times' sake, or was this a hard-nosed entrepreneur recognising a sound business venture? He was to collect the cash from one of her men in three days, same place.

Steve started his grows in Plymouth, where he knew the property and drug markets. He had built up a regular income stream. But after eighteen months, he realised that he would do even better if he moved to London.

The phone rang. A French-accented female voice. One of her conditions for the loan had been that he call her once a month with a progress report. If he didn't, she called him. There was always an undertone of menace even when she was making pleasantries.

'Allo, Steve, 'ow are you getting on down there?'

'Yeah OK, Frenchie. Things are getting established.' He knew it would be wise to give her the minimum of detail, lest she try to lever more advantage out of him.

'Splendid,' said Frenchie, 'jus' remember we 'ave placed trust in you. Don't run away with my money, haha! I do not want to be disappointed. Remember the clock is ticking. Our agreement ends February.'

'No worries, I won't let you down. Promise,' he said, feeling on top of the world.

## GREEN LANES, HARRINGAY

Behind a curtained, grimy shop-window, a pool table stood surrounded by six metal tables and scattered chairs. Two elderly men played pool while others sat, some playing back-gammon, some chatting or drinking tea from small glasses. A TV fixed high in one corner played VHS recordings of a Turkish football match. At the back of the room was a bar counter. And behind the counter, a wall-to-wall mirror, and a door. This was the Topkapi social club. Beyond the door, Mustafa Igli sat behind a large desk from which he ran the Topkapi organisation. Since arriving in London twenty years before, he had gained in weight as well as years, though he could still boast a full black beard and shock of hair. Today he was wearing a paisley shirt with the gold chains that he had worn throughout his adult life. But appearances could be deceptive and beneath his flamboyance, he had a reputation for violence and ruthlessness. Across the desk before him stood a tall skinny figure, close-cropped, clean-shaven and a face like a skull, in a long leather trench coat, his first lieutenant Kemal, Denzil's cousin.

'Tell me Kemal, what's the traffic like today?' Mustafa asked in Turkish.

'Pretty slow through Clapton and the Blackwell tunnel, boss,' replied Kemal with a rictus grin, 'yeah, melons from Mardin due this evening to the warehouse.'

The Edmonton warehouse, where Onur worked, was a modern hangar on an industrial estate. Incoming shipments were sporadic, so it did not require much staffing. Onur was employed as a permanent presence while more muscle could be brought in, as and when required to unload deliveries. The premises also provided a secluded venue for other gang activities when necessary.

'Keep me posted. I promised to call H as soon as it's arrived. Any beef from the Blacks or Albies?' Mustafa always asked for updates on street tensions with other local drug gangs, the Jamaican yardies who largely traded skunk and the more directly competitive Albanian gang that had recently been carving itself a niche in the cocaine market over the marshes in Walthamstow. Cocaine had become Topkapi's central business since Mustafa had been approached some years ago by representatives of a Colombian business enterprise seeking a logistical partnership. Their traditional transatlantic routes were becoming less secure and they had been investigating alternative ways into the UK for their product, one of which involved a diversionary land route via Turkey.

Topkapi had caught their attention due to its established trucking and warehousing facilities, a shared understanding of the importance of discretion and their local reputation. A pilot run had been successful, hiding the cocaine in secret compartments within specially crafted plastic watermelons buried at the bottom of a cargo of real ones. In return for the transportation, the Colombians gave Topkapi a preferential price on enough product to supply and control this corner of north London, with options for expansion. Mustafa did not know what the Colombians did with the remaining bulk of the cargo once they had collected it from his warehouse. But he was always vigilant for potential competitors, anything that might threaten Topkapi, particularly the Albanians: new in the neighbourhood with a reputation for violence rooted in regional warfare and selling cocaine across the Marshes in Walthamstow. Who was supplying them, Mustafa wondered? Were the Colombians riding both horses?

'No boss, all calm. I'll keep you posted. Saw them yardies Dwayne and Ellis yesterday near Downhills. No beef, even sent me a nod. Albies are keepin' east of the Marshes. Errr, boss, you remember my cuz Denzil, been runnin' errands and his bro' Onur, sitting the warehouse? They're keen to move up, prove themselves. You said you might give 'em a chance, something bigger?'

'Yes, I remember. Let's give 'em a try. We need more soldiers. Call them. Send 'em in when they arrive.'

An hour later, Denzil and Onur walked into Topkapi. They always felt conspicuously young in this place of elders who had grown up in the motherland and been pioneer migrants to London. They knew they owed them respect and thought it strange how the British disregarded and cast off their own. A couple of wizened men looked up momentarily as the young ones crossed the room before returning to their game. Denzil knocked on the door by the bar and they were buzzed into a smoke-filled office.

'Denzil and Onur,' Mustafa greeted them.

'Mr Igli, sir,' they replied shyly in Turkish unison.

'Kemal says you both want some more responsible work.' He paused. 'Topkapi knows how to offer trust, but we deal harshly if we are disappointed. Are you sure you want it?'

Locking them in eye contact, each in turn, he paused, waiting for their reply.

'Yes, boss,' they replied almost in unison.

'Alright then. You want tea? Kemal, get tea. We're giving you a trial. Next level up. Sales. You will take a package. Inside is 250 grams of cocaine. You will weigh it, bag it one gram one bag. You will sell it. Better to people you know. Or their friends. Recommendations. Charge £60 a gram. Bring back £15,000.'

Denzil almost asked how much they would be paid but thought better of it. This was their big opportunity, a trial, and he would do it for nothing if it meant more status in the gang.

'No problem, chief,' Denzil assured Mustafa, taking the bag.

They drove to Onur's house and sat in his bedroom. Mehmet was still at school, so they had the room to themselves. The package sat on the table.

'At £60 a gram, it's a neat profit for Mustafa,' said Denzil in English. Of course, he knew nothing of Topkapi's sources or arrangements but carried on. 'I bet it costs him half that, the volumes he brings in. Easy money for him, and he's not even takin' the street risk. That's on us. I reckon we're owed somethin' more.'

'What, you sayin' we sell it over £60?' said Onur.

'The Pembury crew down Clapton sell it for £70.'

'No bruv, he'd get to hear,' replied Onur.

'Well, we could make the weight go furver. So long as he gets his 15 grand. He won't know if we cut the stuff. Increase the weight and keep the difference.'

'I don't know, man. If it got out...' protested Onur. 'What if it got back to Mustafa that the quality was cut?'

'Who's gonna complain to Topkapi?' went Denzil, confident that he could outsmart the gang. 'This is the street, not Sainsburys. It's cool. I'm goin' shoppin'. Back soon.'

An hour later he returned with some shopping bags from which he pulled out a plastic washing-up bowl, two plastic spoons and a packet of Johnson's baby powder.

'Not too much, I'm not greedy,' said Denzil, cutting open the cocaine bag, pouring it into the bowl and carefully stirring in the talc, 'just about 25g. That will give us £750 each.'

Onur looked on. He wasn't so sure this was a good idea.

# Chapter Ten

**WEST GREEN**

Brenda and Lloyd called round at Crossfield Road. Monday night was five-a-side and Lloyd was here to pick up Lucas, leaving Brenda for an evening with Mollie. Lucas loved the run around, the game, the camaraderie. He never missed it and Mollie was always pleased to see him get some 'mates time' away from the family. The women were going to watch a movie together from Mollie's growing collection of DVDs.

Men out the door, Mollie opened a bottle of wine while Brenda thumbed through the DVDs.

'*The Princess Bride*, I loved watchin' dat. It's one dat has somethin' for every age group. Like dem Disneys dat build in jokes for da parents dat da kids won't get.'

'Yes,' replied Mollie. 'My favourite is *Lilo and Stitch*, just a kid's story about family and being left out, but there's another level for adults about children with disabilities.'

'You can be so deep, Mollie! By da way, how's Lucas' ghost story goin'?' she asked hoping the joke would be appropriately received.

'Yeah, it's giving me goosebumps,' replied Mollie, bouncing

the joke, and thinking of the kids' horror books that Ned and Mark used to love. 'He's told me a bit more. There's this guy from the past who's turned up. He says it's just upset him, being forced to remember his teenage punk haircut. Things he's not proud of and tried to move on from. That's all.'

'Yes, we all 'ave t'ings we'd rather forget.'

Meanwhile, on the Park School Astro Turf, Lucas had hoped the football would prove a distraction, but much as he tried, he couldn't stop thinking about Steve Jerrish and the blackmail. It affected his game. He missed loads of passes and failed to score an open goal. 'Lukey!' they had shouted at him. 'Relegation, mate!' Lloyd had called out, though Lucas knew it was in jest.

Two hours of cardio was always followed by a pint in the Goat just a few doors down the West Green Road from Stanhopes.

'My round. What are you drinkin'?' Lloyd was their goalie. It was Lloyd who had brought Lucas into the team. They had been mates ever since they had met at the school gates, bonded by parenthood and their sons' friendship. Lloyd was a big man who made himself bigger by twice-weekly stints at the gym on top of his Monday night knockabout. He ran a successful plumbing firm which he had built up steadily since his own apprenticeship twenty years earlier. He now ran three vans, employed three other plumbers and was training three apprentices. Brenda might have the church, but these were his Holy Trinity, he joked to himself. People were always going to need plumbers, especially in an area of ageing housing stock and gentrification. It was a well-paid trade and Lloyd had been successful. He was much liked and highly respected within his Jamaican community, a good father, husband, and loyal friend with a thriving self-made business.

The team bantered and drank for an hour, made their apologies one by one and slipped out, returning to their home lives until the next Monday meet-up. Lucas and Lloyd were the last remaining.

'Whazzup, Lucas? You seem a bit preoccupied tonight,' asked Lloyd.

Lucas hesitated to reply. He had got to know Lloyd well over the last five years and they had frequent family get-to-gethers where Lucas and Mollie had enjoyed tipsy adult time with Lloyd and Brenda while the children played. But their friendship had remained at that level. Lucas wasn't sure how far he could trust Lloyd or how he might react to Lucas' current problems.

'Whatever it is, Lukey, I can handle it. A problem shared is a problem halved, you know.' Lucas decided to risk his confidence.

'I've got a problem. I don't know what to do and I'm not sure you can help.'

'Try me.'

'Someone is threatening me. Blackmailing me,' said Lucas. 'Threatening to hurt my family. I can't go to the police.'

'What?' said Lloyd. 'What 'ave they got on you? Look Lukey, I know we're both decent family men, but I'd been aroun' the block a few times before I met Brenda. I know 'ow these things work. Trus' me. Maybe I can help.'

'How could you possibly help?'

'Well, why not start by tellin' me who dis is and what they got on you.'

Lucas paused, calculating how much he could tell Lloyd, what the benefit of disclosure would be, how Lloyd might be able to help, and decided to tell more.

'Someone from my darker past. Way back I ran with a bad crowd, something bad happened and I got blamed. I didn't do it. But I had to escape. That's why I came to London. This guy's showed up two months ago, recognised me, is threatening my family unless I cover his rent. On four flats he's renting from Stanhopes. I didn't see any choice. The first couple of months have cleared me out.'

'Why don't you go to da police? You're holding back,' said Lloyd.

'It's not straightforward. He's from a dark world, got dark friends, all well dodgy. The rentals are meant to be for relatives studying in London. I've checked and... well...' Lucas paused. This was the moment when Lucas's trust for Lloyd would be tested.

'Yeah, what? I can guess somet'ing else is going on. Safe housin' escaped cons? Bomb makin'? Prostitution? Gamblin'? Cultivation of cannabis? Am I warm yet?'

'One of the above, ... number four actually,' replied Lucas. 'The point is it's illegal, worth a lot of money and I'm sure he's not acting alone. He must be part of an organisation. He's using me to reduce their costs. If I lead the police to him, I'll become a threat to them. A grass. A target. I'll be ... *we'll* be in even greater danger. He knows about Mollie and the kids. He's already threatened me, put a threat on them.'

Lloyd picked up his glass. With elbows on the table he turned it so the last inch of IPA swirled in front of his eyes, as if gazing into a crystal ball while he digested Lucas's story. After nearly a minute of silence he put the glass down.

'You want some help?' he asked.

'Well yes. But how? What are you thinking?'

Again, Lloyd paused.

'I know some people,' he finally answered. 'Scary people,

who can represent for you, stand up to bullies.'

'But they'll be facing organised crime. Why would your people do that? I can't afford to pay them.'

'Don't worry, they can handle themselves. And they'd do it if I ask. They don't like outsiders who come in to make trouble, try to take over, mess with the order of t'ings.'

Lucas was surprised to feel a sense of comfort in the idea that he might have some back-up, some muscle standing behind him. It made him feel less vulnerable, part of a community. Maybe there was a way out of the situation which didn't involve the police and didn't pit him directly against Steve and his backers.

'Let me talk to a few people,' said Lloyd.

The next day at midday, Lloyd met up with some old friends at their special spot in the Italian gardens of Downhills Park. Lloyd loved Downhills and it had been his dream to buy a house on Downhills Park Road. Now he had done so, with a view across the playing field from his bedroom window. He had been raised on Broadwater Farm, and Downhills had been one of his childhood playgrounds, from early days with Mum and Dad on the swings and climbing frame through to his teen years with friends like Dwayne and Ellis, hanging out in the woodlands, chatting on benches. There had always been something about the Italian gardens that particularly appealed to him. Of course, there was the summer beauty of the roses and bedding plants, so lovingly planted by the council gardeners, though now leafless and bleak. But he loved their faded grandeur, their sense of history, a link to the past within the present, a sense of continuity, of permanence.

His parents had seen him through school and college, had always been there for him, encouraging him to aspire and supporting him. His was a hard-working, church-going family of the Windrush generation. As a chirpy and sociable boy, popular at school, he had got to know a lot of people in the neighbourhood and not all of them as respectable and law-abiding as his own family. While he found success in his chosen life, built his family and his trade, some of his old school friends found other forms of success. Dwayne and Ellis had always been bad boys, class clowns, eager to leave education and find their future with the local Jamaican underworld. Fifteen years after leaving school, they were now senior members with influence. But to Lloyd they were still mates. They always came to him when they needed plumbing, met up for a drink every few months or sometimes came round for a family Sunday lunch. Brenda found this a difficult relationship. She had a strong moral code and disapproved of their professional activities. She worried about their influence over Mark. But they were Lloyd's friends, and she did enjoy their company and cheeky humour. She had been pleased when Dwayne started coaching basketball at the community centre two evenings a week, doing something positive for the local youth and she prayed that this would lead him to turn from the darkness. For Lloyd's part, he loved Brenda and knew that these friendships troubled her. But he had no desire to lose these friends. He liked them and knowing that he could always turn to them for help. It was a good feeling. Not only did he have security in conventional terms, his family and career, but he also had back-up on the streets if he ever needed it. From what Lucas had told him, he knew they would consider Lucas's problem theirs too.

'So, dis bomclaat movin' t' our yard, settin' up grows, and plannin' to sell on our street?' Dwayne checked with Lloyd. Dwayne was an average height and build, dressed in a leather bomber jacket, jeans and sparkling white Nike trainers. He was clean-shaven, his hair close-cut on the sides with longer but flat-cut top. The most remarkable thing about his appearance was his bling: gold chains, rings and a gold front tooth. Although all three were born and bred Londoners, this was a conversation that was best spoken as Jamaicans.

'And t'reatenin' my frien' and he family,' added Lloyd.

'Raas,' said Ellis, a six-foot-five, eighteen-stone giant bulging with muscle and steroids. He was dressed in joggers, hoodie and trainers and looked permanently ready for a workout. He wore his hair long in beaded braids.

'We gotta protec' our yard from claffy like he, or every gangsta in Babylon t'ink dey come take Tottenham.'

To Lloyd, these were old friends sat beside him, but he knew they could be an intimidating force when they wanted to be.

'Irie, Lloyd, we'll talk wid' d' bredren an' come back.'

The following Monday night Lucas and Lloyd sat at the same table in the Goat after a better pitch performance from Lucas. The rest of the team had gone. They were alone again. Lloyd was the first to raise the subject.

'I spoke to some people,' he said.

'And..?'

'They think they can make your problem go away.'

'That's good news. And they know I can't give them anything?'

'Yes, they'll do it as a favour. But you've gotta be sure. There will be no turning back once started.'

'That sounds good to me. There's no good can come from having this guy around. I want him gone, final answer.'

'You're sure.'

'Yes, I'm sure.'

'Another thing is after tonight we don't talk about this ever again. You don't ask me any questions. It's like our conversation never happened. Can you promise that?'

'Man, this feels like we're in the script of some killer movie, Lloyd. You don't need to be so dramatic. But yeah, I don't want to ever think or talk about him again. I want him out of my life and mind. So OK, I promise. No questions ever.'

'You're sure?'

'Yes, I'm sure.'

'Well then, I just need three things from you. The guy's name, number, and the rental addresses.'

Lucas got a notepad out of his jacket pocket, wrote the information, tore out the page and passed it across the table. He felt hugely relieved.

'How long will it take? What will they do?'

'Just forget about your problem. It's gone.'

# Chapter Eleven

**27TH NOVEMBER 2001**

**LORDSHIP REC AND DOWNHILLS PARK**

Mark was up early as usual for his paper round, every day before school and on Saturdays. It gave him pocket money. Unlike most teenagers he liked getting up before other people emerged from their homes. He loved the quietness of the streets, even on dark winter mornings. He finished the round, went home for breakfast, and thought about the rest of the day. He had been saving up for a new bike and his dad was going to take him to Bicyclebox on Philip Lane to buy it. In the afternoon he was going to meet Ned in the park to try it out. If Ned brought his bike along too, they could race.

By 2pm Mark and Lloyd were back, wheeling a Carrera 14 speed. The frame was black with some black and white chequered edging, drop bars, Shimano gears and brakes. Uncle Dwayne had told him this was the best he could get within his price range. Both parents were so proud that he had saved up from his round to buy it without any help from them.

He rang Ned and they fixed to meet at 3pm in the Lordship Rec. Ned always loved riding around the street grid of the model traffic area and came on his Raleigh. He knew Mark's would be a better bike and was excited for his friend. The Carrera exceeded both their expectations, and they couldn't help but dance about, doing their football celebrations before saddling up and setting off. Round and round the traffic area street grid they went, Mark trying out all the gears, going fast, then slowing down, trying the brakes, falling off when he jabbed them too fast. Ned spinning along after him but falling behind on the sprints. Then they swapped. Mark let Ned try it out. An hour later they were ready for a rest and change of scene, so headed up to Downhills Park Road and crossed into Downhills Park. Through the gate and turn left and they found a bench in the Italian garden.

'Wow, Mark, your Carrera's wicked,' said Ned. 'You better get a proper good lock for it.'

'I don't plan on leavin' it outdoors, bro. It aint' never leaving my sight!'

'Gonna be your baby!'

'Maybe but more useful!' joked Mark.

'Well lookey 'ere, what 'ave you got boys?' A voice came from behind them. They turned to see Mehmet and a group of his cronies coming up behind them.

'Nice bike. Which one of you's minted then?'

'Yeah, well we're waiting for my uncles, innit,' said Mark, hoping that Mehmet might be bluffed off that they would not be alone for long.

'Well, you gonna let me have a spin? What? You think I'm gonna ride off on it?'

Mark stared at him silently.

'Don't be tight. Just a quick one round the beds,' said Mehmet, stepping closer.

Mark stood up. Ned followed. Mehmet and his mates now

surrounded them.

As Mehmet reached to take hold of the handlebars Mark pulled the bike back and held tight to it. Mehmet grabbed. Ned stepped forwards and pushed Mehmet away. The others turned on Ned.

'Go!' Ned muttered to Mark. In any other situation Mark would have dropped the bike and stood by Ned, but he had to get the Carrera to safety. While Ned distracted the gang, Mark slipped through the melee, wheeling it at a run and then jumping on to it.

'Get out of here!' Ned shouted over his shoulder. Mark lived on Downhills Park Road and knew he could be back in a few minutes.

Mehmet and his gang had got what they wanted, the bully's thrill of power. They could find Mark later. For now, Ned was an easy target. They punched and kicked him to the ground. After two or three minutes Mehmet called them off. It had just been a bit of fun. While he felt the kicks and imagined the bruises that would come, he felt strangely serene. Looking across the tarmac path he saw the world at ground level for the first time. Is this what the world looks like for ants, he wondered? An expanse of rough, hard terrain which was the path, tall stands of leafless and drooping plants overhead like wonky scaffolding, and in the distance, towering above, massive giants with sparse brown and russet canopies which were the trees, shedding their leaves.

'Let's see *your* wheels, chichi boy,' went Mehmet. 'Don't worry. No one wants a ride on that. I might get oil on my trousers.'

His gang seemed to think this was funny, and switching to Turkish they walked away laughing. But then they suddenly all stopped laughing and went quiet. What had happened?

Looking up Ned saw two women walking towards the gang. Mehmet saw his mother, Dilek with another woman.

'Hey, Mehmet,' muttered Necip, 'isn't that your mum?'

'Hello, Mrs Zaman,' the boys mumbled together.

'Hello, ma,' Mehmet offered sheepishly in Turkish, wondering how much of the episode she had seen.

The women took in the scene, the group of boys looking shifty, guilty about something, and beyond them another boy curled up on the pavement, a bike cast aside nearby.

'What's going on?' Dilek asked in Turkish. 'Is that boy alright? Why aren't you helping him?'

The gang were dumbstruck. Surely it was Mehmet's job to deal with his own mother, he was their leader, and it had been his idea to jump Mark and Ned. They shuffled and squirmed in their own ways while Mehmet struggled to think of a reply.

'Yes, ma, he's a boy from school,' he replied in English, feeling that this would give him more power over the adults in this situation. 'He came off his bike. We asked if he wanted help, and he said no.'

'Let me go and see,' said Dymphna, recognising Ned as Arjan's friend. 'I'm a nurse so I'll check him over.'

She walked past the boys and knelt by Ned.

'Hi there. You're Ned, aren't you? Arjan's friend. I'm Dymphna, his auntie. Remember me?'

Ned smiled, feeling safe with her.

'What's happened to you then, Ned? Shall we see if you're hurt? I'm a nurse.'

'I'm OK,' said Ned trying to get up. He hated Mehmet and his gang but didn't want these adults to know about the attack in case it just made things worse. Everyone hated a grass.

'I skidded and came off my bike.'

'OK,' said Dymphna, 'how did you land? Left or right side? Knee? Elbow? Hand?'

She quickly scanned all of these and seeing no grazes or cuts, doubted this story.

'My left knee,' he offered randomly, 'but I didn't get hurt.'

'So how do they fit in?' She gestured discreetly with a nod in the direction of the gang.

'They were just passing. Asked if I wanted help.'

Dymphna looked at the grazes on his face, inspected his arms and legs, and after a few seconds said, 'You know you have to stand up to bullies, Ned, or they will think they can carry on forever. Covering for them, protecting them like this just makes them stronger and the bullying worse.'

He blushed. How could she see through him so easily? Was it so obvious what had happened?

'Come on,' she said, 'let me help you get home,' helping him up.

'I'm OK I'll go on my own, thanks,' he said, trying to ignore the pains in his ribs, arms and legs as he straddled the bike and pedalled off.

She turned back to Dilek, who had sent the other boys away and now had Mehmet alone. Emine had told her about the bullying and now she had seen enough fragments to piece the picture together. She was speechless. She felt overwhelmed by waves of upset, shame, and anger to have found her son in the act. Meanwhile, Mehmet shrivelled with embarrassment. How would he face his mates on Monday after they had seen him cowered and scolded by his mum? How they would laugh at him. At the same time, he felt another creeping shame: he knew that his mother hated bullying and she had caught him. Yes, he wanted to impress his mates, but deep down he also still wanted his parents' approval. A random moment in the park had spun out of control to take on an entirely unpredicted significance in his life as his worlds collided.

# Chapter Twelve

**4TH DECEMBER 2001**

**PARK SCHOOL**

'You can't let this go, bruv. The more they get away wiv, the bolder they get,' said Grey.

It was break-time, and Mark and Ned were with a group of their friends. Ned had a black eye, some cuts and grazes to his right cheek but the rest of his bruises were beneath his clothes and thankfully nothing was broken. His parents had been really shocked and upset when he came home in that condition. They had wanted to take him to hospital, but he had persuaded them that nothing was broken, and that the hospital would just give him paracetamol. He insisted it had been a bike skid although they had been sceptical. Mark hadn't mentioned it to his parents either. He had got home unscathed, the bike safe, and then ran straight back to help Ned. But when he got there, he had seen Dymphna kneeling over Ned, Mehmet standing nearby with his mum and the rest of the gang gone. He had decided to stay away so as not to complicate the situation.

'Grey's right, we can't keep turnin' our cheek. The problem will jus' grow for all of us. That bully's gotta get off,' said Mark.

'So, what then?' asked Ned. 'We can't do nothin' on our own. We need back up, fam. Grey, Dev, Arjan, Billy, Ahmed, Den... are you in?'

Ned looked around at the faces of their friends.

'They need to know if they mess with one, they mess with all of us, innit.'

'This ain't no new t'ing blad,' said Grey's friend Dev. 'Them Turks been beefin' us for years. And their bruvvers beefin' our bruvvers before. Course we got your backs, innit, blad.'

'Mehmet's big bro' Onur, he's with a serious Turkish crew. Proper gangsta. They hate Kurds,' said Arjan. 'Mehmet says Onur's got his back.'

'My big bro, Mike, was at school with Onur back in the day,' said Grey, 'says Onur ain't so hard. An' we got our mandem too. I ain't scared of Mehmet's big talk. Time to stand up.'

'Get up, stand up.' 'Yeah.' 'Yeah.' One by one the boys bumped fists.

Across the yard, Emine complained to Shereen, sitting on a low wall.

'The world's gone crazy.'

They occupied a central spot and so had a good view of the yard. They watched different groups of boys and girls gathered in their usual spots. By the concrete ping-pong table were Mehmet and his group of followers and, further off, by the grass slope that bordered the park, Shereen's cousin Arjan was part of another group. Something was going on. It was palpable in the atmosphere.

'My lil' bro' is such a dickhead. I can't believe the trouble he's makin' with your Arjan's friends. The bullyin'. Beatin' up Ned in the park. Five on one. So cowardly. The upset he's made for my mum and dad. And then my big bro' Onur backin' him up! It feels like the family's fallin' apart, down the middle.'

'It sucks,' replied Shereen, 'and I mean it's so pathetic when other people have to deal with real world problems. Have you heard anythin' from Tulay? She's not been in school for a week and she's not answerin' her phone.'

'No, I'm really worried her parents have locked her up or somethin',' said Emine. 'Maybe taken her phone away.'

'I spoke to Walton. He's gone cool on her. Says he don't want no trouble with her family. Says there's nothin' he can do.'

'What kind of a friend is that? What about Walton's parents?'

'Come on, Ems, what parents are gonna face up another bunch of parents for somethin' to do with their parentin'? And when it's a cultural t'ing too. Walton's Jamaican and his parents probably feel they don't understand a Turkish t'ing.'

'Do you know, did Tulay speak to Ms Poole, like we said?'

'I don't know, but maybe we should go speak to Ms Poole ourselves.'

'Let's go today. You know Tulay's parents are old school, very traditional. You hear stories about those kinds of people? What some of them do if they think their family honour has been hurt? Even killings?'

'If Ms Poole won't help maybe we should go to the police.'

The tannoy signalled the end of break-time, but from the lingering of the crowds it was clear that not a lot of learning was going to happen back in class.

## GREEN LANES, HARRINGAY

Mustafa Igli sat behind his desk. It was 10am and he was suffering from his usual morning mental fug. Kemal came in carrying a tray of coffees and baklava.

'Any news from H?' asked Kemal in English. 'We need our December melons. November's are all pipped out.' He grinned at his own joke.

Mustafa didn't laugh. He maintained his composure but felt a twinge of anxiety. He had not heard from Hasan Güney for over a week. Hasan organised the cocaine shipments from Mardin, loaded them into the hollowed-out watermelons and on to the refrigerated truck. He remembered first meeting Hasan back in Mardin and liking him even though he was a Kurd: straightforward, honest, reliable and with a good sense of humour. Why couldn't all Kurds learn to get along better with their Turkish neighbours like Hasan did? When Mustafa left for England, they had lost touch. But ten years later, Mustafa made a return visit to Mardin and found Hasan now running his own truck across Europe and wanting to expand. Mustafa had seen an opportunity, offered to invest and they had been partners since. Since the Colombian arrangement, the monthly watermelon shipment had become central to Topkapi's prosperity, so Mustafa insisted on weekly status updates from Hasan. He often also asked for updates on his own family gathered from gossip. He preferred not to call them himself. His parents were old and annoying; his brother Bulent was so uptight, no sense of humour. All of them were so conservative, living with them had been stifling. And how often they would ask him about his love life. Why didn't he have a girlfriend? When would he give them grandchildren? He couldn't tell them he was more interested in men than women. Homosexuality was not acceptable in Mardin. But London had been more open-minded, and this had been an important reason for his move, although he told people it had been for the economic opportunities.

Why this two-week silence from Hasan? He looked for possible explanations for a disruption but surely he would have heard if there had been a police swoop or trouble with a rival firm. Mustafa pulled out his Nokia and dialled. Hasan picked up. He started in Turkish.

'Hasan, my friend, how are you?'

'Well, well, it's the Englishman. Hello Mustafa. How is the rain treating you?'

'I am drowning in it. At least the grass is green over here. It's been two weeks. How is Mardin? What news of my family?'

'Mardin is tranquil, business is business, I hear that your parents can't stop talking about your new house in Payas and how proud they are of you. Last week the builders finished the windows and this week they are moving on to the electrics.'

'When it is complete you will be my first guest, Hasan. And my brother Bulent? How is the army treating the grumpy dog? At his age surely, it's time for a desk job?'

'I hear he is in good health, and they have moved him. Now he is a recruitment officer. But the new job makes him an unpopular man. Imagine, knocking on doors in uniform looking for young men to fight Kurds in the mountains, in a Kurdish town! He will need eyes in the back of his head.'

'It will make him even more unpopular than he is already! Well, it must be safer than the frontline. I should know better than talk politics with you. But about business. What can you tell me about my fruit and vegetables? Are they still growing in Turkey or have the farmers given up?'

'My friend, everything is growing, and I am still sending deliveries. But my drivers are stuck in traffic too much and the tacho tells them to rest.'

'Come now, Hasan, that's why we send two drivers. You tell your tacho men if they don't get here by tomorrow, they won't be making a return journey.'

'Leave it with me and I will call you back.'

Mustafa hung up. This was typical of him. One minute, joking and bantering, the next threatening the violence that always sat just beneath the convivial surface. His unpredictability kept everyone he worked with permanently on edge, never knowing when he would turn.

'Just sit tight,' he answered Kemal. 'H has it under control'.

'About that other thing, boss,' said Kemal, 'my cuz Denzil and his spa, they've moved the weight and are here with the money.'

'Mmmm,' went Mustafa, giving Kemal a brief sideways glance. 'Show them in.'

He knew this wasn't going to lighten his mood, but toying with these two greenhorns might provide a distraction. Kemal went out and reappeared with Denzil, who looked pleased with himself, and Onur in tow.

'You have the money?' asked Mustafa, using Turkish to emphasise the jurisdiction of Topkapi.

'£15,000 as you expected, boss,' Denzil replied respectfully, keeping in language, swinging a holdall on to the desk, striking a pose somewhere between a nonchalant gangster and obedient soldier. He was really pleased with himself and expected Mustafa to be impressed. They had passed the test with 100%. Mustafa unzipped it and, satisfied that it contained cash, passed it back to Kemal who, as usual stood behind him.

'Kemal will count it later. But now I must tell you a sad story. I heard it from one of your customers. Let's call him the mystery shopper. Usually, I send him around London to check the competition. He tells me about the quality of product and prices around town. This helps me set my street price. Well, last week he scored off you. And he was disappointed with the merchandise. I told him I knew what I had supplied. It was good. 90% pure. He says it was cut. How do you explain this?'

Denzil and Onur each felt a rising surge of anxiety as they realised they had been found out. This story was going in the wrong direction. Denzil risked a sideways glance at Onur. He could not see a way out. They had taken responsibility for the package. They would not have been forgiven for allowing anyone else near it so there was no way to blame anyone else. To call Mustafa's source wrong would be equally rash as Mustafa might trust the source more than them. Denzil spoke.

'Boss, it was Onur's idea,' switching to English, 'to mix it just a bit. Just 25g. To give us a reward for shifting the weight. We reckoned no harm. You still get your fifteen grand. Was that wrong, boss?'

He hoped this last note of innocence and ignorance might save them. Onur risked a sideways glance. He couldn't believe that Denzil would drop him in it like this, blatantly shift the blame when it had been Denzil's idea in the first place, and he had warned against it. But he could say nothing that might portray himself as disloyal or weak. He stood and listened silently while Denzil portrayed him as Topkapi's traitor.

'What do you say, Onur?' Mustafa's eyes scanned from one to the other like a searchlight.

What could he say? Denzil had been with Topkapi longer, was higher up the food chain and a good liar. He had to take the blame, hope that he would be seen as strong and honourable. He replied in Turkish to signal his respect and subservience.

'Like Denzil said, boss, it was my idea. It seemed no harm to the house. Now I see it was a mistake. Wrong. I am ashamed and ready to take punishment.' While he looked directly at Mustafa, he could detect Denzil smirking from the corner of his eye.

Mustafa opened his desk drawer and produced his machete. He laid it gently on the desktop as he continued. So it is true, Onur thought, remembering what he had heard about Mustafa's punishment.

'Reputational loss is as bad as financial loss, Onur. Denzil, it may have been Onur's idea but you went along with it, so you are equally responsible. Do you think I can have soldiers who try to deceive me?' He reached for the machete and holding it in his right hand, ran the thumb of his left hand across the blade.

'Well? Do you?'

The air was thick with menace. Denzil and Onur had both turned ashen. Kemal was shifting nervously, torn between loyalty to boss or family and embarrassed at having vouched for his cousin.

'Now, go away,' Mustafa surprised them all, not pressing for their response, 'and think hard about what Topkapi means to you and why I should allow you to keep walking the streets. You will hear from me when I am ready.'

As the pair shuffled out and closed the door behind them, filled with shame and fear, Mustafa looked at Kemal.

'Kemal, you brought them to me. Now what would you

have me do?'

'Sorry, boss,' Kemal stuttered,'but you know, they are young and think they know everything. Let them stew. Then I would give them one more chance to redeem themselves. Good soldiers are not easy to find, and I think they will turn out good.'

'Hmmm, I'll think about it,' replied Mustafa, continuing to play with the machete. There was a job he had in mind, something dangerous that might involve taking casualties. It could be the perfect test for them, and should it go wrong, they were expendable.

Leaving the cafe and walking down the Green Lanes, Onur was charged with mixed emotions. It felt like he was reaching fresh air after being trapped in a mine shaft. He was filled with anger, resentment and disillusionment with a 'friend' who would drop him in trouble like that, and fear for what Mustafa might do to them and their families. Everything he worked for and his hopes for the future had been put at risk. Denzil wasn't smirking anymore. He was slowly realising that although he had saved his own skin, he had lost his friend.

'I didn't know what to say,' Denzil stuttered. Onur had nothing to say back.

# Chapter Thirteen

**20TH DECEMBER 2001**

**WEST GREEN**

Steve had set up the grows and was now playing a waiting game while nature took its course. He had set up lighting to force 24-hour growth, but with no irrigation system in place he was making daily watering visits. He was just about to set off on his maintenance rounds when his phone rang.

'Mr Jerrish?' The voice sounded formal, official even. He detected a Caribbean accent.

'Yes, who's that?'

'Mr Jerrish, I'm callin' from Stanhopes estate agency to say your rents are overdue.'

'I think there must be a mistake,' he replied, feeling alarmed and surprised. 'I've been dealing with Lucas Fairbright. I made it clear I would pay him directly in cash. It's him you need to check with.'

'There's been some changes in our office, Mr Jerrish. Mr Fairbright is indisposed, and I will be acting as your new point of contact,' came the voice. Jerrish was rapidly switching into alert mode as his adrenaline kicked in. He listened attentively for any clues to the caller's identity.

'I'd like to meet you at 15a Carlingford Road for an

inspection, is that alright?'

Something wasn't right. Jerrish needed time to check out what had happened to Lucas, think this through and clear out the grow before this new agent came round.

'Today isn't convenient. Tomorrow, OK? 1pm.'

'I can do that,' the voice replied. 'See you there.'

Jerrish hung up. What was going on? Lucas was a partner in Stanhopes. Surely no one could tell him what to do. Without direct contact, he would lose his leverage over Lucas. Then he would have to pay the rental costs for the grows. It would eat into his profits. He didn't like this.

He would have to clean up today before tomorrow's inspection. Three hours later he parked a rental van outside 15a and let himself in. A new aroma immediately hit him. The smell of cannabis smoke. Entering the living room, he was overwhelmed with surprise. The room had already been cleared of all plants and light stands. It was empty except for two Black men standing in the middle of the floor, sharing a joint, one of them resplendent in gold bling and, Jerrish noticed, a gold front tooth. The other was a mountain of muscle, with braided long hair.

'Mr Jerrish,' said Dwayne, 'we t'ought we come a bit early and surprise you. A pre-inspection inspection 't'ing.'

'You from Stanhopes? You don't seem like Stanhopes kinda people,' came out of Steve's mouth before he realised what a stupid thing it had been to say.

'No shit, Sherlock,' said Dwayne. 'But we be Tottenham kinda people. And we feel strong 'bout rules. One rule say you canna use dis flat for illegal purposes, so we save you da trouble of clearin' your t'ings. Another rule is particular for *your* kinda people.'

'My kinda people?' asked Jerrish.

'Incomer who t'ink dey can boss I yard. In Tottenham, Jerrish, you jus' a pickininny. No one grow without we say so. You can na sell on da corners, no t'reaten our bredren. Now, we come for ya rent, £2,400.'

'Yeah,' Ellis added in a deep threatening voice to reinforce the message.

Jerrish tried to process his predicament. Yesterday he had been feeling pleased with himself. He had successfully set up four grows and eliminated any rental costs by blackmailing Lucas. He estimated earning enough to pay off Frenchie and walk away with a fat profit. Today all that had all fallen apart. The crop was gone, the free rent ride was over, and he now had beef with a local gang. Not only were these yardies stealing his crop and threatening him, but as if that wasn't enough, they were putting him in mortal danger from Frenchie by robbing his only way of repaying her loan. He felt washed over by competing waves of anger, fear, failure and betrayal. It must have been Lucas. He must have tipped off the yardies about the grows, knowing they would act to defend their own business interests. Lucas was a dead man if Steve caught up with him. But right now, he had to calm himself. He had to think clearly if he was going to get out of this situation. He concentrated on his breathing and tried to slow his racing heartbeat. Clutching at straws, he imagined that if he could sound like a solicitor, as if the law was on his side, this might somehow disarm these gangsters, given that they clearly out-muscled him.

'Gentleman,' he said adopting a calm and deliberately ironic tone of formality. 'There appears to have been a misunderstanding for which I must apologise. You see I represent a large and influential organisation for which I simply follow instructions. I can see that some local rules may have been transgressed, but surely a negotiated compromise might be reached. My associates would hate to find themselves in a dispute with any community in which they hope to operate. But I must make it clear that they are always prepared to follow things to the end of the road when it proves impossible to resolve disputes.' He hoped that his last sentence would leave a shadow of menace in the minds of these men.

Dwayne took two steps towards Jerrish, Ellis just behind him. Jerrish could feel the power of the presence, the physical intimidation of proximity, their fearlessness and strength. Dwayne's face was inches from Jerrish's.

'I can see da end o' the road may be a body in a bush, Mr Jerrish, but I don't t'ink it be one of ours. You reconsider your business 'ere. If you stay, you better pay attention to your new tenancy arrangements. We'll be back tomorrow for the inspection and expec' the rent. Got it?' And with that Dwayne and Ellis left.

Steve stood, feet fixed to the floor, weak at the knees and the blood draining from his head and torso towards the bottomless pit opening beneath him. His operation was finished, his investment lost, his mission failed, and future credibility with Frenchie damaged beyond repair. Frenchie would punish him and that was if the yardies didn't get him first. Why hadn't it occurred to him that his grows might ruffle some local gangster feathers? He took deep breaths, counting to three on the in breath and five on the out, as he had learnt from a hippie surfer long ago in Newquay. It helped to calm him. Don't panic. Think. He needed to take back control of the situation before Frenchie found out.

His phone rang.

' 'Ello Steve. You didn't call this month so 'ere I am.'

He couldn't believe the timing of the call, as if Frenchie

was watching the room with a hidden camera, right on cue when he was at his most vulnerable.

'Yeah, sorry I didn't call. I've had some complications.' He didn't know how else to camouflage the situation without lying, and that was something he could not do to her. She could always tell and that would be fatal.

'Tell me, Steve. What complications?'

Steve's mind felt scrambled. He had to maintain Frenchie's confidence, but he didn't know how he could salvage the operation without her help. She could summon the muscle he would need to push back against these yardies and recover the product. Then he remembered Lucas. It might swing in his favour if he told her that he had found Spikey. She could finally get retribution for the *Sea Queen's* skimmed block. It was a gamble. He threw the dice.

'Well, there's good news and bad news. The good news is that I've found the rat who skimmed us in '79. I've got ways we can get him to pay back for what he done.'

'Mmmm, that's interesting. Go on, the bad news?'

'Frenchie, I've got some beef with some guys round here, Jamaicans who think I'm competition. I need some of your muscle to return a message.'

The line went quiet. Frenchie was obviously thinking things over, weighing the good news against the bad. Steve's emotions hung by a thread.

'I'm glad you found our old friend, Steve, and we can arrange our reunion later. But this other thing, I am disappointed. My only interest is to secure my loan. I 'ave no cause for conflict with your Jamaican friends. My only argument will be with you if you do not 'onour our agreement. You 'ave two months left to pay me back. Or you do know what will 'appen, don't you Steve? You 'ave seen 'ow I deal with broken promises, 'aven't you? I 'ope for your sake you don't let me down. I'll be in London in February to collect.'

She hung up. Steve stood rooted to the spot, unable even to put his phone down. He had gambled everything on this venture. He had known the stakes, the fatal consequences if he failed Frenchie. He had messed up and he couldn't see a way out.

## BRUCE GROVE

Dilek found the repetitive actions of the sewing machine meditative, even therapeutic. Sometimes it helped her drift among her thoughts and daydreams and she left the radio off. This morning, she was agitated. She couldn't settle and was irritated by her work. She felt so distressed about her sons. At 11am she stopped and rang Cetin.

'Cetin, I need to talk to you. I am so worried about the boys. Please come home for lunch.'

He arrived at midday. They settled in the kitchen with glasses of tea and a small plate of börek, spinach and feta pastries. They spoke in Turkish.

'I am so worried about the boys, Cetin. I can't take my mind off them. It stops me working. It stops me sleeping. Onur spending time with Denzil, getting mixed up in …I don't know what. That boy, he's no good. A bad influence. It will lead to trouble, imagine…maybe prison.'

'He's been on this path since he was at school. He made the wrong friends. But come on, Dilek, we both know you can't choose your children's friends for them.'

'Maybe it's our fault, Cetin. Maybe we should have moved to another area. A different school. Maybe we should have stayed in Mardin, with our families around us to help the children keep straight. And now Mehmet. I am so ashamed. To find him with a gang beating a boy. Is this the honour of a man? To bully, five on one? Is this the future we want for our boys? Lives of crime and bullying? And Emine says also he is hateful to a Kurdish boy. Isn't this prejudice part of why we left Mardin? And now to find it here, within our own family.'

Cetin did not know what to say. He shared his wife's feelings but felt a responsibility to present a positive or hopeful response, to pull her away from her gloom although he shared her worries.

After a moment of silence he ventured, 'We've got to remember Mehmet is still young. It is his age. At thirteen, boys all want to impress their friends and think it is funny and makes them powerful to hurt someone who is different, or weaker. If we were still in Mardin he would probably be doing the same. But he will grow out of it. Grow up to be a kind and thoughtful person.'

'And Onur? Has he grown up to be kind and thoughtful? He goes down a bad road and Mehmet follows him.'

They sat in silence, each focused on their tea glass, each wondering where they had gone wrong, wishing for an inspiration, something that would make everything better. Dilek broke the silence.

'We must focus on Onur. Where Onur goes, Mehmet follows. Maybe we should send him back to Mardin, to live with the family, away from Denzil and those people.'

'But this is his home,' he replied. 'Born and bred here. He has never been to Turkey. He does not know our families. He speaks Turkish like the London Cypriots around him. Just imagine how it would be for him. How difficult.'

'Many things look impossible in the beginning but turn out well in the end. Remember how difficult it was for us to come here but look at what we have built over time. He could live with my family, get to know them. My Papa could give him work in the business or there is your old friend Hasan. You said you had heard he now has his own transportation company. Learn about our culture, improve his Turkish. Have a new start, a decent, honest life away from bad people. Now, *that* would be a good example for Mehmet to follow.'

Cetin reflected before replying.

'My love, Onur is now twenty. He is not a child. He must make his own decisions. But I agree, we can explore this option for him. Perhaps he will like this idea. But about Mehmet, he is too young to leave us and must finish school. Maybe if he hears that Onur has a better new life, Mehmet will follow his example.'

'A separation will be hard for them both, they are so close. But we must do something. We are their parents.'

Cetin took his phone from his jacket pocket.

'I will call my old friend, Hasan. I have not spoken to him for years, but I can see if he may help.'

He dialled the number. The line rang for thirty seconds, then was answered.

'Hello, Hasan, this is Cetin Zaman, how are you?'

'Cetin? Cetin from Osman's? Good to hear from you. Long time! How are you?' Hasan asked.

'Yes, it has been a long time. You remember Dilek, of course? We now have three children and we have prospered. Mehmet is thirteen, Emine fifteen, both at secondary school, and Onur is twenty and working in a warehouse. He could do better. I am a running a supermarket. What of you, my friend? I heard you are now a businessman!'

'Well, I'm doing OK. I have my own trucking business now. Better than changing oil in our garage, heh? Yes, I am trucking all over Europe, sometimes to London too.'

'And your family?'

'Well, maybe you remember my son Rasheed wanted to go to London too. And he is there now. He has a good job as an engineer, married to Dymphna, remember her? They were dating already before you left? She was a nurse here in Mardin. They have a daughter, Shereen. My sister Fatima in Qamishli is suffering the hardships sent against the Kurdish people. She lost her husband and daughter in an army incursion two years ago. The army crossed the border to attack the town. They say they were "punishing terrorists." Then Fatima sent her youngest son Arjan to London. He is living with Rasheed in Tottenham.'

'He lives in Tottenham? Praise be, we also live in Tottenham.'

'Ha! Maybe he goes to school with your thirteen-year-old? We should arrange an introduction so they can be friends.'

'Maybe, but there are many schools in Tottenham. Hasan, I am calling to ask something. My older son Onur wants to visit Mardin, stay with his grandparents, spend some time finding out about his roots for a few months. Tell me, what are the prospects for work these days? He has experience in a warehouse and drives. And of course, he speaks English as well as Turkish.'

'It is always difficult to find work, same as always. It depends on who you know. Dilek's family business is still very successful. I am sure they would help him, especially if he is living with them.'

Cetin was surprised that Hasan did not extend a spontaneous offer of help. Of course, Cetin thought, it is only to be expected. A phone call out of the blue after so many years.

'Let me think about it, Cetin. Maybe I'll think of something else to help. I'll ask around and call you in a few days if something comes up, okay, on this number?'

'Thank you, until then.' He hung up and turned to Dilek.

'Not as promising as I hoped.'

'I will call my family,' said Dilek.

## GREEN LANES, HARRINGAY

Onur's phone rang. Mustafa wanted to see him. Denzil was already there when Onur arrived at Topkapi. They both stood in front of the desk, feeling like naughty schoolboys facing their headmaster. Behind Mustafa, as usual Kemal stood looking menacing. To their surprise, today Mustafa chose to speak to them in English.

'It is fortunate for you that we have decided the damage you have caused is limited, so after much consideration and with respect for your cousin Kemal, I am giving you a second chance, Denzil. And because you came as a team, I extend this to you, Onur. Before we go any further, Denzil and Onur, do you both want this opportunity?'

'Of course. We'll do anything, boss,' said Denzil, looking at Onur.

'And you, Onur, will you do anything?'

'Anything for the house, boss,' Onur replied.

Mustafa paused, as if considering whether the two were up to the task he was about to give them.

'There will be no way back from this one. If it goes wrong, you will be finished here. I warn you this. So, before I say more, I offer a final chance to turn away, leave the cafe and leave Topkapi forever. We will only expect you to keep your silence about us on the outside.'

In the minds of both, Topkapi was the future. It would

give them money, power, and respect. It brought excitement, status and meaning to their lives. Surely this was better than humdrum work in a warehouse all day and watching DVDs every evening.

'Anything,' repeated Denzil. Onur nodded despite his recent reservations about his friend.

'OK,' said Mustafa, opening a desk drawer, pulling out a handgun and putting it down in front of them. The sight of it set their pulses racing. He continued in English as if to emphasise that this was London business.

'The Albanians are standing on our toes. They may be brothers in Islam, but they are not behaving like good family. When they first came to London, we helped them find homes, work, like good Muslim brothers, in Walthamstow. There, we told them, they can make business. Like us, they want to sell cocaine. No sweat. No competition with us in Walthamstow. But now I hear some of them are greedy, want to move to Haringey and Hackney. To take our business. It takes the piss. So, we must send a message. You will deliver it. No one gets hurt, but they must see we are serious. A warning. Show them this. Just show. OK? I heard already they try selling in Tottenham Hale.'

Mustafa had indeed heard from reliable sources that a Walthamstow-based Albanian gang was pushing its operations westwards across the Marshes. But he had a bigger anxiety: who were the Albanians getting their product from? Were they working with his own Colombian connection? If so, might this indicate that the Colombians were cultivating the Albanians as an alternative logistics and distribution partner? He needed to send a signal to the Albanians across the Marshes: be grateful for our hospitality, know your place and respect our boundaries. It was always best to start politely, with a light touch. Usually this was enough, and if it wasn't, it allowed for escalation. He would send these dispensable rookies and if this proved enough, he would know the Albanians were nothing to worry about.

Standing across the table, Denzil behaved as if he had won a school prize as he picked up the handgun and put it in his jacket pocket.

'Thank you for this opportunity, boss. We won't let you down, I promise,' he fawned.

Onur nodded along. He didn't understand where the Albanians had come from or how they had grown to be such a feature of the landscape in recent years, but he knew they were a new crew on the block, armed and dangerous. These men were children of the 1990s Balkan war and no strangers to violence and death. Even before that war, the mountainous land of isolated tribal communities had a long history of violent feuding, banditry and smuggling. Now in the UK, Albanian gangs had already established a strong grip on the cocaine market in some cities and seemed to be moving in here.

They left Topkapi. Onur drove. St Anne's Road, the High Road, Tottenham Hale, Ferry Lane. He was uncomfortable with Denzil and couldn't shake off the bad feeling of betrayal and loss of trust, but tried to maintain a friendly demeanour because he knew Denzil's cousin Kemal could make or break his future career. Denzil cradled the gun with a nervous excitement.

'This is serious big time, blad,' Denzil said like an excited child. He'd never carried a gun before but covered his anxiety with bluster. 'It's a test, innit. If we pass it'll be another level for us.'

'We just gotta do what Mustafa said: tell them Topkapi run

the ends, they're newcomers and owe respect. And let them see the strap.'

'Yeah, and if they get lairy...' bragged Denzil, aiming his fingers at the street, 'boom, boom.'

# Chapter Fourteen

**13TH JANUARY 2002**

**PARK SCHOOL**

It was difficult getting back into the rhythm of school after a two-week break, especially Christmas with all the family festivities, gift-giving, and movie-watching. But the inevitable had come, reality taken hold and here they were back at Park School. It was mid-morning break time and Emine and Shereen sat on a low wall in the yard.

'Christmas seems like ages,' said Shereen, 'but it's only two weeks. Ain't fair how time flies when you're enjoyin' yourself but crawls when you're not.'

'True say, but mine was so dry though,' replied Emine. 'My yard is so dead. My parents are so pissed with both my bros. Upset wiv each other. Hardly talkin'. My bro's ignorin' me 'cos I told on Mehmet's bullyin'. Need to get outta there! I'm gonna get my grades, go sixth Form, go uni soon as.'

'Poor Ems. What's wrong with your bros? I don't understand it 'cos I've got no bro'. Well, I've got Arjan but he's a sweet, kind boy, helpful, so we're lucky. Our biggest problem's our yard's too small. Hey, did you hear anyt'ing from Tulay over Christmas? Ms Poole said we should go see her if we ain't heard nothin'.'

'No, still nothin' since December. I reckon they sent her back t' Turkey, to a fixed-up marriage. I don't know what's worse, that or being locked up in her bedroom here.'

'At least in London she knows there's people thinkin' 'bout her and trying to help. Come on, let's go see Ms Poole.'

Ms Poole's door was always open to her pupils, and they knew it. Everyone respected her and many turned to her for help. They found her in the Drama Studio preparing for the next lesson.

'Hello girls,' she greeted them. 'Have you come to help me set up?'

They laughed. 'No miss, it's about Tulay.'

'Ah yes.' She stopped still, gave them her full eye contact, and gestured them to the seating area.

'No news since we last spoke?'

'No miss.'

'Well, I did file a report when you first flagged up her absence. Thanks for bringing it back. I'll follow it up.'

'What will you do, miss. Will you call the police? Shall we call them?'

'Leave it with me for now. The police will take this more seriously coming from me than from you. You've done what you can. Just keep trying to ring her and let me know if you hear anything.'

'We think they might send her to Turkey, miss, to get married. Can they do that, miss? Send her abroad if she doesn't want to go?'

'I don't think they can. It might be considered abduction and to keep her locked up in the flat could be considered false imprisonment. I'll get on it again today.'

The day wore on. The last lesson for the boys in 9PC was French with Ms Deason in G24, top of the building just off the atrium. As soon as they were dismissed, most of the class rushed down the stairs as usual to get into the school yard. But Mark, Ned and Arjan hung back as planned. The holiday break had not stopped them remembering their pledge to stand up to Mehmet. They were all chewing gum. As the tide of teenagers rolled down the stairs, the three friends leant on the banister looking down. They had been planning small acts of vengeance which they hoped would send a simple message. Grey and Dev had reached the bottom and were in position, casually leaning against a wall chatting. As Mehmet and Necip reached the bottom they peeled off and started chatting with them, holding them back with small talk. The boys above took aim and spat their gum over the banister, then pulled out of sight. Necip reached for his head, feeling something wet. He found the gum with his fingers, but it was stuck to his hair and the more he fiddled, the more entangled it became.

'Bro, what the fuck?' he said to Mehmet.

Meanwhile Arjan had scored a direct hit on Mehmet who was going through a similar effort to pull a gooey blob out of his curls.

'Oh shit, dat's deep man!' laughed Grey. 'Looks like you been bombed, boy. Allow dat!'

Mehmet swore at him in Turkish, turned and walked away quickly, both hands fiddling with his hair, trying to unpick the gum followed by his shadow, Necip, who was doing the same. But the more they fiddled, the more the wet warm goo spread and stuck. Other pupils were now looking, pointing and laughing at them.

'Hey look, Mehmet's got fleas!'

'Scratch, scratch!'

'New hairstyle, Mehmet?'

It wasn't nice being the object of jokes. As Mehmet and Necip reached the corner they looked back at the laughing crowd, Grey and Dev among them. Then movement caught Mehmet's eye up at the second-floor landing of the atrium. Mark, Ned and Arjan had stepped back to the railing to watch the mockery below. The penny dropped. Mehmet pointed up at them.

'I see you, fam!' He shouted, 'I'm comin' for you, watch me. Friday after school you're gonna get done.'

## FERRY LANE, TOTTENHAM

For Cetin and Dilek, Christmas had been a chance to catch Onur's undivided attention. They talked persuasively about taking a break to Mardin, the chance to meet his grandparents and relatives, to see the beautiful town, to be treated like returning royalty, the work opportunities, the beauty of the girls. His grandparents, they told him, were excited at the prospect of meeting him. It could open a new chapter in his life, the possibility of work in the family's leather business or Hasan's haulage company, certainly better prospects than the Edmonton warehouse. They had been pleasantly surprised to find him open to the plan and wondered if perhaps Onur's ambitions were shifting. Was he finally growing up? Onur himself quickly saw that the suggestion offered him an escape route, an insurance policy should Topkapi's second chance go wrong. Besides, he could imagine the adulation and respect that he would get from the youth of a small Turkish town, being the big man from London, and deep down he was also curious to find out more about his family roots.

Denzil and Onur's search for the Albanian gang had been

delayed by Christmas. Even Muslim gangsters, it seemed, took time out during the seasonal closedown, perhaps to visit relatives or friends, to party or to rest. But now Denzil had found out where the Albanians liked to meet. The Ferry Boat Inn on Ferry Lane looked curiously like a quaint country pub on the inside, all dark wood and roofing beams but outside it was far from rural. As a solitary building sandwiched between the very noisy Ferry Lane and Walthamstow Marshes, it was a desolate location. Its very isolation, however, was part of its attraction. The low level of passing trade reduced possible risks, a car park gave easy access and its location between Walthamstow and Tottenham gave it strategic reach, a bridgehead into Topkapi turf.

Denzil and Onur arrived at 7pm, well after dark. They sat at a corner table on dark wooden chairs. A slow but steady flow of customers came in from the cold, damp winter evening, hats and coats, collars turned up, small numbers, never enough to fill the tables. Some builders in high viz and hard hats, a group of women perhaps en-route home from work, a few solitary, wizened old men carefully sipping from the evening's half-pint. Bad 1970s pop music and a sticky, swirly red carpet counterposed the rustic, varnished roof beams. After two hours a couple of guys came in, big, trim and dressed for clubbing. Onur could recognise spoken Albanian as easily as an English person might recognise French, without understanding it. They stood at the bar, scanning the room, making themselves visible and available before moving across to a vacant table. A few moments later, the pub door started to open with greater frequency. A new clientele dribbled through. Some bought a drink and loitered for a while before approaching the Albanians, some went straight to their table, and some to the toilets with a passing signal for the dealer to follow. Every now and again, one would answer his mobile phone. There was no doubt, they had found part of the Albanian operation.

The reality of the situation struck Onur. For all Denzil's bluster, neither of them knew what they were going to do next. Onur felt like he had landed a fool's errand with a proper fool for company. But he felt strangely calm knowing that Mardin was waiting for him.

Denzil caught Onur's eye and gestured for him to follow outside to the car park. They didn't have a script other than to send a message to the Albanian gang. Above all, it was important for them to prove themselves to Mustafa. It was cold, damp, and dark in the car park. They had not dressed for the outdoors. Taking cover behind a black BMW in a shadowy corner, they shivered, watched the door, and waited.

'What'll we do, Onur?' whispered Denzil, the damp night air chilling his panic.

'Dunno, we'll see when they come out,' Onur replied, not used to being their decision-maker.

They waited for an hour, watching the steady flow come and go before the two big guys emerged, paused in the portal to light cigarettes, and scan the space.

'Let's go,' went Denzil, checking the handgun in his waistband seeking reassurance that it was really there, then leading Onur towards the doorway while remaining in the shadows. At about twenty metres they stopped.

'Yo blad,' Denzil called assertively across the space, keeping in the shadows and trying to hide his nerves. Onur was worried. He could already see that hiding in the shadows and projecting authority did not mix and that this was not going to go well.

'You're not from round these parts. We ain't seen you 'ere

before,' Denzil continued.

The Albanians looked up, surprised to be addressed like this by a couple of strangers.

'Who are you?' returned one of them. 'Come where we can see you.'

'We're Topkapi, Tottenham,' Denzil called out, remaining in the shadows.

'Ha,' the Albanians turned to each other, spoke in Albanian and started laughing, while one of them replied in English. 'What's this Topkapi? A school gang? What you children want with us?'

Onur's panic was returning. The appearance and self-assurance of the Albanians left no doubt that they were of another league and that Mustafa had sent them on a test too far. He had not expected this humiliation and knew that Denzil was not just out of his depth but in danger of drowning. Denzil had never been good at dealing with teasing and now responded to it too easily. Onur saw him pull the handgun from his waistband and point it. Even in the dark the Albanians could evidently see it because they stopped laughing and raised their hands halfway to their shoulders. Things were escalating too fast. The gun was supposed to frighten them, to make them cower. The Albanians had raised their hands but were still smirking.

'What, you gonna shoot us?'

Onur knew he had to help Denzil out of this rapidly deepening hole, de-escalate and extract them both with face and success.

'Brothers,' he called out in Turkish, grasping at straws and hoping that an appeal to some common cultural bonds might defuse the situation. Many Albanians worked in Turkey and Onur hoped that these ones might understand some of the language. 'We are all Ummah. We ain't beefin'. But the message is stay east of the Marshes. Don't come up our ends or there'll be trouble.'

The Albanians continued to smirk.

'Ummah?' one of them replied. 'We lost religion under forty-five years of communism. We come to Britain, free country. Winston Churchill. We free to go anywhere. Albanian have no fear for your gun. Maybe we come see you in Tottenham.'

Denzil lost it. He pointed the gun at their feet.

'You come to Tottenham, you will get more of this,' he said as he fired. One of the Albanians crumbled, crying out in pain as the bullet went through his calf. His companion immediately pulled a gun which had been concealed in the back of his waistband and fired back at Denzil, while crouching to check on his fallen companion. Denzil and Onur dodged back between parked cars as more bullets tore into metalwork.

'Out of here,' said Onur, as they made a crouching running exit towards the darkness of the Marshes. They could come back for Onur's car later. They had delivered a message, but was it the one Mustafa had intended and how would the Albanians respond?

# Chapter Fifteen

## 14TH JANUARY 2002

## PARK SCHOOL AND DOWNHILLS PARK

Not much learning was going to happen that day. From 8.45am without intermission, everyone at Park School was focused solely on what would happen at 3.30pm. Word of Mehmet's challenge had spread, so by that morning everyone had heard. Mehmet had been busy messaging every Turkish teenager he knew on MSN Messenger, in his school and others: Highgate Wood, Northumberland Park, White Hart Lane and Greig Academy. The message went out that Black kids were picking on Turks and back-up was needed. Everyone had said they would come, to stand for the Turks against what Mehmet spun as racism, though some of them knew Mehmet well enough to see there was probably a twist to the story.

Emine and Shereen knew full well that Mehmet himself was the main purveyor of racism in the school yard, whipping up the Turkish boys against everyone else, especially Kurdish, and Black kids. They understood that standing up to Mehmet was actually the way to fight racism in the school. Mark, Arjan, Ned, Grey and Dev also understood and were mobilising a rainbow alliance of Black, White and Asian Year

7s, 8s and 9s who knew about Mehmet's bullying, and others who resented those Turks who bossed everyone else. This was a moment to stand up.

The day's lessons dragged on. Teachers struggled to keep their pupils' attention. Break and lunchtime in the school yard were electric. At one end, practically every Turkish teenager clustered in a huge group. Rumours spread that others were coming from all over Haringey, hundreds of them, that Onur and other big brothers were coming. Turkish honour would be upheld. At the other end of the yard, a similar-size group of almost everyone else. Different people were chipping into the excited crowd that they'd spoken to friends, big brothers and older friends who were going to come and pull the Turks down a peg or two. Only a small number detached themselves from the conflict and found themselves for once spoilt for space. The scene resembled the lead-up to a medieval battle, like the movie *Braveheart*, with generals on each side rallying their troops. Every few minutes a chorus of chanting would emerge from one side or the other. Teachers knew something was afoot and moved in force to clear the playground at the end of break and lunch. The crowds of pupils returned slow-walking to their classes, but everyone was chanting 'Blacks v Turks'. The head teacher rang the police, who agreed to send a presence to the school gates for 3.30pm, in the hope of deterring trouble.

Friday period 5 was always a struggle but today it was a total write-off. Teachers were satisfied with simply containing their pupils inside their rooms; they hoped to reduce the tension by staggering the release of classes, but this did nothing to calm the corridors or school yard.

Two police cars were parked at the gates, their officers sitting inside watching the teenagers, Blacks, Turks, and everyone else mixing on the pavement. Nothing was going to happen with this police presence. 'Park! Park!' some of them called and the mixed crowd drifted along the West Green Road to the Downhills Park entrance. Because they followed the road route and had to share the pavement, the opposing sides had to walk as one, the point of the conflict strangely suspended. But the atmosphere was electric and intensified as someone shouted out, 'Greig are here!' pointing up at the top level of a passing bus where some teenagers in Greig Academy blazers were sitting. As they approached the park there was a faltering in the crowd. For many, what had seemed so exciting and compelling in the school yard now seemed dangerous. Mehmet was a loudmouth bully and many Turks only stood with him to save face and the notion of Turkish honour, but was it worth police trouble for *him*? Boys and girls peeled off in small groups or on their own with a snowballing effect. The crowd was thinning, and by the time it reached the park gates it had shrunk. Where were the Greig Academy Turks? Just Greig uniforms on the bus heading home? Where were Onur and the other big brothers? Soon it was down to the hardcore – Mehmet, Necip and his usual gang of about fifteen – but facing them was a much larger group, a rainbow of Black, White, Asian and Chinese Year 9, 10 and 11, who were all united in hatred of this bully.

'Where the fuck is everyone, man?' Necip muttered urgently to Mehmet. 'There's bare them.'

'The feds must've stopped 'em,' said Mehmet, desperate for an explanation.

'Oi, isn't that your sister Emine over there?' asked Necip, pointing towards the opposing crowd.

'What's she doin' there? With Shereen, Arjan's sis. Whose side is she on?'

Soon Emine, Shereen and the rest of the group started a chant: 'Turk and Kurd, Black and White, unite against the racists!' The chanting gathered rhythm and intensity.

'What we gonna do?' asked Necip.

Mehmet stepped towards the rainbow crowd and called out, 'Alright, you got the numbers so this ain't gonna be a fair fight, obviously,' receiving a response of laughter and derision.

'Where's your big bro now, Mehmet?' someone called.

'Where's your big mouth now?' called someone else.

Mehmet regained his composure.

'Let's finish this one on one. Any one of you and me. Here and now.'

A lot of the crowd had their own reasons to step up and settle a score with Mehmet, including Arjan and Ned, but it was Mark who was first to step forward. He was incensed about the bike and what had happened to Ned. 'Go on, bro!' went Grey and a cheer went up from the others behind him. Mehmet went for him. They sparred around, throwing punches for a while, before Mehmet moved in close to grapple and the two were now wrestling on the ground. One minute Mehmet was on top of Mark, the next Mark had flipped him over and was sitting on Mehmet. What happened next took everyone by surprise. Mark cried out and fell off Mehmet, clutching his thigh. He was bleeding. Mehmet was holding a knife.

'Mehmet, stop it!' shrieked Emine over the crowd noise.

Then the sound of a police siren was heard as a squad car drove towards them through the park gate.

'Feds!'

Everyone scattered, even Mehmet. But Arjan, Ned and Grey clustered around Mark.

'This takes it to another level, cus, they better watch out,' went Grey. 'It's gonna be blood for blood.'

## GREEN LANES, HARRINGAY

Denzil and Onur arrived at Topkapi. Mustafa sat behind his desk scowling. It had not been a complete surprise that the mission had gone wrong or that the Albanians had not been deterred. They came from tough stock. But he was shocked by the extent of his boys' incompetence and the damaging turn it had brought about. On reflection, he was annoyed with himself for sending them. He should have sent more experienced soldiers.

'What have you done?' he spoke Turkish so quietly that it was almost a whisper.

'We shot one of them,' boasted Denzil in English, thinking this would win approval.

'Who is 'we'? Both of you fired the gun?'

They both looked down sheepishly. Mustafa pointed to the corner of the room where a large sheet of rolled industrial plastic lay on the floor.

'What's that, boss?' asked Denzil.

Through the sheeting they started to make out a severed pig's head, a gross insult as well as a clear blood threat.

'This is how they reply,' continued Mustafa, with a chilling level of control in his voice. 'It arrived this morning. Why did I receive such a gift? From who? I am guessing an Albanian postage stamp. Maybe you fucked up. What did I tell you? Guns are to frighten, not to use for so little reason. First you must use your brain, your words. Not your gun. Once you shoot an animal and don't kill it, you make it angry and more dangerous. The animal will think you are weak. Now you force us to have a war with these goat fuckers. Leave the gun.' He gestured to the table.

Denzil was dumbstruck. He had thought he would be congratulated. Onur understood that once again he was caught up by Denzil's foolishness and could say nothing lest he commit the greater crime of disloyalty. They had been given a second chance and Denzil had messed it up again.

'The gun,' Mustafa gestured to the desk again. Denzil drew it from his jacket pocket and put it on the desk.

'Now go home, do nothing and wait for me to call you.'

Blushing with shame, heads lowered and shoulders bowed, they slunk out of the club and walked away. All was lost.

In the back office, Mustafa turned to Kemal.

'First, they steal from us, then they fail to deliver a simple message. Instead, they bring a war. I put them under your watch, Kemal. They go nowhere without you knowing. I will think what to do with them.'

'My cousin brings shame on the family, boss. I am your soldier and will do whatever you decide.'

Mustafa had to tread carefully with any punishment. What mattered was his long-term strategy. He had learnt the importance of controlling his own instinctive urges, like the violent punishment he now felt like dispensing. 'Act in haste, repent at leisure,' he had heard the English say. He needed to recruit more soldiers. That was why he had given these two a chance. He needed to build Topkapi's image, its attraction, among the Turkish youth. Rumours of harsh punishment would scare them away while measured discipline would look fair. Perhaps if he sent these two to Turkey for a while, they would be out of the way and could do no damage. Who knows what might happen to them over there? He already had some ideas. Yes, he thought, I will make some calls, some enquiries, before discussing this further with Kemal. Could he even trust Kemal, being as he was, Denzil's cousin?

# Chapter Sixteen

## 1st FEBRUARY 2002

## GREEN LANES, HARRINGAY

For months Mustafa had been worrying about the smooth running of his melon supplies, the long-term security of his Colombian relationship, the Albanian threat to his street market and the possibility that they might take over his Colombian connection. But since the Ferry Boat incident his anxieties had turned to Topkapi's reputation. In his youth, the only reputation that had mattered to him had been for toughness, ruthlessness and strength. This guaranteed security from his enemies – and deflected any rumours that an unmarried man of his age might be homosexual. This would have been fatal to his authority. He had been careful, over the years, to keep his penchant for younger men strictly contained in the Soho club that he periodically visited. Meanwhile, he reacted aggressively if conversation in Topkapi approached romance, relationships or sex, until those around him learnt that business was all he wanted to talk about.

Over the years and as the business had grown, he had broadened his reputational concerns to include reliable delivery, prompt payment and quality of product. But in recent weeks he had once again been reassessing what mattered to him, and had begun to worry about his reputation in the community. He wondered if he was going soft or starting to worry about his legacy. How would he prefer to be remembered? As a machete man, or as an elder who had advanced the London Turkish community? He liked the idea that future generations might remember him as a champion for the economic opportunities of young Turks, like Kemal, even if this had sometimes involved crime and violence; that Topkapi was a family that looked after the community, much as the Casa Nostra looked after Italians. Perhaps he needed more velvet glove for his iron fist.

He still had to clean up the Ferry Boat mess, stop the Albanians, and punish Denzil and Onur. But he had to think smart about how. He would arrange to send them to Turkey. Then, whatever else happened, their families would not think their sons had disappeared and would not call the police. He would tell them that the boys were the first successful candidates for a new Topkapi initiative, an international placement programme to promote opportunities for Turkish London youth, that would provide work-based skills while strengthening their association with the motherland. He hoped it sounded respectable, benevolent. Surely it would win over the families. He would talk to them, starting with Denzil's. They should be easy. They were simple, uneducated Cypriot village people who spoke poor English. They would appreciate Topkapi making opportunities for their son, and they would trust their nephew, Kemal.

## LORDSHIP LANE

Mustafa and Kemal arrived at Denzil's mid-afternoon.

Denzil opened the door. Startled by this unannounced visit and disconcerted by the collision of his worlds, he opened it no more than a crack. Though his parents knew Kemal worked for Topkapi, they did not know exactly what this involved and had no idea that Denzil worked there too, alongside his Kwik Fit job.

'Mr Igli, sir,' he managed.

'I've come to speak with you and your parents, Denzil,' replied Mustafa.

'I am afraid my father is sick and my mother …'

'Who is it, Denzil?' His mother's voice called in Turkish from the kitchen and got louder as she approached the front door.

'Sir, they do not know I have been working for you,' Denzil whispered urgently.

'I see,' Mustafa paused, considering how to adjust his proposal to the parents. 'Don't worry, Denzil, you will not be compromised,' he whispered in reply.

Denzil opened the door as his mother reached it.

'Kemal!' She exclaimed, seeing her nephew standing behind.

'Auntie!' he exclaimed, 'how are you?' stepping forwards and giving Denzil's mother an embrace.

'Kemal, what a surprise,' returning the embrace and continuing in Turkish. 'What brings you here? And won't you introduce your friend?'

'Auntie, this is my employer, Mr Igli, managing director of Topkapi Enterprises. May we come in?'

She led the way to the living room.

'Oh my,' she replied, 'my husband is upstairs. Denzil, go help your father come downstairs. I am sorry, Mr Igli, Denzil's father has a little difficulty with stairs these days. Let me make tea. Kemal, please make Mr Igli comfortable.'

She disappeared into the kitchen and Denzil went up the stairs. A few minutes later he reappeared helping his father and they repeated their respectful introductions. When all were seated and the tea poured, Mustafa began.

'Excuse my intrusion, but I come at Kemal's suggestion. He has worked for me since he left school. Maybe he has told you a little. Topkapi Enterprises is a successful export-import business specialising in trade between Eastern Turkey and London. It is hard for young Turkish Londoners to find good jobs. Many employers are prejudiced, and so it is important for successful Turkish businesses to help them. I am starting a scheme for promising young people and Kemal has suggested that your Denzil would be a good candidate. He tells me that Denzil has a job at Kwik Fit. Perhaps he can do better. I will send successful candidates for my scheme to spend two months in Mardin, Turkey, to learn about the import-export business. It is sad that many young London Turks have not even been to visit the motherland. If Denzil is successful, he will learn much about our culture and I will then offer him a good job when he returns. All expenses paid. Maybe this will lead to a new career for Denzil.'

Denzil's parents listened, enraptured. From the little Kemal had shared with his own parents, the family knew he worked for a mysterious Turkish entrepreneur who paid him well but expected discretion in return, so they asked no more questions. Kemal always had money. That was good enough for them. But now Mr Igli was here explaining the business and offering Denzil an opportunity.

'Well, that sounds like a fantastic opportunity, Mr Igli,' Denzil's father replied. 'Our family are from Cyprus. We know nothing of Mardin. Is there a chance that some unexpected expenses may arise that we will have to pay?'

'What kind of work will Denzil learn? Where will he live?' added Denzil's mother.

'I personally guarantee there will be no costs,' replied Mustafa. 'He will learn about double-entry bookkeeping, logistics, international tariffs and trade...' Mustafa rattled off as many impressive phrases as he could think of, doing his best to conjure the impression of a successful and fully legitimate businessman.

'He will live in a guest house.' He turned his attention to Denzil who sat listening, grateful that Mustafa had not given away his existing involvement and puzzled by this show of favour so soon after his disgrace and dismissal.

'Denzil, what do you think of this offer?'

'Yes, Mr Igli, it sounds very exciting.'

'Perhaps you will give us some time to think about it,' his father interjected, anxious in case there were any possible catches to this too-good-to-be-true offer.

'Yes of course.' Mustafa rose, followed by Kemal. 'If you decide to agree, Denzil can send a message through Kemal.' And with polite nodding and handshaking, they left.

'That went well,' Mustafa commented to Kemal as they got into the car. He was confident that Denzil would go for this. The roasting he had given the boy after the Ferry Boat must have left him puzzled by the apparent forgiveness: the boss offering a new opportunity to remain within Topkapi and the prospect of an all-expenses-paid visit to Turkey. Surely, he would think it was his lucky day. The parents had seemed awestruck by the scheme and blinded by this opportunity for a new career for their son.

'Yes, boss, I think they liked it,' Kemal replied.

'I'll drop you back, Kemal. I'll go to Onur's on my own.'

## BRUCE GROVE

After dropping Kemal back on the Green Lanes, Mustafa drove on to Onur's house in St Margaret's Road. He had a feeling this might not be as easy as Denzil's family. He knew they were educated and from Mardin too, so might have heard something about him and Topkapi. It was early evening when Mustafa knocked on Cetin and Dilek's door. Cetin opened it, just home from work.

'Hello, can I help you?' he asked in English.

'My friend, I am Mustafa Igli,' he replied in Turkish. 'I run a business, import-export, maybe you heard of Topkapi Enterprises. Your son works for me, in my warehouse. I believe you are from Mardin, as am I, though I have been living in Tottenham for many years. May I come in?'

Cetin was momentarily speechless. He had known the Topkapi social club since his first days in London and had heard that a gang was run from the premises, but when Denzil helped Onur find the warehouse job, he had no idea it was connected to Topkapi... until this moment. These were dangerous people doing bad things, not what he wanted for his son. And now their chief was standing at his door, asking to come in. His adrenaline was pumping as he quickly recognised the danger of the situation. He also remembered the name Mustafa Igli from Mardin. His old friend Hasan used to go every day to the Igli tobacconist and had heard that the man had gone on to become a gangster in London. But this was the first time they had met.

'Yes of course, Mr Igli,' was the only possible response as he led Mustafa to the living room. Cetin was grateful that the children were all out, but hearing their voices, Dilek came from the kitchen. 'My wife, Dilek,' he introduced her. 'Please sit. Some tea?'

'No thank you. But please, we should talk. About your son Onur. I will be brief. He is a reliable employee and has a bright future. I want to promote him to manage more logistics and am starting an overseas placement scheme for promising employees. Two months in the first instance, all expenses paid, in Mardin. Our shared city. Has he ever been there?'

'No. He was born here, and we never took the family to visit.'

'So, this will be a good opportunity for him. Good work, money and a chance to discover his roots.' Mustafa paused, seeking any reaction in their faces.

'Yes, Mardin. A beautiful place. Good people,' replied Cetin.

'Mr Igli, this is a coincidence,' Dilek broke in. 'Over Christmas we have also been talking with Onur about going there to spend time with our families, to get to know them and learn about his motherland. And he wants this too. He was planning to give you his notice this week. How funny that now you should come to suggest this.'

'A coincidence indeed.'

'He already has an offer of work in the family business,' added Cetin.

'Is that so? Well of course, where he works would be up to him,' replied Mustafa, a little taken back that this detail of his plan had drifted off course. But gathering his composure, he recalled that his objective was to get Onur out of London and his family were arranging this without him having to lift a finger or spend a pound. The second part of his plan, punishment, could still proceed regardless.

'I see. Well, what a lucky young man to have opportunities

coming from all directions. I wish him great fortune with your family. But please, let him know of my offer and if he prefers it, with your blessing, let me know.'

And with that he stood up, bowed with a smile and Cetin escorted him to the door. As he closed it, Cetin hoped they would not meet again but was not so sure.

# Chapter Seventeen

**13th FEBRUARY 2002**

**WEST GREEN**

Lucas had never forgotten a Valentine's Day, though he and Mollie always celebrated it a day earlier. They both agreed that it was silly to pay the hiked prices restaurants always charged on the 14th, and they were grown-up enough make their own special date. So, every year, Lucas had given Mollie a card and taken her out on 13th February and, however shabby and worn-down family life made her feel, this simple act of love and recognition always gave her a boost. But this year he forgot. Of course, she was upset. But more than that, she was concerned. He had been distracted, withdrawn, not himself for months now.

'Happy Valentine's-minus-one,' she greeted him when he came down to the kitchen to make tea and prepare lunchboxes. His jaw dropped.

'Oh no, I forgot. I'm sorry. I've had so much on my mind. But the day isn't over yet.'

'No worries,' she replied, 'but I am worried about you, Lucas. You've been so distracted recently. Is there something I can do to help?'

He digested her offer while he pottered in the kitchen, put

the kettle on, laid out the sandwich-making on the counter – bread, margarine, cheese, pickle, lettuce – operating a practised routine.

'It's true. I've been distracted. I'm sorry. It's not your fault and you shouldn't have to pay for my worries. I'm sure things will settle down.'

'What things? Is that old face from the past still worrying you?'

'No, I'm over that,' he lied, anxious that she shouldn't be drawn into his problems. 'Maybe it's just a mid-life crisis thing. You know. What am I doing with my life? What have I achieved over my years? What am I missing out on? All those clichés.'

Mollie knew there was something else going on, but she wasn't going to press him. If this was how he wanted to respond she would respect that. He clearly wasn't in the mood for sharing.

'Maybe we can talk this evening,' she replied.

'Yes,' he said, 'I'll book us a table to celebrate. Malay sound good? Penang Satay House?'

Half an hour later the whole family was out the door, boys to school, Lucas to the office and Mollie heading for Turnpike Lane station. It was her college day, and she had some lectures to attend. Although there were quicker routes, she liked to walk by Downhills Park, turn right on Langham, a left and then a right down Carlingford Road. She had always liked Carlingford for its tranquil atmosphere, the regularly spaced trees and its Victorian and Edwardian houses, each built to make its own small statement: tiled paths, corniced bay windows, alabaster cherub faces or floral arrangements embellishing the rendered brickwork around window frames. Some even had pillared porticoes. Like most of

Tottenham, the street had been built by an assortment of small developers, each buying a plot and building a run of four, five or six houses designed to share a common set of decorative features reflecting the developer's taste. Although most people might just see a terraced row of houses, to Mollie's trained eye the net effect was to create little blocks of varied styles which made the streets interesting. She had loved London Victoriana from the first, having been brought up surrounded by a landscape of modern Swiss architecture, and drew inspiration from it in her studies.

But she had an additional reason for taking this route today. Lucas had told her that his ghost from the past was renting 15a and her curiosity had got the better of her. As she reached it, she paused. How people decorated and furnished their homes could tell her a lot about them. Who was this ghost? What was he like? Why had he so troubled Lucas? Maybe the flat would offer some answers. She imagined a grey corduroy-covered sofa and armchair, a TV table and big screen, mature pot plants, an oriental floor rug, a small table and upright chair. She couldn't resist. There were net curtains in the window but there was a gap where they had not been pulled together properly. She turned off the pavement, walked up the path and hesitated. If he was in and saw her looking through the window… She rang the doorbell. If someone answered she could ask if Michelle was in, surely this was the address she had been given. Then she would meet the mystery man. That might give her some insight. But there was no reply. So, she stepped off the path and gingerly around the bay window. She peered through the gap in the nets. No corduroy sofa, armchair, TV, pot plants, rug, table, or chair. Nothing. The flat was stripped empty. Was the mystery man gone? So, what was bothering Lucas?

## WEST GREEN ROAD

It was early evening. Kemal and Denzil walked along the West Green Road. Denzil had agreed to Mustafa's placement proposal, with his parents' blessing. He had been told to pack, leave his bags at Topkapi and be ready to go at short notice. He would travel overland with the next returning truck from the warehouse. It could be any day now. He had already said his goodbyes to family and friends. Meanwhile, he had been rolling the streets under Kemal's tight supervision. Mustafa wanted to keep him where they could see him, not leave him on his own. For his part, Denzil thought he was the cat who had got the cream. Despite creating two major fuck-ups with Topkapi, he was still standing. Mustafa must have believed that it was Onur rather than him who was responsible. He hadn't spoken to Onur since the Ferry Boat. They had been forbidden from communicating, but Kemal had told him that Onur was restricted to the warehouse. Kemal must have spoken up for him, he thought, if he had been selected for this new placement scheme.

Tonight, Mustafa had received a tip-off. A group of Albanians were cruising West Green pubs. He sent Kemal and Denzil to check it out. The Goat was their first stop, then KK McCools. In each pub they ordered a drink, found a table with a good view of the bar, and sat for a half an hour, watching and listening before moving on. Kemal briefly chatted with familiar faces. Yes, some told him, Albanians had been in recently and yes, they were approaching people.

'I need some air,' said Kemal as they approached the Black Boy pub. 'Let's go park.'

The pub was located immediately next to Downhills Park, stomping ground of both throughout childhood and adolescence. They knew it as well as their own bedrooms: the playground, playing field, bushes and thickets. As teenagers they had come to know it at night, an exciting place, a world away from adult eyes, where mates could meet and mess around, smoke blow, jump strangers, feel powerful; the gates which never closed; poorly lit Midnight Alley; the perimeter paths with alternating patches of light and swathes of dark; the safest benches where you could most easily hear people coming and the dodgy corners where you could hide. Now they were adults, their tough teenage pranks seemed to merge with their memories of childhood. This park held neither surprises nor fear. They went in through the West Green entrance. Path lighting soon gave way to shade as they crossed the playing field into the dark, cold and damp midwinter night. Trees loomed as massive dark shapes bordering the field, the ground was an invisible squelch underfoot, quiet surrounded them but for the constant hum of background traffic, pierced by the occasional police siren. They walked in silence for five minutes, making a wide circuit of the field. Denzil's phone rang. It was Mustafa.

'Where are you?' came Mustafa's voice.

'Just outside the Black Boy, Mr Igli, sir. We already checked the other pubs.'

'Okay. Listen. The truck has arrived at the warehouse. We are unloading and the drivers are resting. But you will be off very soon, travelling back with them. Probably in the morning. I will send your bags to the warehouse and Kemal will take you there later tonight. OK?'

'Yes, Mr Igli, sir.'

'Pass Kemal over,' said Mustafa.

'Yes, boss, it's Kemal.'

'After the Black Boy, get Denzil to the warehouse, OK?'

'So, he's leaving tomorrow?'

'That's it,' replied Mustafa. He hung up. Kemal had expected more of an explanation and was surprised by his shortness. Why didn't he sound more encouraging? The boss has a lot on his mind, thought Kemal, maybe it's up to me to big it up.

'This Mardin t'ing sounds good, cuz,' he said to Denzil. 'Mustafa must rate you, 'specially after the mess Onur got you into.'

'I'm excited, but between us I'm a bit scared. I mean, I never been Turkey. Don't know what to expect.'

'Don't worry, man. You'll love it once you get used to hearin' Turkish all the time. They'll treat you like the top man. And with t'ings gettin' messy with the Albies here, you'll be well out of it.'

They looped around the playing fields and walked back towards the lights of the park entrance, back to the West Green Road, Denzil trying to keep his apprehensions at bay. It was an offer he could not refuse. He had to prove himself to Mustafa and Kemal, to step up as the man he wanted them to see. But without back-up, someone like Onur to fall back on, he was frightened, like he had felt on his first day at secondary school.

The Black Boy was warm and welcoming after the park. Denzil took a table while Kemal went to the bar. As before, they sat quietly, watching customers come and go. After half an hour they were just getting ready to leave when three men came in. Denzil pulled Kemal back into his seat.

'The one on the left,' he whispered, 'he was at the Ferry Boat.' Kemal nodded, turning away from the new arrivals and reaching for his phone. He made a call.

'Boss, three just come in the Black Boy. Denzil's ID'd one.'

'Sit tight,' Mustafa answered. 'Follow them if they leave. I'll send soldiers.'

They watched the newcomers settle at another table. After five minutes the Ferry Boat survivor got up and walked across the pub. He stopped at a couple of tables and seemed to have brief conversations before turning and heading for theirs. Denzil was terrified, although he thought he had kept himself in the shadows of the Ferry Boat car park.

'Good evening,' he said to them both, with a stare that lingered on Denzil.

'Yes, it is,' replied Kemal.

'Brother,' the Albanian continued in English. 'You guys like coke?'

Denzil sat speechless, taken aback by this brazen cold-calling approach and terrified that he might be recognised.

'I ain't seen you before,' went Kemal, keeping a poker face.

'No? But maybe I seen you?' he replied with an ironic smirk, flicking his eyes from face to face. 'Take free sample. I come back tomorrow 8pm. Free delivery service now coming to Tottenham. If you like, £60 gram.'

The Albanian slid a bag across the table hidden under his hand. Kemal nodded and took the sample. He cast a glance at Denzil and another across the bar to the other Albanians as this one straightened up and returned to his friends. Then he reached for his phone and texted Mustafa 'Def selling. Three big leather jackets.'

Instantly a reply arrived. 'Sit tight. We're outside. Message their exit.'

Ten minutes later the Albanians got up and left. Kemal sent the text. A second later he received a reply. He looked up at Denzil.

'Mustafa says send you out, cuz, I'll be seconds behind ya,'

Kemal said.

Denzil stood up, legs like jelly.

'Mustafa says you gotta prove yourself, Denz, you're the front man. Don't vex. Mandem's outside, bro, and I'm behind ya. In the mornin', it's off to Turkey and 'appy days, innit.'

'True dat,' blustered Denzil, standing up, and heading for the door he went out into the cold night.

# Chapter Eighteen

## 14th FEBRUARY 2002

### DOWNHILLS PARK

Ned, Arjan and Shereen met at the park gate. It was 8.15am. They were shivering under their puffer jackets in the February chill on their way to school.

'What 'appened last night, den?' started Ned. 'I smashed GoldenEye. What abou' you, Arjan?'

'We watch TV, *Brookside.*'

'Oh yeah, my mum an' dad watch that. And how many Valentine's cards did you get then Shereen?' Ned teased.

'One more than you,' Shereen parried back, and they all laughed.

'How's Mark? Any news?' Shereen asked.

'He looks like the Mummy or somet'ing, all bandage an' crutches!' Ned told them. 'His dad is drivin' him to school, chauffeur service!' They all laughed.

'That Mehmet,' she continued, 'he's like a child, jus' not realisin' the mess he's got 'imself into.'

They passed through the brick gate pillars on to Midnight Alley with its old spiky railings, a hundred years old, installed who knows why, now rusting and gapped like an old man's teeth. It was a landscape they had seen a thousand times before. To the left, the familiar, massive, leafless hornbeams and planes shivered in the cold. But to the right … they could not believe their eyes. It was as if they had crossed a portal into a TV world, something from CSI. A hundred metres down-slope by the old disused changing rooms, white and blue 'Police Do Not Cross' tape, police vans and cars, a white tent, flashing blue lights tingeing the early morning light and figures in full white forensic suits. Outside the tape, a crowd of dog-walkers and joggers mingled with uniformed teenagers distracted from their journey to school. Shereen spotted Emine with some other girls and left the boys to join them. The atmosphere was a heady mix of shock and thrill. A dead body in *their* park.

'My days, Ems, what's 'appenin'? Is this a murder, for real, in Downhills?' went Shereen.

'Scary or what!' Emine replied.

'Can you see it? The body?'

They stood on tiptoe to see over the crowd.

'Nah just a white tent t'ing, must be coverin' it up.'

'There won't be no learnin' in school today, for real.'

'Nah, dem boys 'll be high as kites.'

In the crowd nearby the boys were excited.

'Someone got capped,' said Ned. A silent understanding passed between them.

A policeman patrolling the tape perimeter approached the crowd to disperse them.

'Nothing to see here, ladies and gents, move along please. Come on young 'uns, you'll be late for school.'

They took their cue and reluctantly continued their journey across the park, high on a mix of intense emotions.

The school yard buzzed with excited chatter as word of the crime scene spread like wildfire. Everyone had a theory.

Imaginations ran wild. Anyone who had walked through the park that morning was quickly surrounded by others quizzing them for details. What had they seen? Did they see the body? Could it be someone they knew?

# Part Three

# DUST
# SETTLES

**2002**

# Chapter Nineteen

## 18th FEBRUARY 2002

### DOWNHILLS PARK

February is always the hardest month, thought Mollie as she jogged around the park perimeter. Resilience to winter wears thin, health gives way to illness, age to death, depression to suicide; yet every year the snowdrops manage to push through the cold earth and challenge the gloom with the first promise of spring. In the early morning light, she jogged as she did every day, rain or shine. The air carried chill and damp. Downhills Park was bleak, bare and trampled. She passed the old changing rooms; blue and white police tape still fluttered around the crime scene, left behind by the forensic team and its travelling circus days earlier. Blue and white tape in the bleak and desolate parkscape, the only memorial to an unknown victim. She felt a stab of sadness as she passed by, for the waste of life, lost opportunities and stolen dreams dashed by violence. It felt to Mollie that apart from her own pulsing blood, life had drained away from this place, retreated into the woody skeletons of trees, migrated to warmer climes while people just stayed indoors.

Back home, she put the kettle on as Lucas came downstairs. 'Good run?' Lucas asked.

'Park feels different, like it's been violated or something. Police tape still flapping around the changing rooms.'

'It'll take time for it to feel the same again.'

She sat at the kitchen table and looked at the *Advertiser*, the local newspaper that came through her door every Wednesday. The headline read "Park Valentine's Massacre." She read the article aloud.

'"Police have launched a murder investigation following the discovery of a body in Downhills Park on 14th February. They have revealed that the victim was disfigured and this is hampering identification. They would like to hear from anyone concerned about a missing family member or friend."'

'Someone must know something,' Lucas responded.

'It's just so scary, something like this on our doorstep.'

'Look, it's not like something like this is going to happen to us.' he reassured her. 'We don't move in such circles. The police will sort it, and everything will get back to normal. You'll see.'

'I suppose you're right.'

With that they returned to their daily routines of rousing children, breakfast, making packed lunches and getting out the door. But there was only one thing on Lucas' mind. An hour later, he arrived at Stanhopes. Jack Job was studying a copy of the *Advertiser* spread across his desk.

'"Park Valentine's Massacre",' Jack read aloud. 'Bloody great. Just what we need for house prices.'

'And no clues on the victim,' said Lucas.

Jack pointed to the *Advertiser*. 'The police say that a corrosive chemical had been used to disfigure the victim's face and fingers, making fingerprints impossible. I reckon it's a turf war thing. Drug gangs. Someone wants to send someone else a message, like, "watch out, we're new bosses on the block" or fending off a newbie, like "don't try messin' in our patch."'

'You could be right, Jack,' said Lucas, keen to speculate and spin any theory that he could believe himself and which distanced him from the corpse.

'Yeah, drug gangs,' said Lucas. 'I saw this documentary about Albanian gangs in the UK. Since the Balkan war, a lot of them have been coming and they're not shy of violence. Could be Albanians showing their power, or a local gang trying to keep them out. What about dental records or this new DNA thing?'

'DNA will only help if there's a matching sample somewhere for the victim,' replied Jack. Lucas was impressed with his apparent knowledge of forensic science. 'If you don't know what family to ask or if there is no family, DNA can't help. There's no central database for dental records either. Each dental practice owns its own records. I found that out when I tried to change my dentist. My old one wouldn't transfer my records to the new one, so I had to have loads of new X-rays and start my records all over again. The police could only use dental records to ID a suspect if they already had a name to check. And what if the victim has just arrived in the UK and only went to the dentist in another country like Albania, or never went to the dentist at all.'

Lucas was deeply troubled. He had been round to 15a Carlingford and found it empty. Cleaned out. The other flats were the same. He had heard nothing from Jerrish. The man seemed to have vanished. Lucas had wanted Jerrish gone, he didn't care where to; and he was gone. Part of him was relieved. He didn't care where to. He had protected his family. But another part of him just couldn't help feeling a creeping sense of guilt about the disfigured corpse. He had thrown out this speculation about Albanians to distract himself from his anxieties and was grateful to Jack for picking up this thread. An Albanian turf war was a safer and more comfortable narrative and if enough people believed it, the more real it would become. An alternative in which the corpse was Jerrish, and the police connected it to him, could send him to jail. How would Mollie and the boys cope? It could be even more damaging than the blackmailing had been. Had he made a terrible mistake?

# Chapter Twenty

School Tuesdays were calm. The weekend had passed, and the next one seemed far away. But in the school yard, all talk was speculation about the body. Ned, Mark and Arjan were sitting on a bench watching some other boys showing off their football skills.

'It's still all over the news, man,' Ned told them. 'They were talkin' about it on the radio earlier and it's in the papers. One story said the face and fingers were burnt with acid.'

'That's deep, man,' said Arjan.

'Yeah, the feds made a statement yesterday, innit.'

'How was he killed?' asked Mark.

'They said he was shot.'

'So maybe the bullet will lead to the gun and the killer,' said Mark.

Across the school yard, Mehmet sat alone with Necip. Their posse was nowhere to be seen. After the fight in the park the police had arrested and charged Mehmet with actual bodily harm and possession of a bladed object. It was the first time he had been arrested. He had thought this would make him look big and impress Onur and the gang, but the custody

suite had scared him, made him feel small, alone and vulnerable. He had been suspended from school for two weeks and
referred to the Youth Offending Team where he now had
to go twice a week after school. His Juvenile Court hearing
was set for June. At first, he had been relieved that it was so
far away, but the six-month wait had started to increase his
anxiety and he now just wanted to get it over with. Worse
than this was how upset he had made his parents, the stress
and shame he had brought on them.

The Youth Offending Team, social services and school had
all agreed that the best thing would be to re-admit him to
school. But in the yard, he had become a shadow of himself.
Gone was the bravado and bullying. He avoided others,
except for Necip. And others avoided him. There had been no
triumphalism or counter-bullying from his past victims – not
even Mark, who hobbled around bandaged and on crutches.
It was as if the climactic fight had shaken everyone out of a
hysterical dream and back down to earth. The school yard
had felt different to everyone. The atmosphere of edginess,
fear and tribalism had faded. The invisible gang boundaries
across the yard lessened their force field. People moved more
freely, venturing into unfamiliar yard spaces.

'Onur's gone Turkey, went airport early this mornin',',
Mehmet told Necip as they sat on a low wall. 'It's bare weird
without 'im bein' here.'

'What's he doin' there, man?'

'Gone to stay with our grandparents. Holiday,' replied
Mehmet. 'I'll 'ave no one to talk to.'

'I'm still here, you know,' replied Necip feeling a bit
snubbed that Mehmet didn't count his friendship as a sub-
stitute. He'd not seen Mehmet this quiet before. If the truth
be told, Necip was going off Mehmet. He used to be a laugh,

powerful. People followed him. But without that, the gang had no one to follow and had fallen away. Now Mehmet just moped around feeling sorry for himself. Necip was getting bored. School was no fun since the fight: no jokes, no beefing. He wondered if someone else might step up as a new leader to follow.

After school Shereen went back with Emine to St Margaret's Road. The radio was usually on in the house, but today the only sound was the rapid clack-clack-clack of Dilek's sewing machine. They called out 'hello' to her as they went upstairs without stopping for a reply. They were both upset about Tulay. But on top of that, Emine was distraught about her own family. Onur had left that morning for Turkey and, since Mehmet's arrest, her parents had been devastated, ghost-like shadows of themselves. It was hard enough for her, and they were just her brothers. She could move on with her life. But her parents couldn't do that. Raising the family had been their life's work and it was as if they had lost their sons.

'Onur's gone Turkey, just after that body turns up in park. Do ya think he had something' to do with it?' asked Emine, realising as these words came out how her disgust for Mehmet's bullying had spilt over into suspicion and distrust of Onur. Her brothers seemed like two peas from the same pod since Mehmet modelled himself on Onur.

'But your parents had this planned for ages, bought the ticket and everything, before the murder.' Shereen tried to maintain rationality for her friend.

'Yeah, but he still could have been involved, 'specially knowin' he had an escape route set up.'

Shereen put her arm around Emine.

'Involved in what?'

'I dunno. Well, some of his friends are well dodgy. Denzil. I heard he runs with some hard nut Turkish drug gang. What if they got Onur to be a trigger man, knowin' he was leavin' the country? Paid him, bigged him up or even t'reatened him?'

You can't be t'inking like that. Don't jump to conclusions. We have to wait and see what the police come up with.'

'And Mehmet!' Emine continued. 'He gets carried away. T'inkin' he's proper gangsta too, all front. It goes 'gainst everyt'ing our parents taught us.'

'It's really tough on them,' replied Shereen, 'to see their sons goin' down that path. But maybe it will be easier with Onur out of the way. Mehmet won't have a big brother to show off to. And Onur will get a break from the bad'uns himself.'

'You're lucky, Shereen,' said Emine, 'your family ain't fallin' apart. Your parents and cousin are all sound. Well, I know my parents are too, but my brothers…'

'I'm lucky and I don't ever stop countin' my blessings. Arjan knows it too.'

'But my brothers, oh my days, they have no idea.'

'Put them in a war zone, like Arjan, and maybe they'd change. Appreciate livin' in a peaceful country and make the most of it.'

They sat in silence for a while, each deep in thought. Shereen broke the spell.

'And Tulay's gone.'

'Yes, Ms Poole says police and social workers went round but her mum told 'em she left the country. Gone Turkey with her father.'

'That's the worst.'

'Said the police would contact the Turkish police to

investigate her safety, but ya know, I bet they'll turn a blind eye. Like, "Immoral English girl, getting what's coming to her."'

'It's shit. The system. I mean, if they'd gone over when Ms Poole first reported it, not four months later, they would've found her. They could've forced the parents to send her to school.'

They sat together in silence for a few minutes.

'I don't get it,' Emine continued, 'like, all our parents come to England to make a better life for their children, and then send 'em back! I mean, Onur, Tulay. I heard Onur's mate Denzil's gone Turkey too. What's happenin'?'

They fell silent again for a while, till Shereen shoved Emine.

'Come on girl. That's enough. We ain't gonna let nobody drag us down.'

'Ha, you're right, Shez.' Emine shoved her back, got up and crossed the room. 'Come on. I know what we need.'

She pulled a Destiny's Child CD off a shelf and put it into her ghetto blaster. The pulsing syncopated rhythm, the catchy melody, the background harmony of the music filled the room, shifted their mood instantly. In seconds they were both up, dancing and singing along with Beyoncé.

## WEST GREEN

Lloyd and Brenda were watching the BBC evening news, having a rest before their Friday night community centre quiz. There on the screen was their park.

'Look, Lloyd, look!' urged Brenda, although Lloyd was as transfixed as her to the screen.

How strange it was to see a familiar part of their world on the TV. It was library footage of the Downhills Park entrance, a cut to the changing rooms and then a shot of blue and white police tape at the crime scene, just 100 metres from their home. You could see the roof of the changing rooms from their bedroom window.

'Shh woman, listen,' he said.

'It has been over a week,' said the presenter's voice, 'since an unidentified acid-burnt body was found in Tottenham's Downhills Park. The police have now revealed that the victim had been shot before being disfigured with acid and left in the park. They continue to be unable to identify the victim, and are appealing to the public for information about any missing persons. If someone you know has disappeared recently, please call this number ...'

'What you t'ink, Lloyd? Some mad 'atter or sadist, like 'urtin' people? Or a gang t'ing?'

'Da gun, dat sound gang. Could be Turks, Albanians pushin' in on dem... either one way or other...'

'Maybe da police ballistic will lead to da killer.'

'Not so easy, Brenda. Der's plenty o' rent-a-gun out der don't belong to no one. Always changing 'ands. 'arder to find, 'arder to pin. Could be one of dem.'

'Oh Lloyd, so sad. For all of us,' Brenda sighed.

The doorbell rang.

'Mus' be Dwayne an' Ellis, said they'd drop by, walk up da centre together. I'll get it.'

Lloyd got up to answer the door. Brenda stiffened, wondering if they might have anything to do with it. She had always disapproved of their illegal activities, but her upset about the murder made her particularly uncomfortable about seeing them.

Lloyd opened the door a crack and gave his friends a quizzing look, but received regular greetings and stony

eye contact in return. He swung the door open and welcomed them. Mark was just coming down the stairs. He was
always excited when Dwayne and Ellis came round to see
his dad.

'Wha'gwan, Mark?' Dwayne offered a high five.

'Love, fam,' he replied. They all headed for the living room
where Brenda was still watching the TV news.

'Who do you t'ink did it, Dwayne?' Mark asked, under the
illusion that he knew everything that happened in London's
underworld. 'It's gotta be a gang t'ing, innit?'

Dwayne and Ellis exchanged a look and Dwayne shrugged.

'Say less. Could be a psycho or terror t'ing. If I knew somet'ing, be sure, I'd be passin' it to da police, Mark,' Dwayne
fibbed, knowing what Brenda would want to hear. 'Der's a
lot of bad'uns out der. What matter is we safe.'

Lloyd kept a deadpan expression as he listened to Dwayne's
declaration of faith in the police but knew better than to open
his mouth. Just as Lucas had sworn to him, he had sworn to
his friends to never ask questions or talk more about their
little problem.

'Don't matter who did it,' she said, 'or who da poor soul
was. Rich, poor, Black, White, Turkish, Albanian, make no
difference. It's a tragedy. For da dead'un and his kin, and da
killer. He don't know yet da damage he done to 'self. Maybe
OK now, even proud, but in da years 'e will 'ave nightmares.
Da guilt of 'is secret will grow. Weigh 'eavy on 'is soul. And da
damage 'e 'as done to our community, our neighbourhood,
now everyone t'ink a 'dangerous place to go. Da damage to
our park, now jus' a murder scene. Dat ain't no way to settle
no beef. No matter about what, killin' cannot be an answer.
Da 'eight of 'uman wickedness.'

They listened respectfully in silence. Lloyd searched

his friends' faces for a reaction but could detect nothing. Between them, they could not find a word of reply.

## GREEN LANES, HARRINGAY

Mustafa sat behind his desk in the back room of Topkapi. The gun lay before him wrapped in chamois leather. He always hired in hardware as and when it was needed. Safer than keeping his own. It was time to return this one to his supplier.

'Kemal,' he called, 'this piece needs returning. Take care of it,' he said pushing it across the desk.

'Sure boss,' said Kemal, picking it up, 'I'll return to sender,' placing it in his inside jacket pocket.

'Any news from the Albanian front?' Mustafa asked.

'Been quiet since the Black Boy. Reckon our message got through this time.'

'Good,' grunted Mustafa. He dismissed Kemal and sat in thought for a while before picking up his mobile. It's time I spoke to my brother, he thought, to finalise matters. He dialled the number.

'Hello, Bulent,' he spoke in Turkish, 'how are you? Aisha and the family?'

Mustafa had only met Aisha, Bulent's wife, once at their wedding twenty-two years before. He had just moved to London but had returned to Mardin for the occasion. They now had a daughter but Mustafa had not yet met her. He could not remember her name and at this moment felt bad that he had made so little effort towards his niece.

'Brother, good to hear from you,' Bulent replied. 'I am well. All is good here. Aisha and Elif are both in good health. Elif is finishing school and wants to go to medical school. Of course, she will get the necessary grades.'

'Inshallah. I heard the army gave you a new job. Too old for the front line, eh? A recruiting officer now, right?' Mustafa could not resist poking his brother but regretted his impulse immediately.

'Good news travels fast. It's a promotion, brother,' Bulent replied with an undertone of indignation. He never could deal with Mustafa's provocative sense of humour. 'In recognition of over twenty years of service. They have acknowledged me as a role model. I am not just a recruitment officer. I oversee all recruitment in Mardin.'

Bulent was proud of his own career success, his medals and family. These things made him, he thought, more successful than his brother. Did Mustafa have a wife or children? As a teenager, Mustafa had seemed more interested in hurting animals than finding a girlfriend. Bulent had always suspected Mustafa was a homosexual and that that was why he had moved to London. And what did he do there? What was his mysterious business that allowed him to send so much money back to their parents? As far as Bulent was concerned, money aside, his brother was a failure who never showed respect and always mocked his achievements. So, he was pleasantly surprised by Mustafa's next comment and change of tone.

'But really brother, that's fantastic. You know I was only joking,' said Mustafa, trying to control his habitual teasing. 'Really, I am so proud of you. I am sure Ma and Pa are too. And how are our parents?'

'Ma and Pa are so excited about the new house and with your last money transfer they have ordered the marble for all the floors and tabletops. A house by the seaside will be such a pleasure!' Bulent was relaxing a bit.

'Yes, it will be good for them to spend the summers there, cooler and healthier. Tell me, as a military man, are we winning the war against Kurdish terror? Are you recruiting all the men you need?'

'Things are hotting up, brother, and we can always use more soldiers, but how could we lose? As for me, I'm still getting used to life among civilians. Instead of enemy bullets, now I'm under fire from dirty looks and insults!'

'Ha!' Mustafa laughed. This was as close to a joke that he had ever heard from Bulent.

'No one likes me knocking on their door to serve them their orders,' Bulent continued, 'but as I see it, the young'uns have a duty to the motherland and should serve just as we all did. Chasing the shirkers is an important job.'

'You're right. And what of the diaspora, the Turkish youth living across Europe? Germany, Sweden, here in the UK? Some have never been in our country. If only you could get your hands on them!'

'If their parents are Turkish, then they are Turkish too and have a duty to their forefathers.'

'It is so sad, Bulent. In London we have a generation of young Turks who never visited the country, don't know culture, don't even speak the language properly and don't understand duty like we do. Twelve months in service would do all of them good, don't you think?'

'Yes, brother,' replied Bulent, enjoying this unusual moment of accord, 'it would help them to know where they come from, to correct their immoral and decadent ways and protect the motherland. It is the law. Mustafa, it is good to hear you have become so interested in patriotic duty. Are you a changed man?'

'Ha!' laughed Mustafa. Was this another joke from Bulent?

He had spun the conversation to get to this point and decided to make his move.

'Ah, well, if I hear of any young London Turks returning to the area, maybe I'll let you know and we can help them to rediscover their allegiance. You could pay them a visit. Perhaps a spell in the army will be a growth experience for them.'

'Of course. We always appreciate information from the public that makes it easier to do our job.'

'Tell me, are things dangerous right now?'

'The way things are going, new recruits are all getting a spell on the front line.'

'I see. Well, it was good to speak to you, brother, and I'll be in touch if I hear anything,' said Mustafa, hanging up with a wry smile. Bulent had always been so easy to manipulate.

# Chapter Twenty-One

## 23RD FEBRUARY 2002

## DOWNHILLS PARK

Cetin and Dilek sat on their bench in the Italian garden, wrapped up against the cold but feeling the sun's rays on their skin. It was an unusually clear Saturday morning. The *Daily Mail* lay on Dilek's lap turned to page five and a headline, "Tottenham murder victim description issued". The police were still appealing to the public for information about missing relatives and, to encourage this, had released a description that was so bland as to be unhelpful: a White male, average build, five foot nine inches tall, black hair.

Since the murder, Cetin had been rethinking events and he was deeply troubled. He had lost trust in both his sons since Mehmet's fight and then finding out Onur worked for Topkapi. Cetin thought back to that night three weeks before, when Mustafa Igli had come to their house with his international placement proposal. It had been a shock to discover Onur was working for him, but a relief that Mustafa had let his son go so easily. His imagination tormented him. If it had been a gang-related murder, might it have involved Topkapi? And if so, might Onur have played a part in it? Perhaps Mustafa had set up his international placement proposal to be an assassin's escape route. Had the family's own Mardin plan offered an even more convincing escape cover? Was Onur the trigger man? What would they say if the police came round looking for Onur?

Dilek broke the spell.

'Let's ring Onur and see how he is getting on,' she said, dialling Onur's mobile. He picked up quickly.

'Ma, it's good to hear your voice.'

'How are you? How was the journey?'

'I'm fine. Yes, the journey was long.' Dilek smiled, remembering how it had taken four days by bus when they had travelled from Mardin twenty-three years before, not the seven hours of Onur's plane journey. 'Grandpa was at the airport to meet me with a sign with my name. Just as well, as I would not know him. The house is beautiful. Much bigger than ours!'

'Your grandparents have worked very hard for many years to build their business, and this has been their reward. I am sure it has changed much since I left.'

'Yes, they told me they built a new room since then. But also, satellite TV, new sofas, beds, it's so comfortable.'

'I am happy to hear this for them as well as for you. And you are meeting your cousins?'

'I can't remember all their names, there are so many uncles, aunts, cousins, nephews.'

'And the business? Did Grandpa take you there yet? Have you talked about work?'

'Yes, a bit. There is so much to learn.'

'Well, keep busy. It will come to you. And stay out of trouble, Onur. The police in Turkey are very harsh. We are all missing you, especially Mehmet, who doesn't know what to do with so much bedroom space! He has been very quiet since new year.'

'I miss him too, all of you. Tell him I will call him. How is Papa?'

Dilek passed the phone to Cetin.

'I am here, Onur. I heard your conversation, and I am pleased for your arrival. But I am worried. You know your old boss Mustafa Igli is from Mardin? Of course, he still has family and business connections there. I do not know what kind of people they are, but it is better you make a clean break from the Igli family. Please, if you meet anyone connected, leave them and stay away. For your sake and for your mother's family. OK?'

Across the park, Lucas sat on a bench overlooking the playing fields. He had stepped out from work to allow himself time to think. Was the corpse Jerrish? The police description was so vague as to fit almost anyone, including Jerrish. So far, they had not found a DNA match. But that did not rule him out. Perhaps he had never had to give a sample, or if he had there may have been a test error. What if it was Jerrish and the police found some other way to make the identification? Wouldn't they wonder what this Plymouth man was doing in London? If they found out about the rentals, the trail would lead the police to interview him. There had been written contracts. The arrangement to pay rent in cash; to deal with Lucas alone; to meet in the properties instead of the office. What if further digging revealed their common past in Cornwall? Might they suspect him as a partner in criminal enterprise? Or if they found out how distracted Lucas had been recently, might they work out the blackmailing and conclude that he had a motive for murder?

He told himself to stay calm, even as he felt a cold sweat and nausea wash over him. Focus on facts not fears. The police had failed the identification so far. Jerrish was a loner. Who would report him missing? Certainly not his gangland associates. If the corpse was Jerrish, no one could make the connection apart from him and the killer. He could tell no one, not even Mollie. This secret would have to go with him to the grave. He had sworn a silence to Lloyd that could not be betrayed. He reminded himself to be happy that the blackmailing bastard was gone, one way or the other. He had nothing to feel guilty about and knew nothing of the circumstances. In time the story would go away. People would forget. News reports of the Downhills murder were already receding into the back pages and would soon disappear altogether, or so he hoped.

It was mid-afternoon when Mehmet left the house and set off for Downhills. He was depressed and hated weekends, feeling lonely and getting bossed around at home by his parents and sister. He had drifted away from his friends at school and didn't know what to do with himself. He hoped he might see someone in the park. How he missed Onur, telling his big bro about his day at school and hearing Onur's old stories even if for the millionth time. He walked down Napier Road and turned right along Philip Lane.

Since the fight and his arrest, his ma was anxious every time he left the house. He knew she thought the streets were filled with danger and dreaded him getting into more trouble. He could see that his parents blamed themselves; that they had tried their best to be good parents and tried to give their children a better life than their own. But he and Onur couldn't help it. They were drawn to excitement like bears to honey.

He had been shaken by his arrest. For the first time in his life, he realised the consequences of his own actions, of trying to be a big man, of running down other kids and getting into trouble with the law. He had never spent time in a police station before. He thought it would give him cred. But it wasn't like that. It just made him feel small. Now he was on tag and curfew, watched by the Youth Offending Team and waiting for a court case which could put him in juvie for months or even years. Without Onur there was no one to praise him for his exploits. And he had been shocked at how upset his parents were. He had thought them invincible. But now he had seen them break, saw they were human. He had taken their love for granted and now he felt their shame. He hated himself for hurting them.

He didn't know what to do with himself. At school the old gang had splintered. Some backed away, looking for someone else to follow. Others, who had only followed him to avoid being his victim, melted into the sea of faces. Even his old friend Necip wanted more than he could give.

Mehmet reached the end of Philip Lane and went into the park. Near the entrance he passed the site of the fight. He froze, electrified by his memories, as if he was experiencing some kind of divine visitation. How could a couple of square metres of tarmac and grass hold such significance for him? He replayed the fight: the gangs, the taunts, the bravado, the grappling, the knife, the blood, the police. Two square metres of ground and five minutes that had changed his life. The spell was broken by the bark of a dog running nearby. He walked on, past the playground and into the Italian garden. He sat down on a bench, exactly where he and the gang had tried to take Mark's new bike and beaten Ned on the ground. His mind drifted here and there, hazy and detached. His mum and dad, how hard they worked; Onur, starting a new life in Turkey, returning where they had come from, full circle; Emine, with her ambition; Necip, his old friend; West Green, all the world he knew.

And then someone was coming, walking towards him. Still fifty metres off but heading directly his way. Was it Necip? He'd like to see him. But no. It was Arjan, the boy he had teased and bullied for three years. He expected Arjan to cuss him. He knew he deserved it. There was no blag left in him. He would take it without resistance. There were no words. In his shame, Mehmet tried to smile sheepishly. As Arjan walked by, he nodded and returned a smile, an expression that conveyed understanding and compassion. As he receded into the distance, Mehmet choked with tears.

Part Four

# GOING BACK, MOVING ON

**2012**

# Chapter Twenty-Two

## MARDIN, EASTERN TURKEY

From the craggy outcrop of rock that overlooked Mardin, Onur scanned the rooftops and the patchwork landscape of green and brown beyond. He often came here for solitude. Somehow, this vantage point helped him find perspective over his own life – past, present and uncertain future. It had been ten years since he had left West Green, yet he still thought of it often, picturing significant places and people clearly: his home in St Margaret's Road, his family, the Green Lanes and Topkapi club, Kemal, Mustafa, Denzil, Downhills Park, the humdrum of the warehouse, the joy of his car, the excitement of Topkapi. How strange, he thought, to have returned to the place his parents had left thirty-three years before. They had come to Tottenham seeking a better life, and now he had reversed the process. Both their journeys, both quests, seemed to connect the places.

He missed Denzil. They had been closest friends, but they had not spoken since the Ferry Boat. He remembered the warmth, closeness and trust they had shared, and the terrible sense of betrayal. He could not help wondering what Denzil was up to: still in London, working the streets of Tottenham for Topkapi, following Kemal's career? Had Kemal vouched for him? The Downhills corpse had haunted Onur over the years; it had given sharp focus to the grim reality of where a Topkapi career might have led him. And strangely, it had felt like a violation of his childhood: the park, his place of play, fun, friendships and mischief; his memories had been stained by the detritus of violent adult abuse.

Looking back, he remembered his apprehension and fear about coming to Turkey and leaving behind everything familiar, but he had known he had to get away; punishment was coming. It had been a jump into the unknown, into the hands of grandparents he had never met, in a town, country and culture he did not know. He had especially missed Mehmet and it had been difficult not speaking English when he wanted to. Although the Turkish here was the same as that of his parents, it was different to what he had spoken with his Tottenham friends. For a long time, he had felt like an outsider.

But his grandparents had done their best: given him security, accommodation, employment, and connected him to a long-lost extended family of uncles, aunties and cousins. They had treated him like a prodigal son, delighted that they now had an heir, a grandson to pass on the legacy of the business which they were becoming too old to manage. They were pleased too that Dilek now rang once a week.

Within a month of arriving, he had received his call-up to the army. A knock on the door. A stony-faced recruiting officer had stood there, letter in hand. A report had reached him, he had said, of Onur's recent arrival and it was every Turkish man's duty to serve. 'Who reported it?' his grandparents had asked, but the officer didn't reply. Onur was to report to the town barracks in one week. He had expected this to happen. Everyone got called up. He had spent two months at a training camp doing a lot of drills, jogging and target practice, sharing a dormitory and shower room with twenty other conscripts. Then they were driven in convoy into the hills close to the Syrian border. There had been fighting. The enemy was the PKK. He had naively told himself that the shots fired at the Ferry Boat would prepare him. But pistol shots in a car park were hardly preparation for the cacophony and terror of a battlefield, of automatic rifle fire and explosions, of carnage and mutilation, of fear for your life. He saw people die, from both sides, but it struck him that because the PKK were dying for something they believed in, Turkish deaths were the more tragic. He survived the full year of patrols and skirmishes.

He had returned from the army to the family business and worked hard to repay their kindness. Nevertheless, their home had felt claustrophobic. He had taken to long walks around the town in the cool of night, despite their concern for his safety. After the army, he thought he could handle himself. At first, he had kept to the well-lit, paved streets of the modern town, browsing shopfronts and admiring cars, especially the Audis, BMWs and Mercedes brought back by 'guest workers' from Germany and proudly driven around, showing off their success. As he became more confident, he ventured down darker tracks into neighbourhoods with street-side workshops and mixtures of homes at various stages of completion or development, breeze blocks and steel rods poking out of the concrete. If there was a full moon, he might explore dirt tracks beyond the edge of town, threading between fields and wasteland. He had met others out walking, seeking space from their crowded homes, enjoying the cool of the night. He had frequently been stopped and searched by the police. But once they saw his ID card, they always let him go. He heard that they were not so easy on Kurds, and after his military service he could see why.

In London he had had no interest in, or understanding of, politics. Labour. Conservative. No one even talked about this on the streets of Tottenham. But here, everyone was interested in what the government was doing because they saw how it affected them, although they could not talk freely about it. In eastern Turkey, you couldn't ignore the state. Armed police and soldiers were on the streets all the time and every young man or woman was suspected of being a PKK terrorist until proven otherwise. He remembered his parents recounting similar experiences. It made him feel closer to them, imagining them as the young people before they had gone to London and had children. Had his father been conscripted? Cetin had never talked of it.

His mind turned to the present. He was in love and all he could think about was Elif; beautiful Elif, almond eyes and sculpted cheekbones, long black corkscrew hair, a smile that warmed any room and a sense of humour to lighten any party. He had been smitten the first time he had met her. She had come into the shop to buy a leather jacket. Then, by chance he had been delighted to bump into her soon after in a nearby cafe. A whirlwind romance had followed, and he could hardly believe that someone as wonderful as her would feel the same way towards him. They had dated for six months, gone to movies and restaurants, for walks and picnics, started talking about their futures together, of getting married. They had even set a date in July. His grandparents had been wary and protective. They asked him about her family, and he had passed on what he knew: her mother, Aisha, was a homemaker and her father, Bulent, a career soldier, well respected within conservative, nationalist and military circles, and now responsible for conscription and recruitment in Mardin. He had not yet met them, but who knows, perhaps it had been he who had delivered his call-up papers years before. The family seemed to have money. They had a seaside home five hours drive to the west in Payas.

But things had been complicated. Early on, when he found out her family name was Igli, he had wondered if she might be connected to Mustafa Igli. He prayed that this was just a coincidence, after all, Igli was a common name. He had tried to put such thoughts behind him. But his grandparents had confirmed his fears. They told him the rumour that Elif had an uncle in London who sent money to the family. Onur had been stunned. The bitter irony of leaving London to get away from Topkapi, only to find himself in love with Mustafa's niece. The information had made him doubt the marriage. How would Mustafa react to the news that he, a disgraced Topkapi soldier, was marrying into his family? Mustafa may have let him go but wouldn't have expected to meet him again, least of all like this. Onur had so many questions. Would Mustafa try to obstruct their marriage? Would he blackmail Onur back into service with the secrets of his past? How much did Elif or her law-abiding father know about what her uncle did in London? What would they think of *him* if they knew he had worked for Mustafa? He considered breaking up with Elif, but they loved each other. He reminded himself that she could not help the family into which she had been born and was not responsible for her uncle's actions. He would go ahead and say nothing about his past associations, lest this result in her father's disapproval.

## CORNWALL

Polperro was Ned and Shereen's favourite place and they visited whenever they could. It was a picture-perfect fishing village, with whitewashed cottages wrapping around a sheltered bay, fishing boats bobbing on the water protected from the ocean by the harbour arm. He read some of the boats' names to himself. *The Jenny Claire, Mousehole Cat, Sea Empress, Saracen.* The fresh, salty breeze, the clang of mast tackle and screeching of gulls, seaweed and tar tingeing the air. It carried Ned's imagination to past days of smuggling, barrels of brandy, redcoats, three-cornered hats and muskets, and when he was not in this historical fantasy, to dreams of travelling beyond the horizon.

Ned was curious to know more about his father's past. Lucas had always been cagey, and this only served to increase Ned's interest. Lucas had let slip that he had spent time in Polperro, so this was an added attraction of the place. For Shereen, Polperro represented a rural idyll. Villagey, quaint, simple, well-ordered, the opposite of the Tottenham world she had grown up in. It was just an hour from Plymouth, so it made an easy day trip by car, and she had one. They sat together on the quay, perched on mooring bollards, watching boats bobbing while they shared a bag of chips.

'Don't let the gulls see,' warned Shereen, reminding them both of recent experiences of aerial mugging in Plymouth.

'Ha, never mind the roadmen, watch the gulls,' joked Ned.

They were in love. Neither was quite sure when it had started. There had certainly been nothing between them at school, given their age difference. Shereen had moved to Plymouth in 2006 to study Social Work at the university, while Ned did his A-levels at City and Islington Sixth Form.

They had had no contact. It had been Arjan who reconnected them in 2008, when Ned had chosen to go to Plymouth University to study Psychology. He had liked the idea of living by the sea, learning to surf and had heard that Plymouth had a rising club scene that offered an opportunity for him to grow his sideline hobby as a DJ.

Shereen had happily become his mentor and guide, showing him around the town, the best spots for food, drink and dancing, how to use the university library and so much more. Their age difference no longer mattered. The more they had talked, the more they had realised that they felt drawn together by their shared past, their common experiences of growing up in West Green, playing in Downhills, going through Park School and all the people they had in common, above all Arjan. They had spent hours talking, working out what they wanted for themselves in life. Most of the other students on their courses had come from less diverse, middle-English towns, so a sense of difference bonded them. It didn't take long for their relationship to turn romantic.

'I've got a gig next Saturday,' he told Shereen. He had been offered a weekly residency at the Three Tonnes, an old pub with yellowing 1970s décor that was trying to catch the new wave of club culture emerging in the city, 'but how about we try to visit Launceston on Sunday?'

'See your grandparents? Have you been in touch? Are they up for it?'

Ned liked to think he had returned to his roots. He wanted to connect with his father's earlier life, to fill the gaps between the bits that Lucas had told him. This desire had only been made stronger by Lucas' reluctance to share. Before moving to Plymouth, Ned had met his grandparents on their annual visits to London and the odd family trek to Launceston, but he didn't feel he knew them properly and liked the idea of spending more time in their home. He didn't understand how Lucas had drifted away from them. While Ned was growing up, Lucas hardly ever called them and shied away from talking about his own youth. Now Ned could discover this history for himself. Meanwhile he had fallen in love.

After graduation, Shereen had found a job as a social worker in Plymouth. She liked the town and wanted to stay there. It was familiarly urban, but interestingly different and she felt like she was making a fresh start in her life, free from any baggage of the past. She had rented a flat in a new harbourside development, a nineteenth-century naval warehouse that had fallen into disuse after the war, been squatted from the 1960s to the 1980s and finally been bought up for renovation as part of the city's regeneration programme. Today Sutton Harbour had become a cool and trendy neighbourhood, a far cry from its origins. She had needed a car for her job so bought one, which she used at weekends to explore Devon and Cornwall. Ned often tagged along and, by the time he graduated, they had become deeply involved. He moved in with her and found work in the local authority housing department, not much of a use for his degree, but it was a job for now.

He liked visiting home, but neither of them wanted to live in Tottenham again. 14 February 2002, 'the day of the dead' as he called it, had ended their childhood innocence and tainted their perception of the neighbourhood forever. It had been traumatic, more than either of them realised at the time, and had a sobering effect on all the tough teenage talk of the school yard. Although they knew, on a rational level, that Plymouth also experienced its share of violence and murder, they had no direct experience of it, so it felt like a safer place. Ned feared for his parents, still living in Crossfield Road. He saw them as oblivious to the potential violence and danger surrounding them in their daily lives. They knew nothing of the underbelly of society, the drugs, gangs and violence coexisting in plain sight. What could they know? Lucas had grown up in a small Cornish market town, Mollie in a Swiss village and both lived insulated from the realities of the street. If only he could persuade them to move away, maybe back here to Cornwall. Shereen's parents had already left, moving to Ireland a few years ago. He lived in hope that they might follow this example.

'Arjan messaged me,' Shereen said. He had been living in Broadwater Farm since graduating and now had the flat to himself.

'He's askin' if we're plannin' to visit any time soon. Says he'd like to make a reunion. Says his mum's comin' over from Syria. She'll be staying with him. That's my great auntie, Fatima. He wants to have a welcome party, maybe a picnic in Downhills or somethin'.'

'That's good news for him. Half his lifetime since he saw his mum. Yeah, I'd be up for that. Catch up with old friends, see my folks.'

'He says in July. A Saturday afternoon.'

'We can stay at mine. My folks will be happy.'

They were both excited at the prospect of the visit. They had gone back many times since leaving, but each time they wondered how they would feel when they got there.

# Chapter Twenty-Three

## 25th JULY 2012

### MARDIN, EASTERN TURKEY

Onur waited at the arrival gate of Mardin's small regional airport. He had not seen his family for ten years and he was so excited that they were coming for his wedding. This was his parents' first return in thirty-three years, and Emine and Mehmet's first ever visit to Turkey. He imagined their apprehension. He wondered how they would have changed. Emine now aged twenty-six, Mehmet twenty-three, his parents in their sixties. He had followed their lives from a distance: Emine going to university, earning good money as a qualified accountant with her own flat; Mehmet still working at the supermarket on the West Green Road; Cetin and Dilek slowing down as their health deteriorated, with his high blood pressure and her arthritis.

The plane landed and, soon after, a stream of passengers came through the gate. Then they were there, Emine walking with quiet self-confidence, Mehmet looking a little lost, and behind them, Cetin and Dilek. He was shocked to see how they had aged, their faces lined and hair flecked with grey, wheeling their bags slowly, wearing their apprehension.

In the car, Emine and Mehmet were full of questions about

what they saw out of the window as they drove through the town. They chatted in English. What was sold in this or that shop, what was the network coverage like, what was the price of petrol, why were there armed soldiers on the streets? Mehmet had never been out of London before. They chatted in English. Onur was happy to respond but floundered with his words at first as his English was so out of practice. Dilek and Cetin sat quietly, gazing at the streetscape that was both familiar and yet changed by the passage of time. After so many years apart from Onur and exhausted by the long journey, they found conversation difficult. Dilek was just happy to see Onur's face. He had booked them some hotel rooms. Her parents' house was not big enough for all of them. Dilek needed to rest, freshen up and recover her composure before seeing her parents again. Onur left them at their hotel and arranged to return in the morning.

The next day, rested from a good sleep, they were ready when Onur collected them. They had two days before the wedding. Dilek could barely recognise the frail octogenarians who embraced her. The joy of reunion was overshadowed by her sense of guilt for having left them. But this was quickly overcome by excitement as Mehmet and Emine met their grandparents for the first time. Everyone was talking at once, full of questions and answers, catching up on the missed years. Communication was not made easier by Emine's and Mehmet's London Turkish and their grandparents' hearing difficulties.

'Tell us, Emine, can we expect wedding bells soon, like your brother?' asked her granny. Dilek had warned her she would be asked about marriage, children and career, so she had prepared her answers.

'Not yet, sorry, Grandma,' Emine replied, as diplomatically

as possible. 'I haven't found the right person yet. And I must work so hard, I am usually too tired to go out at weekends.'

'I heard you are now an accountant,' her grandfather chipped in. 'Did you consider maybe coming to live here, like Onur? There is always plenty of work for people with your qualifications.'

Dilek bristled a little, wondering if her parents' attempt to lure the children back was intended as a reprimand for her departure years before. How ironic it would be if all her children returned to Mardin leaving her and Cetin alone in West Green. But she knew that was unlikely. Emine and Mehmet were settled in their British ways, and she was confident that this visit to Mardin would confirm that for them. Across the room, Onur sat next to Cetin and Mehmet.

'How has Tottenham changed, Papa?' Onur asked Cetin.

'Slowly, you know, some new building work on the West Green Road. A lot of money spent on Downhills Park. House prices going up. More Albanians and Eastern Europeans. The shop is busy. Mehmet is running things more and more, aren't you, Mehm? I take more time out. I'm reading, walking, playing pool.'

'Yes,' chipped in Mehmet, 'I know how everything works now.'

'What of the streets? West Green Road? Green Lanes?' Onur continued.

'More cars, more people,' Cetin laughed. 'If you are asking about the gangs, I don't know. I guess the same. These things don't change so quickly.'

'Papa, did you hear anything about my old friend Denzil?'

'Sorry, son, I have nothing to tell you about that. Hey, there is something I need to do. I'll be back in five minutes.'

As Cetin left the room, Onur turned to Mehmet.

'It's good to see you bro'. Talkin' and textin's not the same. How you been? Sounds like you're keepin' busy.'

'I been through changes since you've been gone,' Mehmet replied. 'Those crazy days in '02 shook me up, bro. Beef with the feds, nearly goin' juvie, losin' my crew, losin' you, upsettin' Ma and Pa, everyt'ing went bad.'

'It's a good thing Pa helped with that, a job in the store. You got a proper future now. I'm proud of you, bro.' He paused, and then continued. 'Did you hear anything about Denzil? Is he still rolling with Kemal and Topkapi?'

'I don't know, Ons, I thought he was here. Same time you left, word was he was coming over too, some Topkapi job. I've not heard nothin' since.'

'I ain't seen him,' Onur replied, 'but suppose Mardin's a big place. Or maybe he's gone some other town.'

Cetin left the room, went down the stairs to the front door and out to the street. He was delighted to see Onur again, now fully grown-up, but he had never felt close to his in-laws and sensed their resentment against him having taken their daughter away to London. There was one person he wanted to see. His old friend Hasan Güney. He must be seventy-two by now. Since Onur moved here, Cetin rang him often. It helped him visualise Mardin and Onur's life. He had enjoyed the renewed contact with his old friend and told Hasan that he was coming for the wedding. Now that he was here, he wanted to meet. He took out his phone and dialled the number. Hasan answered.

'It's me, old friend, I am here in Mardin.'

'I've been waiting for your call. Let's meet in Saladin's, remember it, round the corner from Osman's garage?'

'Good idea, for old time's sake. This afternoon?'

'This afternoon at 2pm.'

Cetin hung up and returned to the family reunion. He tried to join in with the conversation but was restless, waiting for the hours to pass. At 1.30pm he excused himself.

Saladin's cafe seemed unchanged. The tables looked like the very same ones where they had sat and drunk coffee on their way to work thirty-three years earlier. Saladin himself was still behind the counter. Hasan was there when he arrived, older, greyer and more wrinkled, yet otherwise remarkably sprightly, upright and slim.

'Welcome home, Cetin.' Hasan embraced him, 'And congratulations at this happy time. I hear the reception will be at Cercis Murat Konaği, the same place as your own wedding! What a great party that was, and what a happy coincidence, but the best place in town.'

'Thank you, old friend. You look fantastic. What news of your Rasheed and his family?'

'Well, they moved to Ireland a couple of years ago. You remember his wife was Irish. Her parents died, and left her their house, with a garden. They both got good jobs. Their daughter, Shereen, stayed in England, went to university. Now she is a social worker. Plymouth. And Arjan, my nephew from Qamishli, he also went to university and has a good job with computers. Still in London. Now his mother, Fatima, goes to see him. The first time in twelve years.'

'Such stories renew my faith in our old dream, that in London you can find opportunities for a better life. Me, Dilek, Mehmet, Emine, we are all still there. We have what we need. But what irony that Onur has come back here, to where we started! And what of the freight business?'

'It is still going well. More trucks. More lines across Europe. Now I want an office in the west. These western routes are too difficult to run smoothly from here. Maybe

Ireland.'

'Anything to do with Rasheed moving there?' Cetin ventured, sensing the real motivation for this business plan.

'Well, maybe a little. I just wrote to ask if he wanted to work with me. I miss him. It would bring us closer, don't you think? And maybe he would carry on the business after me.'

'This I understand,' replied Cetin, 'as I feel the same about Mehmet. If you can't pass it on, what was it all for? Do you still send trucks to London?'

'Oh yes, at least one a month. One of my oldest and best customers is in London and, by coincidence, the uncle of the bride. Mustafa Igli. Surely you remember the name, Igli. The family owned the tobacconist shop where I bought my Birinci every day on the way to Osman's. Mustafa moved to London soon after you. Built an import-export business. Then helped me build mine with investment for trucks. You will meet him. He is coming here for the wedding.'

Of course, Cetin remembered Mustafa Igli and the tobacconist shop. He also remembered Mustafa's uninvited visit in London. Cetin had surmised that Elif Igli was related to Mustafa as soon as Onur had announced the engagement and told them her name. Hadn't he warned his son to stay clear of any Igli connection in Mardin? If his son had asked his opinion about the marriage, he would have told him to think very carefully; after all, he had come to Mardin to escape this very man. But Onur had not asked, and Cetin knew it would be a mistake to criticise or interfere with his adult son's personal decisions.

'Mustafa Igli, yes, I have met him. Topkapi Enterprises. Onur used to work for him, in the warehouse. Maybe handling the very same goods you were loading on to lorries here! He came to our house once to offer Onur a special work placement opportunity, here in Mardin. But it was too late because we had already made our plans for Onur to come to Dilek's family.'

'Lucky for Onur. In truth, he is better off with the leather jackets, believe me. But my friend, you will meet Mustafa at the wedding for sure and I hope you will be friends. Now you will be family.'

'You must join us at the wedding, as a guest to both sides. You can sit between me and Mustafa. Help us to become friends. I will ask Onur to invite you to the reception.'

'It would be my pleasure, like old times.'

Cetin smiled but he was worried. What was Onur getting himself into? Of course he wanted his son's happiness, but he feared that this family association with Mustafa Igli was dangerous. Would this marriage make them all vulnerable? Would Mustafa try to regain control of Onur? Would he use the marriage to get inside the Mardin leather business or his London supermarket; to bring them under Topkapi's influence? What was Onur getting himself -and the whole family- into?

# Chapter Twenty-Four

## 28TH JULY 2012

### MARDIN, EASTERN TURKEY

The roof terrace of Cercis Murat Konaği was lit up with coloured bulbs and strings of fairy lights. Beyond the balustrades, the house lights of the town glimmered while thousands of stars twinkled in the sky above. A troupe of musicians sat in one corner playing traditional songs, while guests sat around tables eating, drinking and celebrating. For Cetin and Dilek, whose wedding reception had also been here, there was a strong sense of déjà vu.

Emine and Mehmet were welcomed into a crowd of unknown cousins of their age, at a large table. Meanwhile, Cetin and Dilek sat with Elif's parents. They all knew how important it was for the couple's parents to have good relations and were making their best effort.

'You must be very proud of Elif,' Cetin said to Bulent. 'Such a bright and charismatic woman.'

'Yes, and I hope Onur will provide for her as well as we expect,' Bulent replied without humour or grace. 'Ah, look over there. It is my brother, Mustafa, just arriving. Like you, he has come from London for today. A shame he missed the ceremony. But not surprising. Not a pious man but always a party animal.'

It was embarrassing to hear Bulent speak so disparagingly about his own brother. The bear-like figure of Mustafa emerge at the top of the stairs. They remembered him from years before: tall, swarthy, black hair no doubt now dyed, gold chains, dark glasses, slightly comical-looking.

'Brother.' Bulent and Mustafa greeted each other with an embrace.

'Come sit, better late than never.' Bulent invited Mustafa to join them. He would enjoy the power that being the host gave him over his brother. As his guest, Mustafa would have to show respect.

'Same old Bulent, eh?' Mustafa joked, 'A barrel of laughs, a bucket of smiles! I got to commend the army for its social skills training programme! And you, of course are Mr and Mrs Zaman.' He reached across the table to shake their hands in turn. 'Congratulations! Well, you know we have met before.'

'Yes,' Cetin replied, 'I remember you came once to our house to kindly offer Onur a work placement.'

'Indeed, and a curious twist of fate that while he declined that job offer, here he is again, now joining our family!'

Dilek was not sure how to interpret this and wondered if menace was intended, but was quickly disarmed by Mustafa's side-slapping laughter at his own comment.

'Excuse me,' she said, standing up. 'You men must have much to catch up with. I will take a little walk around; will you join me?' She invited Aisha, Bulent's wife, who rose and accompanied her to leave the men together.

Cetin couldn't work out what was going on between Bulent and Mustafa. He had no brothers of his own so did not know how normal the behaviour was, but these brothers were so different and seemed quite disdainful towards each other. He wondered, what did Mustafa think of his niece marrying a former employee? Had he tried to persuade Bulent to refuse the marriage? Thankfully, the tension was broken by a new arrival.

'Look,' Cetin broke in, 'Hasan is here.'

'Hasan!' called Mustafa. 'Over here!'

Hasan made his way across the terrace and greeted the three men with handshakes and hugs. There was genuine affection for his old friends, Mustafa and Cetin, and polite civility for Bulent. Hasan had never formed a friendship with Bulent who, since running the army recruitment office, had become one of the least popular people in town.

Soon the three friends were sitting together, making pleasantries, and catching up while Bulent sat quietly, surveying the party on the terrace. Cetin wanted to find out more about the Igli family.

'I hear you have a villa in Payas by the sea, Mustafa,' he began. 'Your Topkapi business must be very successful.'

'Yes indeed, Cetin. It is mostly for my parents. Sadly, I have few opportunities to go. When I retire, perhaps. But you know, we live so close to each other in London.' Mustafa changed the subject. 'We must get together. A game of pool at the Topkapi club maybe?'

'I'm a bit rusty but thank you for the invitation. And what of your operations here in Mardin? I remember when you offered Onur a work placement here.'

'Yes, we have some activities, if Onur is considering a change of direction or your other children would like to move to Mardin.' The thought of Emine or Mehmet falling into the Topkapi orbit sent a chill down Cetin's spine. 'Now, Hasan, tell us about your business. You know, Cetin, I am his biggest investor.'

'I already told Cetin, I want to set up an Irish office,' said Hasan, 'now my son Rasheed has moved there. I hope he will come into business with me.'

'What a good idea. Ireland is an untapped market that I should also consider,' said Mustafa. 'As your largest share-holder, perhaps I can piggyback your operation and get my foot into Ireland too.'

'I'm not sure my shoulders are broad enough to carry you,' joked Hasan, realising too late that it had been a mistake to tell him. The last thing he wanted was for the venture with Rasheed to be corrupted or railroaded by Topkapi. Mustafa didn't laugh but shifted his attention to the party.

'Where are the happy couple? I must congratulate them,' he said, turning to scan the terrace and spotting Onur in a matter of seconds, standing by the balustrade, talking to a young woman wearing a bridal dress, his niece Elif of course, he told himself.

'Ah, I see them. Back soon.' He rose and crossed the room.

'Congratulations, my dears!' he approached them, confi-dently interrupting their conversation. 'Elif, I am your uncle Mustafa and such a shame your wedding is the first time that we meet. But better late than never.' He embraced her and offered a kiss to each cheek. Turning to Onur, he continued, 'and Onur, of course we have met in London, long ago.'

'I didn't know that you knew my uncle, Onur.' Elif expressed surprise.

'London is a small place, my dear. Onur worked for my business many years ago, so I am delighted to see him again,' shaking Onur's hand. 'We have so much to catch up on.'

Onur blushed with embarrassment. He had hoped to keep his past association quiet until they had been married for a while, in case Elif had heard bad things about her uncle and might then hold this against him.

'Yes of course, I am sure. I must circulate among the guests,' and with a smile, Elif left them together. Once she was out of earshot, Mustafa turned to Onur and addressed him, maintaining his magnanimous smile, but with a chilling tone.

'How strange, Onur, that I find myself welcoming you into my family. The last time we met, I was releasing you from my employment after you and your friend created considerable messiness in my life. I had not expected to ever see you again. But I see you survived military service and now find you running your grandparents' business.'

'Mr Igli, sir, I have felt regret for the problems I caused, every day for ten years. I hope you will forgive me for the sake of your niece.'

'Yes... well… I am not one to bear grudges. Always look forwards, that is what I say. To the future.' He slapped Onur on the back, then put his arm around his shoulder and pulled him close, holding him too tightly.

'So, tell me about the leather business now that you are the boss, or soon will be. Where do you source the leather? Where are your markets? What is your turnover?'

Onur felt overwhelmed by these questions.

'If you want, we can meet in the office next week and I can give you a tour, Mr Igli. That would be a better moment to give you all the information you want.'

'Ha, I'm only making conversation, Onur, but yes, it is your wedding after all, so Monday? Perhaps in the future there will be some partnership opportunities with Topkapi Enterprises. After all, you more than anyone in the family understand what it is I do in London and how there might be a lucrative arrangement for both of us.'

'Of course, Mr Igli,' replied Onur, aware of the need to tread carefully. 'Mr Igli, may I ask you something? You remember my friend, Denzil. I have heard nothing since I left London. Is he still with Topkapi? Is he well?'

'I do not know where he is,' Mustafa replied curtly, before continuing, 'such a wonderful wedding. Welcome to the family!'

## DOWNHILLS PARK

The sun rose at 5am, warming the dew-covered grass and launching the chatter of birdsong. The park teemed with life: colour burst from carefully tended bedding plants, the woodland canopy was dense with foliage and the grass of the playing field grew irrepressibly. Insects and birds feasted with joy.

Mollie was up soon after. By 6am she was jogging her circuit, smiling at familiar faces, other early joggers and dog walkers. It cleared her mind and prepared her for the day. She was happy to have her boys back; the family together, if only briefly. After so many years she knew every footfall: where new sections of tarmac gave way to the old, where tree roots buckled the path. This was her space, to stretch and breathe, and find the grounding that sustained her through each day. But even now, every time she passed the old changing rooms, she remembered that terrible time ten years before. Lucas had been stressed for weeks about the ghost from his past, the tenant in Carlingford Road. He had relaxed a bit after the tenant upped and left, but had never fully recovered his zest, and even now she sensed that he had not told her everything. Perhaps he was living in fear of his reappearance. As she jogged on, the scenery changed and her thoughts returned to her boys.

By midday, the park was heating up and a crowd of spectators had gathered around the basketball court. At the front stood Dwayne and Ellis, still an inseparable team forty years after they had first met at school. Dwayne had brought Ellis on board the coaching team. They were co-coaching the Haringey Hawks under-16 basketball team, drilling the players from the sideline as they hosted London Thunder from Lewisham in the league semi-final. The game was fast and intense. Dwayne did most of the shouting, but had to compete with the enthusiastic cheers and shouts of a few dozen parents and supporters who lined the court.

'Come on, you Hawks!' chanted their supporters, among them Brenda, Lloyd and Mark. Brenda was still a pillar of the community, active in the church and community centre. The game ended with a Hawks victory. The players ran around the court celebrating and high-fiving each other. London Thunder players slunk away, looking disappointed and dejected.

'Come on, boys,' Ellis boomed over the court, 'let's give T'under a Tottenham send-off!' clapping above his head in applause of their opponents. Soon every Hawk was joining in. Lloyd could see how it lifted the Thunder boys' spirits. He knew Brenda liked to see this side of them, though he couldn't help grinning, knowing she was less approving of their day jobs.

'Nice,' he said to Ellis as the two coaches came off the court.

'Well done, fam,' Mark chipped in.

'You boys done a great job,' said Brenda. 'Soon another cup for Tottenham!'

'Course, Brenda, what you expec'?' Dwayne grinned. 'Come we go.'

'I gotta go meet Ned, Shereen and Joe. Catch y'all later,' said Mark, peeling off from his family and heading towards the park cafe.

'Be good,' Brenda called after him, still her baby at twenty-three. Mark laughed.

They left the basketball court and followed the old balustrade, set among beautiful trees, enjoying the stroll and a chance to catch up. It had been a couple of weeks since they last met.

'Y'know, dis place,' Dwayne started, sweeping his arm outwards across the park, 'what it give us. Da memories we 'ave.'

'True dat,' replied Ellis. They followed the path down-slope, towards the gate leading closest to the Durrants' house. In the near distance, a hundred metres further on, stood the old changing rooms.

'Yes, 'appy memories. We built our lives 'round dis park. Its stories are t'readed t'rough us like the weave of tapestry. But every time I see dat place,' said Brenda, indicating the building. 'I remember da murder. Can't 'elp it.'

'Some t'ings maybe better we don't remember,' 'said Lloyd, shooting a glance at his old school friends. 'Come to ours for a cup o' tea?'

While Mark was leaving his family, Ned, Shereen and Joe were making their way across the field, through the flower beds, past the playground and tennis courts to the cafe. They could hear the loud applause coming from the direction of the basketball court. By now the park was packed.

'Look there, bro,' said Joe, nodding at a group practising yoga on the grass. 'Not seen that before in Downhills.'

'The neighbourhood's changin',' Ned replied. 'Did you see the Green Lanes? Another new restaurant. Them Turkish social clubs, turning into smart diners.'

There may have been some changes since their last visit, but in many ways the park was as they had always known it. Dozens of people had come out to enjoy a good-weather Saturday. Rough-and-ready games of footie were played between coat-and-bag goalposts all over the field by groups of mostly males of all ages. Mums and dads were chasing their tots around the playground or pushing them on the swings. Some pre-teens cycled by, full of noise and bubbling with energy. A small group of teenagers sat on a bench slumped under their hoodies, passing a cigarette, supping on energy drinks.

'It's like every stage of our lives, laid out before us,' Ned said to Joe. Where could be better for a reunion with our most important friends?

Ned's phone pinged and he checked the message. It was Mark, waiting at the cafe. They found him sitting under the wooden canopy. 'What's 'appenin', bro'!'

'Long time! Must be a year!'

'Shereen, good to see ya,' said Mark, trying to include her in the boys' reunion. 'Likin' Plymouth? Hey, any word of your gels, Emine and Tulay? You were proper tight?'

'Yeah, I'm in touch with Emine. She got a job as an accountant. Got her own place in London. Jus' now, she's gone Turkey for her bro' Onur's wedding. Tulay went Turkey long time, remember her parents sent her? But things worked out. Her fam didn't force her to marry and even let her go to a Turkish uni. Now she's teachin' English in a secondary school! Istanbul.'

'So her Tottenham years, speakin' English, came in useful.' joked Ned.

'Ha! Tulay a teacher, like Ms Poole!'

They all laughed while Shereen remembered how Ms Poole had tried to be in Tulay's corner and felt sure Tulay would do the same for her pupils.

They bantered for a while. It was good to meet after months apart in their new lives, new towns and new friends. Once together, all distance melted away and they felt instantly back in each other's lives. Shereen felt a little out of place in the boys' reunion and besides, she was keen to find Arjan and Fatima.

'Good to see you guys. I'm on my way to Arjan,' she said. 'Havin' a picnic near the school gate.'

'OK cool,' said Mark. 'tell 'im 'hi', and maybe we'll come find you later?'

'Yeah, do. Arjan wants you to meet his mum and he's got plenty o' food, so come. Laters.' said Shereen, waving goodbye and leaving them to catch up.

'So, what else is new? How's sunny Plymouth? You been ravin' on the beach, surfin' the waves, sailin' a boat?' asked Mark.

'Yeah, you know, Sir Walter Raleigh and all that,' joked Ned. 'Actually it's decent. Calm. Nice to visit back here, but we're happy there. And what about Luton, the Mecca of Thameslink commuters?'

Mark had spent three years studying Accountancy at the University of Bedfordshire and, like Ned in Plymouth, decided to settle there. He had found a job and a flat which kept his parents happy because it was still within easy reach.

'Well, it's quiet. Distractions from study were minimum. And now it's affordable and near my job....and away from my parents!'

They all laughed.

'How's your family?' Mark continued.

'They're good, aren't they Joe? Dad is the boss of Stanhopes now. Took over when his boss retired. He says West Green is the new Stokey! Well, he is always talkin' it up. But there is somethin' in it. Every time I come back, I notice another house or shop bein' done up. More middle-class. Saw some yoga in the park jus' now! Dad says it's good for his business. Apart from work, he still plays footie once a week with yours. He's learnin' sax so the neighbours keep complainin'! No seriously though, he's quite good. Mum is the same. So fit and youthful. Runnin' every day. What about yours?'

'Same old,' replied Mark. 'Dad's workin' hard as ever. Expanded his business. Bought a new van and got extra crews. Playing footie with your dad! Mum still holdin' everythin' together. Church. Community centre. Waitin' for grandchildren! She won't let me forget.'

'I'm so glad we got away.' said Joe. 'It's good to be back, but it's opened a new world for us.'

'True say,' replied Mark.

'Y' know, this place is bittersweet,' said Joe. 'I mean, there's all the good memories but still, it's got a dark side. Remember the murder, that body?'

'Ten years ago.' said Mark, nodding, 'They never did identify it or catch a killer.'

'Right, there's enough dodgy people round these ends,' agreed Ned. 'Remember Mehmet? How 'e used to scare us with 'is big bro', Onur.'

They all laughed, sharing their memories, safe in the knowledge that they had moved on in their lives.

Shereen found Arjan and Fatima, close to the West Green Road entrance. He had brought bags of tasty, sweet and savoury food and laid out the picnic on a blanket. This was a good spot, not far from shops and toilets.

As a child Arjan had felt abandoned by his mother when she had sent him away but had gradually come to understand the bravery and selflessness of her decision; and the open-hearted generosity of Rasheed, Dymphna and Shereen for adopting and supporting him. He owed all his achievements to them: his degree, a good job and an affordable flat. Now he was the adult, he felt the responsibility to look after others had passed to him, starting with his mother. He had sent her money and arranged a tourist visa for her to visit, and hoped he could find a way for her to stay longer. He did not know how, but right now he did not want to think about it. Today was for celebration.

If it were a happiness contest, Fatima would have won first prize: to see her son Arjan again after twelve years, safe, sound, and successful, a university graduate for goodness' sake! To leave the never-ending violence and fear of northern Syria. London felt so safe and Arjan had told her that there were many other Kurds in this area. She prayed he could find a way for her to stay and eventually bring Kalil. Even Hasan from Mardin, though in her heart she knew that if he ever left it would be to Ireland.

As the late afternoon drew on, Lucas made his way home through the park. The afternoon heat warmed his skin. He tried to enjoy the moment. He had reasons to be content. Mollie seemed happy. Ned and Joe were both finding their way. He loved having them both home to visit. Might there even be wedding bells round the corner? Stanhopes continued to do well. He had hobbies and friends. But happiness, that carefree sense of joy, had eluded him ever since that day in 2001 when Steve Jerrish had re-entered his world, endangering everything he held dear, and then vanishing again. Jerrish had been such a significant figure in his life. Now his absence haunted him. He carried a terrible sense of guilt. So long as Jerrish's fate remained unknown, Lucas would not be able to cast it off. Every day, he replayed the thoughts that had been looping for ten years. Was the corpse Jerrish? The police had never made an identification, the crime remained unsolved. Although Lucas had promised never to speak of it, in a private moment back in 2002 Lloyd had quietly let him know that his associates swore they had just scared Steve off and taken his plants, a simple matter of enforcing trade boundaries. If true, he may still be alive, skipped town, returned to Bristol or Plymouth. But what if Lloyd's whispered confidence was part of their alibi? There was also the possibility that it had been Jerrish, but killed by someone else from his shady underworld. Lucas feared he would never again feel carefree joy, bound forever to this burden of uncertainty and guilt.

He looked across to the familiar Victorian villas of Belmont Road beyond the railings. He had been inside so many as an estate agent. How many family histories had each one witnessed? The highs and lows of so many lives, each different yet with so much in common; lives witnessed by their old brick walls. Houses built with great expectations, passed on, subdivided, gentrified or left to decay. And Downhills, at the centre; a place in common, to think and breathe, of nature and renewal. He reached the gate and left the park. Nearly home.

As the sun set and darkness fell, people drained away and the park's night began. A couple of homeless people settled on secluded benches, hoping for a safe sleep. A small group of youth converged on the playground, now a place to sit and smoke. Across the playing field, a few others hung around a bench, ready to toy with passing prey, but eventually boredom drove them all home, allowing nature to reclaim the park in its darkness. Foxes emerged and pigeons scavenged the ground for scraps of discarded food. The Park. Nature, hiding in plain sight, outlasting the fleeting dramas of human lives.

# Notes from the author

This book is about a place where people's lives have converged in their search for purpose: for some this means
better economic opportunity, career choice, escape from
violence or cultural oppression, while for others it is membership of school or drug gangs, status and turf wars.
Thematically, the characters also struggle over cultural
identity, belonging to family or friendship groups, sexual
orientation and owning language.

The characters represent various aspects of West Green's
diverse and dynamic community, as I knew it in 2002. The
Fairbrights represent a generation of White British incomers
from the 1980s, for whom West Green ticked all the boxes,
not least the relatively affordable property market. They also
feel more comfortable than in the places they left behind.
They have found a fit and made it *their* place. As an estate
agent, Lucas helps us understand urban change by providing an ongoing commentary on historic and contemporary
change, including the gentrification of which they themselves are part.

The Zaman, Güney and Durrant families represent hard
working, honest and aspirational first-generation migrants
from Turkey, Syria, Jamaica, Ireland and elsewhere, seeking
economic opportunity. They bring their culture with them
and continue to be connected to the places they came from,

so shaping London to be the multicultural city that it is. Each family has struggled to improve their circumstances, in the universal desire to give their children a better life than they had. Emine, Shereen, Arjan, Mark and Ned all have career aspirations and that align with their parents' values. In contrast, Mehmet, Onur and Denzil's aspirations come from their own inner-urban experience and the excitement of deviance. They have little regard for their parents, or their sacrifices, though the Zaman boys find redemption. All the young people are caught between the culture and aspirations of their family heritage and their own lived world experience; their search for identity and belonging, for example between Turkishness and their Britishness is an ongoing theme.

Meanwhile, a destructive underworld hides behind and preys upon the community, luring the youth with promises of power and easy money. The relationship between community and underworld is complicated The Zamans fear Topkapi as a contaminating and dangerous force which threatens to take Onur and Mehmet, yet the gang has become a feature of the Green Lanes landscape. Mustafa is a complex and multi-faceted character. He is a ruthless, violent and unpredictable gang boss while also being gay, a flamboyant dresser and affable when required. Towards the end, he surprises us with a newfound desire to be seen as contributing to his community. Similar tension exists between Lloyd and Brenda over Lloyd's connection with the Jamaican underworld friends, Dwayne and Ellis. These lovable rogues are welcomed to the Durrant home as extended family, although their gangland activities present a moral conflict for Brenda which is partially compensated for by their basketball coaching. None of the Turkish or Jamaican gangland characters are caricatured baddies, they are layered people. Despite their criminality, each of them seeks validation from their community. In contrast, Jerrish, Frenchie and the Albanians have no such saving graces. They represent invasive and destructive criminal colonialism. They have no connection with the neighbourhood or community but seek to exploit and control it. They symbolise a threat to the ecosystem of the community, which has no choice but to defend itself.

The Zaman, Güney, Durrant and Fairbright families are all connected through their children. The children's teenage struggles and the associated parenting challenges form a significant part of the book. Friendships, bullying, racism; working out who they are and where they belong; reconciling their home cultures with the world around them. All the young people are aspirational in their own ways and by the end, many have moved on and out. Among them, Arjan, a child refugee, stands out: he has experienced trauma beyond anything known by the others and on top of this must endure Mehmet's racist bullying; yet through it all, he shows resilience, adaptability, emotional maturity and compassion far exceeding his years. Ironically, Mehmet experiences his own Damascus Road experience and their silent park encounter, weeks after the school fight, is a powerful moment, a mutual recognition of the other's suffering and their common humanity.

Although Bulent occupies a background role, he has a clear sense of belonging. His humourless conservatism reminds us of the intolerance of the Turkish state. The contrast between the Igli brothers, despite their shared lineage, is a theme we see repeated in the differences between the Zaman children.

Although Hasan is a background figure through most of the book, he occupies a pivotal position within the spiderweb of plots: he worked with Cetin in 1979, is father to Rasheed, uncle to Arjan and business associate of Mustafa. He connects the Zaman, Güney and Igli families and anchors them to their geographical roots. He has faced his own adversities, as a migrant, widower, single father, and double outsider. Yet he has overcome these through courage, humour, and the avoidance of public controversy. He seeks safety as Mr Average and manages to get on with everyone, while having no qualms about participating in Topkapi supply operations. He is a survivor and in this he personifies the spirit of a troubled region. He is a symbol of constancy, and a dependable rock who reminds us that belonging is not about place but a state of mind.

As its title conveys, this book is as much about places, West Green and Downhills Park, as it is about its fictional characters. The title 'On West Green' has an intended double meaning. It is intended to evoke 'the Green' on which much action is centred, while also being a treatise on life in the neighbourhood.

I hope the descriptions succeed in conjuring up their London landscape. The remnant of a historic West Green survives at the junction of West Green Road, Philip Lane, and the southern entrance to Downhills Park. Though this is a small landmark, the name has become attached to the wider area surrounding it. But as with all places, it has no sharp boundary.

When I think of West Green, I think of Downhills Park. It is physically central to neighbourhood, emblematic, highly visible and used by many residents for different purposes. It is the urban village green of West Green, where much action takes place. It is also part of the characters' collective experience and environment. They share this space, although it has different significance for each of them. It binds them together, despite their differences of age, gender, social class, ethnicity, or cultural background. Urban parks are important and under-valued social as well as environmental assets, which can play a pivotal role in community-building and urban regeneration.

How we define 'place' is a much-discussed geographical question. Most people intuitively understand the word, but few interrogate it. The well-established geographical definition presents any given place as a 'bounded locality,' somewhere with borders within which we find a distinctive sets of characteristics: landscape, economy, population, ecology. One problem with this approach is knowing where to fix the boundary between one place and another. Unless there are clear physical boundaries like a railway line or river, this can prove difficult. The landscape blurs from one place to the next and people may have different ideas about where to locate the dividing line. Another problem with this definition is that the people, economic flows, and wildlife move from one place to another all the time. There are constant and ongoing interactions across boundaries, wherever you decide to put them. So, an alternative way of thinking of 'place' abandons this 'container' approach. Instead, we might think of 'places' as nodal points, locations into which people, economic activity and wildlife may flow from other places, near and far, before flowing out again and on to other places. In every place that these flows converge, they shape and flavour the physical space, much as the ingredients of a cooking recipe. For example, Turkish migration has shaped the streetscape with shop front language and colourful displays; should the Turkish community move on 'en masse' to an outer suburb as the Greeks have done, this streetscape will change again. Similarly, gentrification has affected the housing stock and population profile. In this way, places are dynamic, and shaped by these flows. This is one reason why the book begins and ends far away from West Green, in Cornwall and Mardin before moving to Tottenham. These far-off locations and Tottenham are integrally connected by people and shape each other.

Our relationship with nature is another significant theme and while Tottenham may be an urban environment, nature is easy to find in its parks. Until the 1860s, the area was largely rural, and nature remains sleeping beneath the concrete. 'Sous les pavés la plage' (beneath the paving stones, the beach). Many of the characters retreat to nature for mental space. As well as flora and fauna, nature is present throughout in the form of the seasons. They are a force of constancy, something solid, enduring and recurring which contrasts with the brevity of human drama. Nature will remain long after all the characters are gone. Natural ecological systems have also influenced the structure of the book. The chapters follow the progression of the seasons, with related landscape changes and timbre of human drama.

The inter-connections between the characters reflect the inter-dependence that can be found in ecosystem food-webs, while the plot moves from a fragile equilibrium of social order, through disruption and destabilisation by events, back to a new equilibrium ten years later, just as a 'climatic climax' forest ecosystem would eventually re-establish itself after a devastating fire. In the re-calibrated equilibrium, Onur 'comes home' to Mardin, Ned to Cornwall and Dymphna to Ireland; Zaman-Igli and Fairbright-Güney families bond through love; and in the final park scene, Dwayne and Ellis are victorious basketball coaches, young friends catch up, and Arjan is reunited with Fatima. Order is restored …until the next disruption.

I lived in the area for twenty-three years and raised three children there. Like all parents who want to do their best for their children, I stepped in where I could. I served as a school governor and became a committee member of the West Green Resident's Association. We were frequent users of Downhills Park which, at the time, needed some loving care. There were no park wardens, no public toilets, play equipment was vandalised and in decay, broken glass and other detritus was rarely swept away. It often felt like a 'no-man's-land'; but also, 'everyone's land'. I was struck by how the same physical space seemed to have different meaning for its very different users: young, old, children, parents, teenagers, disabled, rich, poor, male, female, Black, White, Turkish etc. With like-minded people, I helped to set up the Friends of Downhills Park which worked with the Council to secure more funding for improvements. We also organised clean up days, Art in the Park events, campaigned for improved playgrounds, new basketball and tennis courts, and above all for a cafe and toilets which could provide a hub for people to hang out and reclaim the space. I left London 2003 with many memories and emotional attachment to the area and park and have been delighted, on return visits, to see how well kept it is now; and that the cafe has become reality.

### Haringey and Harringay

Most of this book is set in the London Borough of Haringey. For readers who are not familiar, it is in north London. To its south are located between Hackney and Islington, to its north is Enfield, to its west is Camden, and to its east is Waltham Forest. According to the local authority, it is the fifth most culturally diverse borough in the United Kingdom with 190 languages spoken in its schools. It also presents a diversity of urban environments, from inner-city to suburb with an east-west gradient from poorer to richer households. West Green occupies a mid-point and has much in common with other inner-city areas economically and demographically, for example in serving as a supportive destination for new migrant arrivals. At the turn of the 21st century, Kurdish and Turkish incomers were among the most significant of its ethnic minority communities.

The London Borough of Haringey was only created in 1965 and should not be confused with the neighbourhood of Harringay. Note the different spelling. Harringay was another early 19th century village to the west of West Green and is now a residential area centred on a network of residential streets known locally as 'The Ladder' and the shopping street, Green Lanes, which features in the book.

### Languages

This book is written in Standard English. Where dialogue takes place in Turkish, Arabic or Kurdish, I have made no attempt to include token vocabulary. But I have deliberately dropped a few prepositions or conjunctions in the speech of the second-language English speakers and have tried to indicate the use of some dialects spoken, principally Multicultural London English (MLE) and Jamaican English. As these have no formal written convention, I have conjured up voices by use of spelling and grammar. I apologise to anyone who thinks I should have just stuck to Standard English or that I have failed to adequately convey dialect.

I love languages and wanted to convey linguistic diversity, language mixing and code switching as part of the environment. Many of the characters are bi- or multi-lingual and move between dialects according to context, for example moving between MLE with friends and Turkish with parents or MLE or Jamaican and more standard English within a single conversation, so allow for intentional inconsistencies.

# Acknowledgements

Thanks to: Annie McMullan, Joy O'Neill, Gerhard Wolf and Gergely Stewart for reading drafts and offering feedback; Jessica Norrie, author of the *Infinity Pool* and *The Magic Carpet* for inspiration and advice; Sandra Staufer for advice and Malcolm Kemp for the cover design; Shay, Levi, Sid and Seb for remembering their school days in Tottenham; Dr Stephen Whittle, stalwart West Green activist for decades of tireless work for the neighbourhood; many people I have known, too many to name who have helped me to imagine the characters.

If you have enjoyed this book, please leave a review on Amazon so others might be encouraged to read it.

Printed in Great Britain
by Amazon

46476789R00148